Afterthoughts

Afterthoughts

Sherrard C. Foster

VANTAGE PRESS
New York

FIRST EDITION

Published by Vantage Press, Inc.
419 Park Ave. South, New York, NY 10016

Manufactured in the United States of America
ISBN: 978-0-533-16137-9

Library of Congress Catalog Card No: 2008908469

0 9 8 7 6 5 4 3 2 1

For all my best friends at the dog park in Arlington, Virginia

Contents

One	A Fantasy Dies in Seattle	1
Two	Detective Clemsen Rises Again	33
Three	On the Road	46
Four	Thar She Blows	58
Five	Sounding	81
Six	Cleaning Up	103
Seven	Safe Harbor	113
Eight	Settling In	145
Nine	Charlie Cool	157
Ten	To Save a Whale; to Break a Heart	167
Eleven	Back to the Pod	182
Twelve	Swimming Free	202
Thirteen	Waves and Undertow	223
Fourteen	Natalie's Interview	241
Fifteen	Dropping Anchor in Settled Waters	250

Afterthoughts

One

A Fantasy Dies in Seattle

Suzanne Douglas sat alone in a booth by a window inside a very pleasant café in the downtown Seattle marketplace, watching more than occasionally the locals go about their routine daily business. Having told the waitress that "a friend" might be joining her for lunch, she sat across from a second place-setting and menu. As early wore on into mid-afternoon, she began to regret having said anything at all. She felt noticeably alone, and striking the pose of self-assured independence was not all that comfortable to her. She could do it alright, but didn't like it, and having to pull it off for the benefit of total strangers, who in all likelihood were completely oblivious to this mini-dilemma, made her angry and a little resentful. The reality, of course, was that this was not even a mini-dilemma and absolutely no one was paying attention to her in any event.

Nevertheless, to help cover her "nothing to do and no one to talk to" appearance, she opted to strike the pose of the successful and elusive author (or what she thought would appear like successful and elusive author behavior), making a few cogent notes now and then on scraps of paper she dug out of her purse. A "few" soon became "several," as the day's inevitable progression closed in on 3:30 P.M. It was time to go, but where?

There was one thing she could pretty honestly say about

1

the apparently short and not-totally satisfying relationship with Pete: all of it was prompting her to write more—a lot more than she ever had before. Of course, everything she wrote was self-absorbed, but at least she was writing. If nothing else, it was good practice. *You never know,* she thought; *someday the stuff she was writing just might be noticed by some incredibly influential agent who would think she was a fabulously interesting and talented writer.* And she really thought she could live with being rich and famous.

So, what to do? By now, it was almost 5:00 P.M. She had scribbled down everything about which she could conjure up even a remote thought. Good God, it was getting close to "happy hour." It wouldn't be long before office workers began to filter in for a couple of drinks, or a possible pick-up. She had to get out of here. Catching the waitress' eye, she paid her bill, left an overly generous tip, exited the café, and sooner than she had expected, actually, found herself on the sidewalk surrounding the pedestrian-filled marketplace.

It was crowded. She began to walk west toward the center of the business district, perhaps not-so-unconsciously hoping to see Pete come out of his office building. How could she still hope to see him, especially after he *had* stood her up? Lord, she was hopeless, couldn't even think independently, let alone act it. She passed his office building from the opposite side if the street and looked straight ahead. By the time she came to the next street corner, she had pretty much decided she should just go back to the hotel, get up to her room, order room service dinner, watch some TV and go to bed early (to kill time before her flight home the next morning). *God,* she was boring. She wondered if other loners from out of town were like this.

The light changed at the corner, and she crossed the street. While waiting for a taxi to appear on the horizon to carry her to anonymous safety, suddenly she saw Pete step into an open space in the small group of people standing on the other side of the street waiting for the "walk" signal. She sort of panicked; a significant part of her didn't want him to see her, and of course a perhaps equally significant part of her wanted desperately for him to see her. So she just stood there and waited, not knowing what to do. *How typical,* she thought. She hoped she looked good, anyway.

Before she could change directions and escape from view into the increasingly crowded sidewalks, Pete *did* see her, and shouted her name from across the street, raising his arm in a wave. Well, now she had something to do: she more or less had to respond. Looking around from where she had been heading, to the other street corner, she calmly waved back and smiled. Smiled as if she was *supposed* to be there. Now she *really* wanted to disappear. What on earth could her plausible story be? Why was she there? There *was* no plausible story; she was trapped in her obsession, and he knew it. He had to. *Get me out of here; I don't need this,* she thought to herself. She quickly decided to keep going down the street away from the corner where Pete was about to step into the crosswalk, rather than wait for him to catch up to her. Maybe he wouldn't even do that; maybe he would in fact head in the other direction, away from her. Maybe he had, in fact, *nothing to say for himself, no excuses.* Son-of-a-bitch. *I hate him; I hate me. You are such a jerk,* she silently lamented.

What is the matter *with you? Why did you let this get totally out of your control? What makes you think you ever had any control? Did you think he was just some sort of mindless plaything? What ever made you think this entire thing was about control? What* did *you think would happen anyway?* A million unanswered questions flooded her brain as she finally found a vacant taxi at the corner of the next block, and directed the driver to the hotel on the other side of town where she was staying.

Once safely locked into the back seat of the taxi and headed down Union Street toward the university district where her hotel was located, she sighed deeply and shuddered a little. "I'm probably going to die for this stupid act of defiance, and no one will care." She had played a good game of complete self-assuredness and independence, but the other half of her psyche was making itself evident now. This was the half she couldn't control. How many times had she had this same conversation with herself? Thousands . . . She wanted *something* so much, but defining it precisely was such an elusive and intermittent fantasy. Even defining it *imprecisely* was not easy. For almost two years she had actively nurtured this fantasy love affair with Pete. Push had finally come to shove; the face-to-face affair had lasted approximately five hours; maybe one of those hours actually taken up with lovemaking, or more accurately, copulating. And after all the build-up and unveiled descriptions of what would or could happen, it hadn't been that good. In fact, looking back on it in short hindsight, it can't been very good at all. *Why* then, did she want to see Pete again? *Why?*

"Because you still think you're unfulfilled and unhappy, and you can't get your own life together, that's why," she quietly muttered to herself once she was inside her small, stuffy hotel room. Without really caring, she ordered something from the room service menu, and started looking at the pay-for-TV movie options. Ten dollars a pop for first-run or porn movies. She wondered somewhat bitterly if Pete would (or could) bestow a little more enthusiasm on her and on his lovemaking efforts if she had paid *him* ten dollars . . . Come to think of it, ten dollars a fuck was pretty damn cheap; some of the whores on 14th Street made better than that. (On the other hand, how would *she* know?) At least she could take solace in the fact that he wasn't anywhere *near* as good as his verbal descriptions had been leading up to their disappointing encounter yesterday afternoon. In fact, Pete was a big disappointment, a *big* one. Too bad, too. She could have shown him the time of his sexual life, and their affair could have gone on for years. (Oh, really?) She suddenly felt sorry for his wife, and had some empathy for the woman's desire (at least according to Pete's account) to leave him. Here was a man who, at age forty, was still trying to decide what to do with his life. Not that that was a major failing; it was apparent she wasn't very clear on what she was doing with hers.

*   *   *

The food arrived about thirty minutes later, and she ate the meal dispassionately, as though it was an assignment. The only way to not think about how wounded and used she felt was to lose herself in mindless television presentations which filled nothing but time. He never called that evening, even though he had said he would. It took a long time for her to fall asleep. Her thoughts were interspersed with half-conscious fantasies of Pete being there with her because he *wanted* to be there, not because he felt he had to pay off one some long-standing obligation, or answer some implied dare. Even though in her fantasies he did a *much better job* of arousing and fulfilling her sexual appetites, they were not, of course, even remotely close to reality. And the self-gratification she indulged in was just not the same as the real thing . . . duh. How come he *talked* such a good game, and when the real thing was right in front of him, obviously eager to be both an enthusiastic pleasure giver and willing object of his sexual fantasies, he didn't (or couldn't) even get excited and hard?

Was it so sinful and complicated that he was incapable of enjoying the moment? She knew she wasn't the first out-of-marriage liaison he had been involved in; even he had told her that. So, she didn't buy for a heartbeat any possible proclamations of fidelity. Right now, he just pissed her off. Right now, she didn't even want to see him. She resented his ruining her fantasy love affair. After *years* of both long-distance and at-hand flirtation, this was supposed to have gone on for years, with no complications; no expectations. No one was supposed to get hurt. However, "Mr. Everything"(or at least "Mr. A Lot") had stumbled badly coming out of the starting gate, and had only barely made it to the finish line. *Well,* she silently surmised, *she had only herself to blame.* Somehow, she should have known better. And now, she had only to go home.

*   *   *

The next morning, she (like always . . . so predictable) packed the rest of her clothes, hauled her stuff down to the hotel lobby, paid her bill, and inquired about getting a cab or shuttle to the airport. All she wanted now was to get out of town quickly. It was obvious that Pete wasn't going to call, and that even if he did, there was no future to the conversation. After all, given how things had gone, what did she *want* out of this interlude, anyway? A friend? A part-time, long-distance lover? She knew she was being unrealistic when she thought about continuing to see Pete off and on over the years. Right now, she sure didn't want to continue seeing him. Still in all, part of her hoped that somehow, yesterday evening had been just an aberration of nerves on his part. Part of her hoped *a lot* that somehow, something would happen to cause everything to turn around and start over. She knew, of course, "something" wouldn't happen. There was no way. She hated bad endings.

Largely because there was nothing else to do, she arrived

at the airport well over two and a half hours ahead of her flight's departure time. There was one thing you could say about her, she followed directions well. She checked in at the airline counter and took a seat in the waiting area next to the gate. She adjusted neatly her carry-on belongings, and began leafing through a magazine from her tote bag.

"What were you doing downtown yesterday?" Pete inquired. Startled (and caught completely off guard), she bolted up from her chair, and stammered something like, "Oh, not much; just taking in some sights before I left town." (God how inane). "Did you want to talk to me?" she asked, trying to recover her composure.

"Sure, I wanted to at least talk to you before you left."

"Well, what did you want to say?"

Pete looked at her intently and said, "I was going to call you last night, but I had to spend some time with Anne and the kids."

"Yeah, sure, she thought. *Of course you were going to call me. I don't even want to hear this, let alone have to respond to it.* She really was quite annoyed with him Without thinking, she plunged ahead.

"I don't care that you 'had to spend time with Anne and the kids.' I *never* in any way implied that I expected you to spend time that you don't have with *me*, did I? What I *did* expect, Pete, was that whatever time we *did* spend together would happen because we *both* wanted it to, and that no hurt or guilty feelings would result. Did I ever give you the impression that I expected some commitment from you? That was never what I wanted. I find it hard to believe that you would ever have gotten that impression, especially from anything I ever said. I guess, in spite of all your magnificent verbal assurances, that it was just too much for you to handle, huh? I have to say that I am really disappointed, and I am more than a little hurt. I thought we were better friends than this; I thought we were close enough to be honest with each other."

Pete just stood there, looking at her, like maybe he didn't know what to say. How ironic that a trial lawyer would find himself at a loss for words. *What a jerk,* she thought, and what a jerk I am for letting myself believe that I *and* my stupid feelings meant something to him.

"Will you be in D.C. this fall?" he asked, as though he hadn't heard any of what she just said. "There's a trial lawyers conference scheduled for the third week in October, and I would really like to see you again. Maybe I could make it up to you, and we could spend a longer period of time together."

As much as it hurt her, she managed to respond, "I don't think you ever could, Pete. How can I ever believe you again?" She picked up her tote bag and headed for gate five, where her plane was beginning to board. Grabbing her arm, Pete said in a whisper, "Hey, don't go. Let's talk about it."

"I don't think so, Pete. You let a really good thing fall by the wayside, and now you're going to walk all over it again? How come you are incapable of realizing that I have feelings, too? You know, I feel like I bent over backwards to be careful of your feelings and your obligations, and your needs. I never imposed on your time; and what time I did have with you, I tried to be sure it was enjoyable. I never asked for more; I never expected more. But I *did* expect you to be honest. I guess this whole thing was just a bad idea." In a shot of anger, she said, "I'll let you know if I test positive." She could feel the heat moving quickly up the back of her head. The feeling made her scalp tingle, and she could feel little tiny beads of sweat breaking the surface, among the strands of her hair. Turning away from him once more, she picked up the tote bag from the floor and headed for the short line of passengers moving toward the flight attendant taking boarding passes at gate five.

Pete quickly grabbed her by the arm again and said, "You can't go; we've got to get this straightened out."

People in the boarding area were beginning to look at them now, including the flight attendant taking boarding passes. She wondered how often flight attendants witnessed this kind of gut-wrenching scene at airport terminals?

"No, we don't, Pete; we don't *have* to do anything. I think everything is pretty straight right now. As long as you're happy, what's the problem? You know, you shouldn't have stopped me. In fact, it's probably a good thing this plane is leaving now, 'cause if I had another half an hour or so, I suspect I'd tell you more than you ever wanted to hear from me."

She didn't know where the words were coming from; they just came. She could feel herself losing control emotionally, and it was the last thing she wanted to do. Not a good closing image. *And,* she thought, *make no mistake, this* is *the closing.*

"Why don't you go pick on someone who is as self-absorbed as you are? You know, even up the match. That's all it is to you, isn't it? I never thought I'd be saying this, Pete, but I feel sorry for you. And I'm *really* sorry that I let myself kind of believe all those things you said to me over the past two years. Am I supposed to be grateful for all the time you spent building up this charade? It was never a charade to me"

With that, she quickly got to the front of the ticket line, and the slightly bemused-looking flight attendant took her boarding pass and directed her to "seat 17D, on your right."

"Thanks," she muttered, and without looking back, she passed through the open door to the covered hallway leading to the "belly of the beast", as she had always thought of it.

It was hot inside the plane, and it seemed to take forever to get everyone loaded and seated. She was grateful for the window seat, as it allowed her, once settled, to put chin in hand, and gaze out the small window to the runway pavement below, and to the backside slope of the jet's wing, and to immerse herself in contemplation. *Finally*, the attendants closed the plane's loading door, and the friendly beast began to slowly back up, as though it was unsure of which way to go. Once the beast had lined itself up at the end of the take-off runway, and started to gather its engines for the still improbable (to her, anyway) climb through air to the clouds above, she began to relax a little. This was her favorite part of flying: taking off. Hopefully, this takeoff would leave on the ground someone broken-hearted, or at least incredibly remorseful for the pain he had caused. *God, what's the matter with you, anyway? You are* so better *than this.*

*   *   *

Monday morning, she returned to work, filled with the realization that absolutely nothing had changed in her life as a result of her sojourn in Seattle. Nor was it likely that anything *would* change. Her life would just continue as before, as though none of this ever happened. Thinking about it made her think how little the world cares or is even aware of what people do and say and think. Somehow, she didn't think it seemed fair. It was funny; now, when she gazed at her diamond wedding ring she thought about what a good man her husband was, in spite of all his faults. Even if he *was* often aggravating and boring in bed, at least he was steady (except for when he was drunk), and she knew that he adored her. She never had to worry about him stretching or breaking the marriage vows; there was certainly something to be said for that. With a perceptible sigh, she turned to the pile of paper on her desk. She realized now, too late, how stupid extra-marital affairs are. Even if they were physically and emotionally satisfying, there were always consequences. Sometimes those consequences were fatal. How could that *ever* be worth it?

10

And yet, people continue to cheat on their spouses all the time.

And *another* thing—she hated her job these days. Even if the job *had* allowed her to get to Seattle for this little (and short-lived) affair, she still hated the undeniable fact that, after over ten years of working overtime and almost single-handedly getting a politically controversial project finished and agreed to by a less-than-friendly Congress, she was still not getting promoted. She got lip service from the head of the agency. Big f—- deal, right? Well, no one had ever said that the Federal Government would be an easy place to work, especially when you were working for a small, under-funded program that had few political supporters. Sigh . . . Well, in spite of it all, she certainly was a joyful individual; no doubt about that. The big problem with the job, she had decided, was not so much her performance (*although a serious attitude adjustment was clearly in order*); it was the job itself. There just wasn't that much to do anymore. The challenges were mostly gone, and pretty much all that was left were planning and revision tasks. Boring. *So* she thought to herself as she aimlessly shuffled through the stack of aging management plans piled on the corner of her desk: *I've got to find a way to make this job more meaningful, especially to myself.* Either that, or find a way to get out and go to something better.

*   *   *

Around 11:30 A.M. Jodie stuck her head inside Suzanne's cubicle and said, "Hey, how was the trip? Good to see you back."

Jodie had pretty consistently been a good friend, but there were times (like this one) when she drove Suzanne nuts. She was perennially upbeat and cheerful, often for no particular reason (none that Suzanne could discern, anyway). She had always been a little suspicious of people like Jodie; they were usually either largely clueless, or were aggressively trying to fill some personal agenda. Suzanne could never figure out which extreme drove Jodie. Sometimes, she wondered what kind of drugs Jodie was on (*and if she could get any for herself*). In any event, you could never tell Jodie everything, unless you were for some reason interested in having it repeated throughout the office.

"Oh, fine. I'm really beat, though."

"Yeah, you *do* look tired. Hey, you missed all the excitement last week. You should *see* the new political hire that's working here now. God, is he gorgeous! I think he's a friend of the White House, did a lot of work on the last Presidential campaign, you know?"

"Great, just great. Just what this program needs. Another 'don't-care-about-it' son of some big political contributor who can't find his own job."

"Boy, you *did* have a good time in Seattle, didn't you?"

"Sorry Jodie; I'm just feeling kind of disenchanted. So where's this gorgeous boy-wonder sitting?"

"Down the hall next to Charlie's cube. I'm going to ask him if he wants to go to lunch today. Wanna join us?"

"You mean he's got the one remaining window office? Damn, Daddy must have contributed *big* bucks. There's just no justice, is there?"

"You know, the funny thing is that since the day he got here, senior management seems to have been sort of nervous," Jodie continued, not waiting for an answer. "You know, like they're trying to hide something."

"Like what? What do you mean?"

"Don't know. All I know is that 'Heartless' and a couple of the branch chiefs have been disappearing together from the office a couple of times a day for the last week or so."

"Heartless" was the code nickname that she and Jodie

12

had long ago attached to Jim Hartford, their boss. The name didn't really have anything to do with his magnanimous nature (or lack of it); it just seemed to fit their feelings about James T. Hartford, Division Chief, career Federal bureaucrat and, in at least Suzanne's personal opinion (she wasn't really sure Jodie had much of a real opinion about anything relating to the Sanctuary Program), totally removed from the realities of the work environment, including the abilities, desires, or work habits of his small staff. (Maybe staying "removed" was the secret to happiness around here.) "Heartless" was also so named for his seeming complacency regarding most everything within the scope of office activity. Well, it certainly appeared that the arrival of the political hire was quickly eradicating that complacency. Suzanne wondered to herself what was going on here. No point in asking Jodie; she wouldn't even have thought about it.

"Thanks anyway for the lunch invite, Jodie; I think I better stick around the office and get through some of this piled-up mail."

"Okey-dokey," Jodie chirped, turning on a dime and moving out of her (windowless) cube.

By twelve noon she had worked through to the bottom of one pile of documents, and decided to get out of the building and get a quick carry-out lunch from the café in the lobby of the office building.

On her way out, she walked down the hall in the direction of Charlie's cube. *Gotta check this new guy out,* she thought. As she rounded the corner onto the hall where Charlie's cube was located, she was almost knocked over by (as previously described) a gorgeous, tall, lean and slightly tanned young man, headed in a hurry up the hall in the opposite direction.

"Whoa, watch out!" she exclaimed as she side-stepped the speeding new hire, narrowly averting a direct collision.

"Ooh, sorry," the handsome blur muttered as he barreled on through and around the corner, not missing so much as a beat.

What a handful, she thought. *He looks entirely self-absorbed; just what we don't need any more of around here. Well, I think I've seen enough* she thought to herself, and moved on until she reached the end of the hall and out the door to the elevators (and temporary escape).

Finally outside, it was gloriously warm, sunny and un-characteristically not humid for this time of year in the Washington, D.C. area. Days like this were rare treats, and she decided to take advantage of it by finding a spot for herself in the sun by the small fountain and pool, where she could watch both her co-workers and the "higher-ups" come and go. She quickly got a sandwich, chips and soda (having beaten the bulk of the noontime crowd at the deli). Someone had turned on the water in the fountain, and it was actually working. She found a spot on the grass near there, where she could observe most everyone else from the four high-rise buildings that comprised the work "campus" as they came and went from the deli, or the larger cafeteria, located in the building next to hers.

As she sat on a small grassy area near the fountain steps, she saw the new hire emerge from the building with Heartless and two other guys she didn't recognize. They were deeply involved in conversation, and the new hire seemed to be trying to make a point.

"I really think we better coordinate this proposed policy with downtown," the political hire was saying, as the small group hurried past her and the fountain. Heartless, in particular, did not look happy. In fact, he looked notably aggravated, *very "un-Heartless-like"*, Suzanne thought. The group quickly moved in the direction of the escalators to the subway, and soon disappeared from her sight.

That was weird, she thought, as she finished half of her sandwich and all of the chips, pitching the remains into the trash can as she went back into the office building and punched the elevator button for the 11th floor. *God, I hate this job,* she thought, as the elevator car reached her floor.

Upon reaching her own cubicle she immediately noticed the message light blinking on her phone. *It's too much to even hope for,* she thought out of habit, as she reached to retrieve the voice-mail.

"Hello, you gorgeous thing," the familiar deep voice almost whispered. Part of her almost could not believe Pete would be calling. The unabashed gall of this guy; what could he possibly want, anyway? She had at least tried to give him everything she had in Seattle. There wasn't any more.

"Do yourself a favor," the suggestively compelling voice continued. "Next time you're in the rest room and you have your panties down, put two or three fingers inside and think of me probing every inch of you, wanting to touch and stroke every recess of your body. Hey, give me a call if you've got some time this afternoon. I really miss you, and I'd like to talk."

Unbelievable, she thought. *The guy never stops. How come he sounds so good when I know he's not?* "I'm not calling him back," she said to herself; "I don't need this." *I need* something, *but not this.* Even though she didn't really want to, Suzanne erased the message. *I've got to erase more than that,* she thought, *if I'm ever going to get back to anything remotely resembling normalcy.* 'Course, there wasn't anything about her individual "normalcy" that she found very appealing. *But that's my problem, not his or anyone else's.*

The remainder of the afternoon passed without incident. At approximately 4:45 P.M., she collected the remainder of the papers still in her inbox and loaded them into her briefcase.

15

Did she really think she was going to work at home this evening?

*   *   *

While eating warmed-up leftovers in front of the television at home that evening (the briefcase filled with papers remained untouched), Suzanne kind of took in the late news. In a breaking story, a local TV news reporter was describing the scene in an alleyway in the Georgetown area where earlier that day the body of a young man had been found. There was no identification; he had apparently died of gunshots. Certainly, at first blush, although it was horrible, this didn't seem like a terribly unusual story; after all, Washington, D.C. was well known as a high-crime city. She didn't really pay much attention to the reporter's words. *Just another in the seemingly unending series of senseless, opportunistic homicides, committed for who knows what reason,* she thought. About the only thing that made this event perhaps notable was the location of the body's discovery. Georgetown was not normally the site for such unseemly occurrences.

Later that night, she checked her voice mail messages at the office; there were none. "Shit," she muttered to herself as she brushed her teeth and changed into the old, faded over-sized T-shirt that she used to sleep in. *I gotta get out of this place; or at least out of this job,* she was thinking, just as the telephone rang. The ring did not disturb at all Suzanne's sleeping husband; she had always envied Doug's innate ability to fall asleep almost instantly, almost anywhere. Nothing seemed to faze him.

"Suzanne, guess what?" Jodie exclaimed softly. "I think there's something going on with the new guy; he never came back from wherever he went downtown this afternoon with Heartless and the other guys. And I *think* I just heard his name

16

mentioned on the late news, but I didn't catch the story. Did you see it?"

"I saw the early news, with the story about some guy being found dead today somewhere in Georgetown. I didn't think there was any identity of the guy, though; is that what you're talking about?"

"Yeah, I think the guy is Justin, from the office," Jodie responded. "I can't believe it." Suzanne muttered thanks to Jodie and turned the TV back on, just in time to catch the tail end of the late local news. The story was just wrapping up, and by now there was more information on the gunned-down young man in Georgetown. Standing in front of the TV with toothbrush in mouth, she listened, transfixed as the local reporter filled in some details to the victim's identity: Justin Kennard, recently moved to the D.C. area from his home state of Wisconsin to work as a Presidential intern at the Department of Commerce. There was not much additional information on motives or circumstances of the shooting. And at this point, no suspect.

Damn, Suzanne thought. *This city is getting worse and worse.* It's getting to the point of just not getting caught in the wrong place at the wrong time. (*Like any of us have any control over that, anyway,* she thought.) The police are so overwhelmed they are virtually incapable of even slowing down the flood of violent crime.

Sleep was hard to get to that night; she could not clear her mind of the image of Justin Kennard lying face down in that alley, with a trickle of blood seeping out from under him.

*   *   *

For the next several days, the office was anything but normal. There were police investigators in and out, talking to Heartless and other supervisors of Mr. Kennard. Suzanne

17

learned through office "rumor control" that Justin's parents had come into town to arrange for transport of their son back to Wisconsin for burial.

Heartless seemed particularly nervous, and cut the normal Thursday staff meeting short. Only brief mention was made of Justin Kennard's death, and discussion of staff issues was minimized. At the staff meeting, Heartless initiated discussion of the status of Marine Sanctuaries' reauthorization legislation. As everyone at the meeting knew, the current administration had forwarded a reauthorization proposal to Congress which far exceeded what was generally assumed would be the ultimate demonstration of less-than-firm Congressional support for the concept of protected ocean areas. There was bound to be serious and prolonged dispute within various Congressional committees over not only future funding for the Program, but the future of the Program itself.

During the shortened staff discussion, Suzanne continued to notice the apparent discomfort of Heartless. For someone so apparently comfortable with the status quo, Heartless seemed suddenly out of his element. *Oh, well,* she thought; *I'm sure there's a story here, but do I care? Too much effort to try and figure this out. Especially when I've got all those incredibly exciting management plans to review.*

*   *   *

Back at his office, Detective first grade Charles "Bud" Clemsen scratched at the thinning hair remaining on the back of his head and sighed heavily. This case just didn't make sense to him, and it was beginning to look like bringing it to closure was going to take longer than it should, considering the facts in evidence at this point in the investigation. He was in charge of this inquiry, and so far his team of investigators had determined the following: Justin Kennard had been at the Commerce Department's headquarters downtown several hours before he was shot in the Georgetown neighborhood—a good distance away from 14th and Constitution Avenue. The shooting had also occurred within two blocks of the condominium that Kennard was renting for the duration of his internship. Even though it was probably not important to the case, he still wondered what Kennard was doing at the headquarters office. Still, it *might* be; he probably shouldn't ignore the purpose of Kennard's trip downtown—whatever that purpose was. Clemsen sighed again, as he began to think about the possible political implications Kennard's trip might have had. *And again,* Clemsen thought, *this case was looking for sure like it would take a while to solve.* There had been no witnesses to the shooting, and the incident occurred in a neighborhood not known for such occurrences. *And,* Clemsen thought, *the discomfort of James T. Hartford had also not gone unnoticed during the interviews of Kennard's supervisors. Too many loose ends.* And too few answers. Yeah, for sure, there were a lot more questions to be answered before this investigation could be wrapped up and closed. Reaching for another doughnut from the half-finished box, Clemsen turned his attention back to Hartford.

Why, he wondered, *had Hartford seemed so uncomfortable—even nervous—during questioning that was routine to investigations such as this one?* In looking over the notes taken by some of his team, Clemsen's suspicions that Hartford was hiding something were reinforced. Yeah, Hartford was definitely on the short list of suspects, but what was the motive?

*   *   *

So a week or so had passed since Suzanne's less-than-monumental liaison with Pete in Seattle. Now that some of the anger and disgust (to say nothing of disappointment) with the whole event had dissipated, and in the quiet solitude of her apartment, she thought back to the time when she and Pete had shared common thoughts about the potential importance of the National Marine Sanctuary Program. Those were uniquely delicious times of compatriotism, when Suzanne felt she and Pete were indeed true soul mates. Of course, that was before Pete took his new law degree and new wife and moved to Seattle, where he quickly made both babies and partner at his firm, specializing in bankruptcy law, of all things. *So much for soul mates,* Suzanne thought. But back during those exhilarating and conspiratorial times when she and Pete devised ways to further the goals of the fledgling Sanctuary Program, life was filled with hard work, long hours and an increasingly intense physical attraction to each other. (What husband?)

The National Marine Sanctuary Program was one of a spate of environmental laws that came into being during the early 1970s, but it never enjoyed much supportive recognition either publicly or from the Congress, which appropriated funds that barely kept the Program afloat but certainly did not allow it to expand or flourish. The original legislation authorized the identification, designation and comprehensive management of discrete areas of the marine environment as national marine sanctuaries in order to protect the "conservation, recreational, ecological, historical, research, educational or aesthetic" qualities of those areas. Over the years a small number of sanctuaries had been designated, and few in the public even noticed. Because designation of any sanctuary was an incredibly long and public process the few initially designated sites tended to be non-controversial, in terms of public uses of each site's resources. Although the overall mission of the Program was to identify and protect discrete areas of the marine environment, Pete and Suzanne both knew the Program was destined to run up against the competing missions of other Federal agencies, notably those of the Department of the Interior (DOI). In particular, development of the nation's offshore oil and gas, as well as other mineral resources, were primarily the responsibility of the DOI. And the DOI had a much bigger budget.

In those earlier days, Pete and Suzanne became a team of sorts, taking the message of the Sanctuary Program to the public in ways the Program officials could not. They not only wrote comments on behalf of their respective environmental organizations; they talked to newspaper editors and Congressional staffs, lobbying for additional support for the Program. The goals of the Program were, at least to Suzanne's way of thinking, so potentially beneficial to the national public; what could be more right and far-sighted than providing safe haven for fishes, marine mammals and the host of food resources necessary for their survival? Given the right publicity and public education about such places, she knew a strong public constituency for the Program would rise above the short-range objectives of the DOI. Although she knew it was naïve on her part, Suzanne felt that if she could just get even some DOI officials to experience the wonder of sanctuary sites, there could be significant changes to that agency's policies. It was not necessary to trash sanctuary resources in order to provide gasoline for cars and asphalt for highway construction to the nation's public. Surely, there was accommodation to be made to all interests that would not destroy the fragile and often irreplaceable resources of the marine environment.

Every time the Program came up for reauthorization, there were numerous attempts—some successful—to weaken through amendment the legislation that directed how new sanctuaries could be designated. Typically, the Program would be reauthorized for four-year periods, and within a week after that particular reauthorization was completed, it seemed to Suzanne, plans began to be formulated to further undo the in-

21

tentions of the original legislation. Over the years, numerous amendments had been made to the sanctuary legislation; to Suzanne's dismay, ever weakening the program's original intent and making it more and more difficult to stave off the short-sighted assaults of other agencies. 'Course, she wasn't exactly impartial. Now, some thirty years since enactment of the Maine Protection, Research and Sanctuaries Act, some twelve sites had been designated, and there now seemed to be a significant loss of will to "fight the good fight" by the Program's small headquarters staff. Or maybe the will was there, but the money to support the troops was not.

The shortened staff meeting over, Suzanne returned to her windowless cube. She felt even more depressed than she had at the start of the meeting. She had been at the Program for almost fifteen years, during which time a total of four marine sanctuaries had been designated. Every one of them deserved, in her estimation, the special, national attention sanctuary designation was meant to afford; they were wonderful sites. But additional progress on increasing the number of sanctuaries had gotten really bogged down lately. The sites currently under consideration for possible designation had run up against strong opposition from the DOI and even the Environmental Protection Agency (EPA), which was the agency responsible for the disposition of "dredged" materials, or "spoils", as they used to be referred to. *How ironic,* Suzanne thought. *I thought the Environmental Protection Agency was supposed to* protect *the environment.* Publicly, anyway, EPA certainly agreed with the importance of protecting marine species and their habitat, unless such protection got in the way of their disposal activities. (Of course, EPA never said *that* publicly.) It seemed to Suzanne that "protection" had gotten very complicated; deciding once and for all its parameters and limitations had become endless exercises in negotiation, forever subject to changes in policy (and administrations). *Like shoveling sand against the tide,* she thought.

In thinking about the past development of sanctuary sites, however, Suzanne began to realize that the deeply entrenched, intractable position held by the DOI was now gathering momentum, and actually began in earnest during consideration of waters surrounding the four "Channel Islands" and Santa Barbara Island, offshore southern California. As usual, the dispute in this case centered around development of offshore oil. Originally, NOAA's proposed boundary for the sanctuary had encompassed waters extending from the mean high tide mark on the four Channel Islands and Santa Barbara Island seaward to twelve nautical miles, inside of which protective regulations would be put into effect. However, lengthy and sometimes unpleasant negotiations with the DOI ultimately reduced these buffers to six nautical miles. Among the final protective regulations was a prohibition on any new hydrocarbon activities inside the sanctuary boundary. The islands were strategically located in a transition zone of the Pacific Ocean, where warm and cool ocean currents converged and provided an ideal environment for a rich and diverse array of marine plant and animal life. Extensive kelp beds and rocky intertidal areas supported large populations of sponges, crabs, abalone, lobster, starfish, sea urchins, octopi and squid. Over sixty species of birds were known to breed in the sanctuary. The abundance of life also attracted more than twenty-five species of whales and dolphins; additionally, the islands provided haul-out and feeding areas for one of the largest and most diverse populations of seals and sea lions in the world. Several of these ocean-dwelling species were endangered; making it all the more important that the sanctuary waters be kept relatively secluded and undisturbed. *Small wonder,* Suzanne thought, *the Channel Islands had been one of the first sites NOAA pursued for sanctuary status.*

By the time NOAA began to actively consider additional sites off the Pacific, New England and Gulf of Mexico coastlines, the stakes for DOI and EPA were raised. The battles got fiercer; policy positions became more rigid. And with regard to the one active candidate site off New England, an additional agency entered the picture and further clouded and delayed progress on designation of the site known as Stellwagen Bank, offshore of Massachusetts. Suzanne knew quite a lot about this particular site, as she had worked almost exclusively on its development since 1984. By 1992, the designation was badly mired in disagreements primarily between NOAA and the Army Corps of Engineers (ACOE).

Stellwagen Bank, to Suzanne, possessed everything the Sanctuary Program sought to protect: a discrete and distinct oceanic feature which provided a complex system of midwater and benthic habitats, which in turn supported a vast array of benthic and pelagic species. The Bank itself was a glacially deposited topographic feature stretching for nearly twenty miles between the northern tip of Cape Cod and Cape Ann, Massachusetts. The Bank's rich environment provided feeding and nursery areas for more than a dozen cetacean species, including the endangered humpback, northern right, sei, and fin whales. The northern right whale in particular, was the most highly endangered of the great whales; scientists thought there were probably no more than 350 remaining in all of the Atlantic Ocean. Foraging activity by diverse seabird species was dominated by loons, fulmars, shearwaters, storm pertrels, cormorants, phalaropes, alcids, gulls, jaegers, and terns. Fish and invertebrate populations subject to seasonal and migration shifts included both demersal and pelagic species, such as bluefin tuna, herring, cod, flounder, lobsters and scallops. Finally, endangered leatherback and Atlantic ridley sea turtles used the Bank area for feeding. With all this varied and abundant life, the Bank was a popular destination for commercial as well as recreational fishing activity, and whale watching operations, which thrived during six months of the year. Suzanne had always felt a special connection with the New England region, and with Cape Cod in particular. Indeed, she hoped that when she retired, it would be to some small but comfortable cottage on the Outer Cape, possibly Wellfleet or Truro, or maybe Provincetown. Maybe there were more potential "soul mates" in P'town. She sighed. *Wonder how I'm going to get Doug to move to the Cape with me,* she silently queried.

Although the Bank was composed primarily of sand, it also contained significant amounts of gravel, and the Corps of Engineers viewed the Bank as a prime potential source of gravel that could be developed into asphalt. Of course, excavation activities, regardless of how carefully conducted, would irreparably change the Bank's profile, and substantially alter its productivity. There were, as Suzanne and others had argued, other sources of gravel that the Corps could exploit; sources that would not jeopardize the existence or continuing vitality of the abundant living resources dependent on the Bank. The arguments pretty much fell on deaf ears, unfortunately; and in the end it took an act of Congress to permanently prohibit any alteration of the Bank feature, thus ensuring its safe future.

Even though she felt her agency could have eventually prevailed in the dispute between NOAA and the Corps of Engineers, at least the Congressional act put an end to the prolonged and time-consuming interagency bickering that Suzanne, at least, felt demoralized the Sanctuary Program staff. Having made a number of business trips into New England to promote the Stellwagen Bank sanctuary proposal, Suzanne also had the opportunity to venture out by boat to the waters of the proposed sanctuary, where she on several occasions was rewarded by seeing several of the large whale species. It was always exhilarating, and she always came away from these encounters with renewed passion and resolve to do everything she could to protect this very special environment.

*   *   *

"Find out where exactly Hartford was at the time Kennard was shot," Clemsen barked at the two other investigators on the case. The sugar-high from the doughnuts always put him into some form of overdrive. "I know this guy is hiding something." With those elevated orders, the police returned to Hartford's office and continued to question Hartford and other members of his staff.

Clemsen opened the continuation of questions to Heartless later that afternoon with, "So, Mr. Hartford, we have just a few more questions concerning any knowledge you may have regarding Mr. Kennard's untimely and violent death. According to the coroner's preliminary findings, it appears that Mr. Kennard was killed sometime during the early to mid-afternoon of Tuesday, the fifteenth. Can you tell us exactly where you were at that time?"

Heartless rose quickly from his desk and, looking still flustered, responded, "Am I a suspect in this matter? I had nothing to do with this. Yes, I can tell you exactly where I was on the afternoon of the fifteenth. I was at a meeting with some folks at the Department of the Interior; I was nowhere near the Georgetown area when the shooting took place. Does that satisfy you, Detective?"

"And you can also tell me exactly who these Interior folks were, I'm sure," Clemsen continued. "And also for how long you were at their offices, right?"

"Yes, sure, Detective, I can tell you who I met with and for how long; I don't know what good it's going to do, though. I met with William Ross, a deputy policy analyst at Interior regarding a possible inter-agency agreement between DOI and NOAA regarding marine sanctuaries and potential research assistance at sanctuary sites the DOI might offer."

"What's in it for DOI?" Clemsen pushed.

"Well, the DOI has a much bigger budget than the Sanctuary Program, and a lot more experience with in-the-field research. If we could get DOI to share some of that expertise, we could maybe allow DOI to utilize some of the resources inside Sanctuary boundaries. 'Course, any damage that might occur to Sanctuary resources would have to be restored once the DOI finished its activities. It really was just a starting point of conversation for both agencies."

"Sounds a little bit like the fox messing around in the chicken coop to me," Clemsen said. "So how long were you at Interior that day meeting with Ross?"

"I guess I was there until three-thirty or four o'clock, Detective. Does that answer your questions?" Heartless seemed to relax a little, having answered Clemsen's questions and having substantiated his whereabouts on the afternoon of the shooting.

Clemsen felt a little heartburn begin to kick in (he must remember to take those antacids *before* the pain becomes visibly noticeable to everyone around him).

"Yeah, assuming your story checks out, that answers the questions. We'll be talking to Mr. Ross, just to tie things up."

With that, Clemsen made a few written notations and rose to leave Heartless' cubicle.

"Thank you, Mr. Hartford; we'd appreciate it if you would continue to make yourself available, should we require any additional information."

A faint smile passed across Heartless' face, as he allowed himself to realize that he had successfully gotten past Clemsen's grilling. *I'm home free,* he thought. *What a piece of work.*

The DOI deputy policy analyst was just finishing up a hastily drafted memorandum to his superiors concerning the very favorable potential deal he had arranged with James. T. Hartford, Division Chief, NOAA, that would give DOI virtually free rein to conduct activities and use resources inside marine sanctuaries—activities and uses that would otherwise be prohibited.

Like the smile crossing the face of James Hartford on the other side of town, William Ross beamed and even chuckled a little as he contemplated the praise and maybe even promotion this deal would bring to him. If this deal went through he could easily see himself as the new DOI policy chief. And it wasn't going to cost the agency that much financially, either, just some research and reclamation funds—pocket change, really. If there was one thing Ross was particularly good at, it was his ability to create a "win-win" scenario in his presentations, scenarios virtually impossible *not* to embrace. It was this finely tuned talent that had gotten Ross ahead at DOI, generally endearing him to his colleagues. His colleagues also often felt frustration in the presence of Ross's memos, of course, but Ross never felt threatened by their frustration; he knew they were just jealous. Ross slept well at night, never letting the petty jealousies of subordinates interfere with or get in the way of his well-planned personal agendas.

*   *   *

There was no faint smile crossing Clemsen's face, or chuckle from within him, either. He was pretty much stumped and back at square one, with no further leads to follow. His primary suspect was definitely covered and accounted for, even the apparent discomfort and seeming evasiveness displayed by Hartford had now been explained. "Damn it," muttered the detective, as he slammed the case file down on his desk and reached into the desk drawer for one of the peanut butter cups stashed there. "I was sure I had him; I was so sure. Now I got no idea." The peanut butter cup lay unopened on the desk. "This could get depressing," he muttered. He tossed the case file back on the "open" pile; his visions of promotion within the department quickly disappearing. "All I got is a gunshot victim who was at the downtown Commerce head-quarters a couple of hours before he showed up dead on the other side of town. There's no explanation of why Kennard was at headquarters, or who he was meeting with or why. Damn, this is aggravating."

So the case remained open. Clemsen came out of depres-sion only long enough to open and finish off the peanut butter cups in his desk, and Suzanne went back to fantasizing about her lost soul mate in Seattle. On one more business trip to Gloucester, MA to discuss management plans for the Stellwagen Bank Sanctuary with town officials, she was able to see the sleek black bodies of several humpback whales with their trademark long flippers who had uncharacteristically wandered in close to the town pier. It was not clear why the whales had come in so close to the pier and to humans; Su-zanne believed firmly there was a reason, but she wasn't sure what the reason was. She knew not everybody thought so, but to her the whales were still beautiful and seeing them was still a thrill almost beyond description.

*   *   *

With management plan revisions in hand, Suzanne re-turned to Washington, and resumed her boring paper-pushing exercises. Truth was, all she really loved was the immediacy of the battle for designation; it was what she did best. So the necessary but disagreeable routine went on and Suzanne endured it as best she could.

A couple of weeks later, an all-hands meeting was called for and convened at the Silver Spring offices by the NOAA Administrator and the Deputy Secretary of Commerce. Attendance at the meeting was mandatory, so Suzanne and others surmised this meeting held some important news. Indeed, it did. Deputy Secretary of Commerce Arnold Paulson was introduced by NOAA Administrator Ronald Wilson, and the "important news" soon followed in Mr. Paulson's remarks.

"Many of you have heard about the recent violent death of one of our Presidential interns, Justin Kennard. While his murder remains unsolved, the police are still actively pursuing several leads, and I have every expectation that his murderer will be apprehended soon. I want to address in particular the members of the Marine Sanctuary office, although all NOAA staff are directly affected by these developments, so pay attention.

"On the morning of his murder, Mr. Kennard paid a visit to Administrator Wilson and myself at the headquarters office downtown. What he shared with us that morning should affect all of you in the future; it will affect in particular the Marine Sanctuary Program. Mr. Kennard presented to us a proposed policy being developed in secret by a Sanctuary Program Division Chief and a DOI Policy Analyst. The proposed policy would allow DOI to conduct activities that would otherwise be prohibited inside designated sanctuaries in exchange for DOI money and expertise to conduct research and rehabilitation or reclamation activities to recover lost or exploited resources. Let me say, first and foremost, this proposed interagency 'agreement' between DOI and NOAA is an outrageously ill-founded policy shift. It is one that will *never* be approved. Just because DOI has more money available in its budget does *not* mean that the nationally significant resources of *any* sanctuary can be exploited or destroyed. As long as I am Deputy Secretary, this will never become policy in Commerce or NOAA. I'm sure Administrator Wilson feels as strongly as I do in this matter. The Division Chief at the Sanctuary Program directly involved in this complicity had better start now looking for employment elsewhere. Finally, we all owe a large debt of gratitude to Mr. Kennard for bringing this clandestine policy development to light. Thank you, Mr. Kennard, for saving the Sanctuary Program."

Whatever relief Heartless had experienced following Clemsen's investigation was now gone forever, as virtually everyone assembled at the all-hands meeting knew it was he who had betrayed, really, the mission and promise of the Sanctuary Program. There was nothing he could say to anyone there that would explain his actions; he was ruined.

*   *   *

"Wow, I almost feel sorry for Heartless, you know?" Suzanne whispered to Jodie as the all-hands meeting came to a silent conclusion. There had been no applause following Paulson's shocking statements; the audience was too stunned. As Suzanne and Jodie walked back to their offices, Suzanne commented on the police investigation into Kennard's death. "They don't seem to have a clue, do they?"

Jodie piped in a response that brought her friend to a stop in their short walk. "They never asked me; I would have told them."

"Jodie, you? You? Are you kidding? Why? Are you crazy?"

Jodie's response was uncharacteristic (or so Suzanne thought): "He blew me off for that lunch invitation. He shouldn't have done that; it pissed me off. I mean, who did he think he was, anyway? God's gift to women? The world's better off without him."

Suzanne was still standing there, waiting for some reason to appear to explain this madness. Jodie the clueless. She couldn't believe it.

"Are you going to tell the police?" Jodie asked.

Somewhere Suzanne found the strength to respond, as she looked at Jodie as she never had before. "No, I don't think so. Think I'll just let the detectives spin their wheels for a while." The thought had not so suddenly occurred to Suzanne that her close friend was unstable and potentially dangerous, even to her.

"Good. Then I can trust you?"

"You can trust me, Jodie."

*   *   *

In the quiet aftermath of all that had happened, Suzanne now had the thought that even though Justin may have been "God's gift to women," he was also, or could have been, her soul mate. He believed the right things. He said the right things to the right people. And he was buried somewhere in Wisconsin.

Two

Detective Clemsen Rises Again

The murder of Justin Kennard remained an unsolved mystery, and it still stuck in the craw of Detective Clemsen. In fact, the open case file on his desk, as well as the weekly chewing out by his lieutenant, were constant reminders, and it drove him crazy. He hated that file, hated not being able to bring that investigation to completion and closure. First grade Clemsen had never gotten the promotion he had felt sure was his at the outset of the investigation; he had been so sure that James Hartford (that slimy, devious low-life) was the murderer. *Well,* Clemsen told himself, *that case was history and there was little point in agonizing over it.* Like hell it's history; it isn't over.

"I could've made lieutenant by now, or at least sergeant," Clemsen muttered to himself as he picked up the dog-eared case file and thumbed through the findings and reports for about the one-hundredth time. Well, at least Hartford's secrets with the Department of Interior had been exposed and Hartford was looking for another job, with no recommendations from NOAA forthcoming to assist in his search for employment. By now, word of Hartford's deceit and betrayal had spread throughout NOAA and Commerce, and it was likely that Hartford would have to focus his job hunt on the private sector, or at least outside the federal government. *Got what he deserved,* Bud thought. But the case was still unsolved and still open.

Clemsen hoped that he could re-polish his otherwise unblemished reputation for solving tough cases by finding resolution and an end to what had become known in the precinct as the "asphalt robbery." There was a direct connection between the asphalt robbery and the Kennard murder case and Clemsen had that old familiar feeling about things being hidden from the light in this case, too. Clemsen remembered that part of Hartford's misguided plans for an inter-agency partnership would have involved allowing the Army Corps of Engineers to extract gravel from an underwater sand and gravel bank now designated and protected as a marine sanctuary.

In his rudimentary understanding of the causes and effects of tampering (or extraction activities) on the Bank, Clemsen knew that this would be a bad thing for the health and lifespan of living species dependent on the Bank environment.

Jeez, he thought, *I never figured I would know so much about the ocean.* But he had begun to understand why sanctuaries were so complicated, and why protecting them was so important. *I really don't like being in the ocean; I like seeing it from the shore. But some people are obsessed with it. Go figure,* he thought. Even though there were other sources for gravel, sources not inside a protected area, the Corps had tried their damnedest to get to those found inside the Stellwagen Bank Sanctuary. In the end, it took an act of Congress to prevent them from doing so and changing forever the shape and productivity of the Bank. All this fighting over gravel to make asphalt for roads. Too many cars and too many roads, anyway. They should give it a rest. *Make my life easier, that's for sure,* Clemsen concluded to himself.

After another month had passed and there was still no resolution to the Kennard murder, Lieutenant Shaw got tired of chewing out Clemsen and assigned the case to another detective, Daniel Parker. This angered Clemsen, and when

Parker approached him for the case file and reports, Clemsen was maybe less than hospitable. Bud had never been known in the precinct as a team player.

"Yeah, sure, you can have the case file and investigation reports; take 'em," groused Clemsen. "For all I care, you can keep 'em, too. You're not going to find anything."

"Ya know," Clemsen continued, "the asphalt robbery thing is not really a crime. It's just a lousy policy decision by some federal agency. Gives a whole new definition to 'road rage'; maybe they should call it 'asphalt anger,' " chuckled Clemsen, as he picked over the remaining doughnuts left in the Krispy Kreme box on his desk. Obviously pleased with himself for the clever play on words, Clemsen continued, "I should've been a stand-up comedian; could've had my own show, like Jay Leno or something. At least the pay would've been better than what I'm making here. Ah, hell; who starts over at my age, anyway?"

Detective Parker picked up the case file and reports, and responded, "Yeah, you're right, Bud. Even the ants living in your desk have better taste than that. Thanks for the file." And Parker quickly disappeared down the hall to his desk, where he started poring over the reports. In some ways, Clemsen was glad that Parker had the Kennard case now, maybe he would self-destruct with it and could now move on to other things and find a way to resurrect his reputation as a great investigator and closer. *I should've had my own show, like Lieutenant Colombo, or something. I mean, that guy always figured out what was going on, and who did it. He never failed. He also never got that raincoat cleaned; God, that thing was disgusting, should've been burned.*

Life for Clemsen was filled with "Should've been's and could've been's." Bud always felt he just missed the big time, and the big payoff. Nobody recognized his talents or appreciated his efforts. When these thoughts got to him, Bud also realized that he was allowing himself to become bitter about the way his 'career' was coming to an inglorious close. How many years did he have left on this job, anyway? Maybe ten or twelve? Well, maybe a lot could still be done in that time. *Yeah,* Bud thought, *there's still cases to be solved and bad guys to be locked up. Guess there always will be; no shortage in that department.* He felt better, as he always did when he reached for the comfort of a fresh doughnut or two.

*   *   *

Back at the sanctuaries program office, Jodie had set her sights on new conquests. Now recovered from Justin's death and feeling somewhat assured that Suzanne would not reveal the truth to the authorities, she considered her options for a short-term agenda. There was little to select from in the office; most everyone was married or otherwise attached. Justin had presented a breath of fresh (and handsome) air; *too bad he was so caught up in himself,* she thought, *too bad.* It was his loss. She had carefully disposed of the gun she'd used on Justin; Jodie figured she would not have use for it again. Good thing she had learned about silencers, too; the hit had not made much noise at all.

Jodie Cranson was not a woman to be scorned, as if she had to remind herself, not ever. She was not to be messed with, either. She was to be respected and admired, even envied. And people should never forget it. At least this was the way Jodie analyzed things. As long as everyone understood this, things would play out the way Jodie knew they should. And I'm not sharing my secrets with anyone, ever. Jodie was one smart cookie, that much was for sure. She definitely viewed information as power, and that which she knew was guarded zealously. It was a careful balancing act, appearing to be friendly and helpful while never really providing full answers to direct questions. Over the years, Jodie had gotten good at this act. And over time Suzanne had come to realize Jodie was as phony as they come. Good and true friends were hard to come by, especially in this office, and although Jodie's insincerity was maddening, Suzanne took private pleasure in the total lack of taste Jodie consistently displayed in her dress. She was about twenty pounds overweight, yet that excess weight never deterred Jodie from wearing cheap knockoffs of the type of clothing that should only be donned by models.

Meeow, thought Suzanne. *Some "best friend." Well, at least I got a marine sanctuary designated. That's more than Jodie will ever do. The only things she's good at are eating, being two-faced, and killing people. No class at all. What's next for me, Suzanne wondered idly. Can I take early retirement, and make ends meet somehow and get Doug to move to Cape Cod and find something meaningful (and profitable, hopefully) to do there?* Truth be told, she didn't really care if Doug went with her or not. But that was another story, one that would probably require the insights of a therapist. And that was a road Suzanne was not prepared to venture down. Not now, anyway. Creating the really tough (and maybe unrealistic) goals for herself had always been a notable characteristic of Suzanne's. *But what the hell,* she thought, *I've pretty much decided there's no such thing as "soul mates."* Might as well go for the place you've always wanted to live; what's to lose? Escapism at its finest. Having been at this government job for more than fifteen years, and being more than a little disenchanted with it, Suzanne began to inquire discretely about how to make a final exit, with retirement, to Cape Cod. Her destination of choice was somewhere on the Outer Cape, like Provincetown or possibly Truro. And yeah, she would take Jodie's secret with her. What Jodie had done didn't really matter to Suzanne; she didn't really care. What she cared about was finding her way back to the Cape.

In fact, it didn't even really matter to Suzanne whether she lived on the ocean or on Cape Cod Bay; both were desirable, wonderful places. People always seemed to think that living on shore facing the Northern Atlantic was the only way to have the good fortune of "living on the ocean." Living on the Bay was just as rewarding, and was at least slightly more protected than the oceanfront. And the right whales seemed also to know this; the Bay provided a good feeding area for this most highly endangered of cetacean species. Unfortunately, the bonus to human residents of the Bay had not escaped the real estate market; prices to live on the Bay were as high (or higher in some cases) as living on the ocean.

*   *   *

Mostly because he couldn't let go entirely of unresolved business, Clemsen had made a copy of the entire Kennard case file before handing the original over to Parker. Maybe something in the file would reveal new insights into solving this murder, maybe not. But Clemsen couldn't let the chance for redemption, if there was any, escape. So Bud found himself poring over the same notes that Parker was. He pondered in particular over Kennard's co-workers at the Sanctuary office: had they all been thoroughly interviewed; were there no stones left unturned?

They had investigated the possibility that the murder was a robbery gone bad, but Kennard's wallet was still on him, apparently untouched. And besides, Kennard was only going to be in Washington for about six months; he hadn't really made many acquaintances in the couple of months he'd been here. So the murder appeared to be personal, which led the investigation toward Kennard's co-workers at NOAA. Clemsen again went through the individuals questioned, checked carefully employees' relationships with Kennard and where they had been at the time of the shooting. It seemed that not many co-workers had any relationship at all with Kennard; he just hadn't been there that long. And they all could account for their whereabouts on the day of the murder.

Clemsen got to the interview with Suzanne Douglas. Ms. Douglas was pretty much dismissed as a suspect, since she had been out of town on business until only three or four days before Kennard's body was found in Georgetown, near his rented condominium. She hardly knew the man; certainly there was no particular relationship between the two. Next in his review of notes and interviews was that of Jodie Cranson, who seemed too much of a "space cadet" to be capable of anything like this. And again, there didn't appear to be any relationship at all between Kennard and Ms. Cranson. Cranson had been out of the office, however, during the time when Kennard was shot and killed. She told investigators she was on her lunch hour, but wasn't very specific about where she was during that hour or so. *Maybe we need to pin that location down a little more precisely,* Clemsen thought. He started making notes about follow-up inquiries, even though technically he was off the case.

Clemsen continued going through interview notes of the remaining Sanctuary office staff members, and also those of the Department of Interior and Army Corps of Engineers, looking for any inconsistencies in statements made to investigators. He was looking in particular for any motivation on anybody's part for killing Kennard. After four hours, Clemsen was thoroughly exasperated. He couldn't find any holes or inconsistencies or motivations anywhere. "We must have missed someone, or maybe the killer was someone once employed by the Sanctuary Program office," he muttered to himself. *Nah, I'm getting off the track here. If it wasn't a total stranger, which I doubt since there was no robbery involved, the killer had to be someone Kennard knew, someone likely at NOAA. But mo-tive—that's a problem,* he thought.

"Clemsen, get in here," shouted Lieutenant Shaw. "I got a new case for you, so you can put your investigative talents to some use, instead of stewing over the Kennard mess. By the way, I saw where you made a copy of the Kennard file. You *are* off that case, you know; let Parker have a crack and *you stay out of it,* clear?" Clemsen muttered his understanding, as he closed the Lieutenant's office door behind him. He didn't re-ally want anyone else hearing either the chewing out or the fact that he had made copies of the Kennard file.

"What's the case?" Clemsen deferentially inquired of the Lieutenant. He hadn't heard of any new murder investigation, and he wondered what the Lieutenant was up to.

"Bud, I want you to take some vacation. You need to get away from this for awhile. I checked the leave schedule; you haven't taken a day off in almost two years. I know you've got all those files at home and you're still thinking you can solve the Kennard case, but it's not your case anymore. I want you to get out of here; go somewhere and *relax.* Believe it or not, we can survive without you for a couple of weeks. Consider that an order."

Clemsen must have looked totally crestfallen and de-jected, as his boss added, "Bud, I'm a little worried about you. You're a good detective, but you've let this Kennard case take over your life. I want you to bring those files back here and get out of town for a while. There will be no disciplinary actions taken, but I mean it, Bud, *let go of this case.* Now get out of here."

Clemsen returned to his desk, not knowing exactly what to think or to do. Apparently, he was on vacation, effective im-mediately. He slowly put together the few things he couldn't live without for the next two weeks and, like Elvis, left the building. *Guess I have to return the files to the office, but the*

Lieutenant didn't say when I had to have them back, he thought. Once home in his apartment, and because there wasn't any rush to pack or anything, Clemsen changed clothes, cracked open a diet soda and plopped down on the fraying sofa. It was mid-afternoon; he was restless. What the hell was he going to do with himself for two weeks? *It's not like I have all the money in the world to take some exotic trip somewhere,* he thought. After a hour or so had passed, the thought occurred to Clemsen that he was going to have to relinquish those files and he would not see them again. He picked up the pile of interview notes from the small desk in the living room and dispassionately started going through them again. When he got to the notes from the interview with Suzanne Douglas, Clemsen read a little more carefully. Although she was not implicated in the Kennard murder, the information provided by Douglas reminded Clemsen of the details he had picked up about the Sanctuary Program, and the passion with which Douglas had spoken about the large whales and the other ocean critters living in the protected Stellwagen Bank Marine Sanctuary off the shores of Cape Cod. He flipped through the notes until he found the address and the phone number for Ms. Douglas. Maybe he'd call her and get some information about where to go and where to stay if he decided to visit those whales and the sanctuary office on the Cape.

"Ms. Douglas, this is Detective Clemsen, from the D.C. Police. I was one of the investigators in the Kennard murder case, and I talked to you and some of the others who work at the Sanctuary office. You remember me?"

Suzanne took a deep breath and responded, "Yes, of course, Detective, I remember. Did you ever find out who killed Justin? Did you have any more questions?" She couldn't believe he was calling again; she thought she had told him all she could the first time around. 'Course that was before she knew about Jodie.

41

"Uh, actually, uh, no, we haven't yet determined the killer. But we will. I was actually calling you about another matter."

Suzanne was silent, and waited for Clemsen to go on.

"See, I have two weeks vacation coming, and I was kinda wondering if you could give me some information about seeing the whales at the Stellwagen Bank Sanctuary. Oh, and also about where to go and places to stay and stuff like that. You seemed to know so much about the Sanctuary, and about the whales and all that. I just thought I'd like to see them, and since I've got this time off, you know?"

Quickly, several disparate thoughts amassed, ranging from suspicion and disbelief at the detective's call to profound relief that he appeared to have no more questions about her possible implication in Kennard's murder. But finally, her thoughts settled on the fact that she did know a lot about the Stellwagen Bank Sanctuary and the whales he was asking about.

"Sure, Detective, I can give you lots of information about the whales at Stellwagen and about when you can see them, and whale watching trips out to the Sanctuary, and places to stay and all that stuff. When were you thinking about going up to the Cape?"

"Well, my vacation starts more or less right away, so I guess I could go in the next couple of days or so."

"You may be in luck, then, if you want to try and see the northern right whales; they tend to show up in Sanctuary waters in early spring, usually late March or early April, before continuing their migration further north up into Canadian waters. They don't stay very long. The other whale species usually show up a little later in the spring, some staying through the whole summer, into September or even early October. Of course there are other marine mammals like Atlantic white-sided dolphins and sometimes Orcas or killer whales, and a few pinniped species, like harbor seals or gray seals. You can even occasionally see endangered sea turtles, although they're harder to spot in the ocean. 'Course, they aren't marine mammals. I guess the large whales are the most fascinating things for people to see, because of their size and magnificence, and their activities which may seem like playful antics to us land-bound creatures. And when you think about the long migratory journeys the whales and also some of the sea turtles make, it's pretty overwhelming to think about."

Realizing she had been talking non-stop for several minutes, Suzanne came up for air and took a deep breath. "You still there, Detective?"

"Yeah, still here. Where do I go to see all this? And where can I stay?"

"Oh, there are plenty of places to stay, either a motel or a B and B, or there are a lot of people who'd be happy to take you in for a couple of weeks; I know of several. The Sanctuary office opened initially in Plymouth, which is not actually on the Cape, but now it's located in Scituate, which is further north of the Cape. The staff have much more room there, and it's more accessible to getting out to the Sanctuary."

"Sounds great. Where's the best location for getting out to the Sanctuary?"

"You'd probably be well-located if you stayed in Scituate or somewhere else where there are commercial whale watch boats going out to the Sanctuary. Places like Provincetown, which is at the far end of the Cape, or some of the towns to the north of the Sanctuary and off the Cape, like Gloucester. Most of the whale watch vessels are located on the Cape, though. It's a pretty big business; over two million people go out on those boats every year."

"Jeez, I had no idea. So there's a lot of money in running a whale watch boat, huh?"

"Well, there's more money if you have more than one vessel. But there's always the expense of maintaining the boats, which isn't cheap, and insurance. And paying the boat captains, and interpreters to identify the whales and explain whale behavior to your paying customers. It's a tough life, but from what I've heard, a very rewarding one. And, at least from my perspective, it's not only entertaining, but whale watches provide the opportunity to inform the public in a very personal way about the often precarious plight of these animals, and what people can do to maybe make their existence a little easier."

Suzanne took a deep breath as she silently considered telling Detective Clemsen about her personal plans (not yet approved by the powers-that-be) to retire from the Sanctuaries program and move to the Cape herself. She hesitated, because her experience had been that talking about any desired dream before it happened was sure to doom the dream to failure. She was a great believer in omens; if the Office of Personnel Management did not approve her application for early retirement, there was a reason that had nothing to do with the government.

It was an omen portending some other course of events. She believed she had no control over the course of events, or the course of any set of events. She decided to try really hard not to discuss her early retirement plans with the detective. However, she couldn't hold herself in; and after several minutes of talking about whale watching and marine mammals in general, Suzanne started talking about her plans to retire and settle on the Cape, possibly in Truro.

"You know, Detective, I'm hoping to take an early retirement from NOAA and settle somewhere on the Cape. I would love to live there; I can never seem to get the Cape out of my mind. Unfortunately, it seems the rest of the world has also discovered the Cape and wants to move there, too. The price of houses has gone through the roof and it doesn't show any signs of slowing down. Not sure I could afford it, but it's a good dream. 'Course, everything depends on whether or not the government approves my application for early retirement. You know, I've got some unused vacation, too; maybe I could join you on your trip to see the whales, and I could be looking for places for sale, what do you think?" She could hardly believe all the stuff she had just said to someone she really didn't know at all. *How typical,* she thought. *I never could keep my mouth shut. And what about Doug? Would he be willing to move to the Cape? Big questions, no answers yet. I don't think he's ready to retire, and I know he doesn't really share my passion for whales and New England in general. Yeah, there's a lot of things that would have to be resolved before I (or we) packed up and moved to the Cape.*

Now Clemsen was quiet, not knowing how to respond. After what seemed like an hour or more, he finally said, "Yeah, sure; I could use the company. Not that it's any business of mine, but don't you have a husband?"

"I do, but I don't think he'd be interested in this trip. And besides, to him, this will just be another business trip to New England." Suzanne could feel the beginnings of deceit growing inside her. *Must remember to keep things straight,* she thought.

"So when were *you* thinking about going?" Clemsen asked.

Suzanne allowed herself a half smile and responded, "Oh, I could leave in a couple of days or so."

Three
On the Road

And so it was that Suzanne and Detective Clemsen embarked on a trip together to Cape Cod: he to see the whales of Stellwagen Bank Sanctuary, she to look at houses *and* see the whales of Stellwagen Bank Sanctuary. Detective Clemsen was like a small child, filled with excitement and anticipation at the prospect of seeing the large whales that Suzanne had spoken about. Suzanne also was filled with excitement and anticipation, but not just because of the whales. She was somewhat filled with feelings of guilt because she had left Doug with the impression that this was just another business trip to New England. Ah, well, he wouldn't want to go anyway, she told herself.

They met at D.C. National (she still refused to call it Reagan National), and boarded a plane to Boston. Things had really changed since 9/11; the security at both airports was unbelievable. *September 11th has really put our lives in a different perspective,* Suzanne thought to herself. Once they got through security at Boston's Logan Airport, she shared some of these thoughts with the good detective. "You know, I don't mind all the extra security measures, do you? I think we all took our safety for granted before the terrorist attacks; now I think we all pay a little more attention to what's going on around us, and that's a good thing, don't you think?"

Clemsen answered quickly, "Yeah, I agree. Just hope people can keep it up. I haven't noticed the crime rate decreasing much, though."

They found the car rental desks and soon enough located their assigned vehicle and, with the help of local maps, found their way out of Logan Airport and on the road to the Cape. Clemsen wanted to drive, which was just fine with Suzanne, since she almost always got lost despite the most careful preparations and directions.

Once headed in the right direction, Suzanne asked, "So Detective—can I call you Bud—how long have you been with the D.C. Police Department?"

"Fifteen years and counting. I have to admit, though; I've been giving some thought to retirement."

"So I guess we have a lot in common; both of us been on the job for fifteen years and both of us contemplating retirement. You have any plans about what you want to do after you retire?"

Clemsen shifted in his seat and glanced in the rearview window. "Nah, not really; I want to see more of the country, startin' with these whales, you know?"

Good answer, Suzanne thought. *Me too, pal, me too.*

Traffic was pretty light, and they made good time in getting to Scituate, where the Sanctuary office was located. Suzanne was a little tired after the two-hour trip, but Clemsen seemed refreshed and ready to go.

Scituate was a pretty little coastal New England town. Clemsen marveled at the neat order and cleanliness of it. 'Sure isn't much like D.C., is it?" he remarked as they pulled into the parking lot and headed for the large, low building which faced the water.

"This building used to provide southern New England offices for the Coast Guard," Suzanne explained, "but they outgrew the space and provided it to the Sanctuary Program for, as I understand it, really nominal rent."

47

They entered the Sanctuary office; Suzanne had only been in the new office once previously, so it was also a fairly new experience for her as well as for Clemsen. The office was light and airy, and filled with the activity of the small startup Sanctuary staff. Suzanne was immediately caught up with excitement of the staff, which currently consisted of the sanctuary manager, deputy manager, an administrative aide, an outreach/education coordinator, a research director, and one part-time enforcement officer. There were tons of volunteers swarming around as well.

Suzanne introduced Bud to those staff members she knew, and almost immediately Karen Clapham, the outreach/education coordinator, launched into her well-rehearsed and often-used promotion of the Sanctuary's objectives and programs. "We've only been here for about a year now, and we're already getting tons of local and regional visitors to the office, as well as requests from schools and research organizations for information about what people can do to help further the Sanctuary's programs and expand its influence to the user and interested public. There are many different users of the Sanctuary, you know. Sometimes their interests conflict, but one of the overriding principles of this and of any national marine sanctuary is that all uses be accommodated, so long as those uses don't diminish or destroy the viability of Sanctuary resources. It's often a pretty complicated balancing act."

Suzanne thought to herself, *She's got to come up for air sometime soon.* About then Karen *did* come up for air, and Suzanne asked her about plans for expansion of the staff, particularly in the enforcement program. "Yes, we do need additional help with enforcement of Sanctuary regulations. The primary attraction for visitors to the Sanctuary is the whales, of course, and there are too many violations of approach and distance rules by both commercial and private boaters. Right now, the Sanctuary budget does not allow us to hire as many enforcement officers as we need. So we're doing the best we can with the one part-time officer and lots of public outreach activities to better inform the public about why it's important to give the whales the space and distance from human activities that they need and deserve."

You're beginning to preach now, Suzanne thought. *Although you're absolutely right, of course. And you should preach. Most people don't realize that their activities can be harmful to these wonderful creatures; most people only want to see the whales, not disrupt their normal activities.*

Clemsen had been following Karen's presentation with rapt attention; however, he was beginning to get restless. He really wanted to get out on a boat—a *big* boat—and see some whales. By now, however, it was too late in the day to be starting out on a venture to the Sanctuary. "Hey, Bud, there's someone here I want you to meet." Suzanne took his arm and pulled him over in the direction of Dr. Charles Baio, standing by the research director's desk, engaged in lively discussion of the feeding patterns of right whales.

"Dr. Baio, it's good to see you again; it's been too long," Suzanne said as she extended an arm around Baio's shoulder. "I'm sorry to interrupt this heavy discussion; just wanted to let you know I'm around for the next couple of weeks. We should get together for lunch or a drink or something before you head back to Provincetown. Hey, there's someone here with me I'd like to you to meet. Bud, this is Dr. Charles Baio, Director of the Provincetown Center for Cetacean Research. He knows more than anyone on the planet about whales. Bud has recently become mesmerized by the Stellwagen Sanctuary and the National Marine Sanctuary Program. In his other life, Bud is a detective with the D.C. Police Department. Did you all hear about the murder of one of our Presidential interns last fall? Bud was one of the investigating detectives; that's how he came to find out about the Sanctuary Program. But that's another story. Anyway, after listening to me yammer on and on about Stellwagen, he just had to come see for himself."

"Good to meet you," said Dr. Baio, and research director Mason Weisner also stood up and extended his hand in welcome. *That's the thing about New Englanders,* Suzanne thought, *they're always cordial, sincere, even if they don't spend a lot of energy on talking. That Karen must be from another part of the country.* "Probably too late to get out to the sanctuary today; it's about a two-hour boat trip just to get there," Mason added.

"Well, we'll check into the Pilgrim Plantation Motel and find a place for dinner. We can head out tomorrow morning, okay, Bud?" Suzanne stepped to the front door of the office and took in a deep breath of the fresh salty air. God, it was good to be back; it was where she belonged. She turned around and went back into the office, greeting those staff she knew and catching up on recent developments since her last visit. As she thought might happen, both Mason and Karen offered to put them up for their visit to Scituate, but Clemsen seemed a little squeamish about accepting the offers of staying in someone's home, and Suzanne secretly kind of agreed. So ultimately they decided to graciously decline and settled into the Pilgrim Plantation Motel instead.

"If you're looking for a good place to eat, try the Happy Iguana in town; it's a pretty good Mexican place," suggested Mason, "and you know New England's not noted for its Mexican cuisine."

"Sounds good to me," piped in Bud, "I'm starving."

"Me too. Okay, let's go. Wonder if they can do quesadillas," Suzanne said.

Suzanne turned once again to leave the office and Clemsen happily followed her to the car. "Let's get checked into the motel first, okay? Then we'll go find the restaurant."

The Pilgrim Plantation Motel was a modest, two-level structure with a "vacancy" sign hanging out front. Normally this would make Suzanne a little suspicious about the quality of the accommodations, but after all, it was only mid-March. The season hadn't really opened up yet, unless, of course, you were a northern right whale. If there were any right whales to be seen, this was the time of year. 'Course, to the land-locked, it was still rather cool, probably around forty or forty-five degrees. Nah, to a whale this would be just about perfect weather. Clemsen and Suzanne got adjoining rooms on the ground level, and as soon as they dumped their bags they set off for the Happy Iguana and some margaritas.

Having placed their orders, Suzanne inquired of Clemsen, "So, Bud, did you bring your seasick pills?" Clemsen looked at her with that "oh no, not that" look and said, "Ah, jeez, do you think it's gonna be rough out there? If there's one thing I hate, it's throwin' up."

"Well, Bud, it *is* the open ocean, you know. Even on calm days the ocean is always moving. 'Course, it doesn't bother some people. You ever been on a boat before? If you can keep your eyes on the shoreline it helps; you know, a stable point of reference. Helps with the equilibrium."

"Man, the only boat I ever been on was a harbor patrol motor boat, and we never got outside the harbor, know what I mean?"

"Well, don't worry; the motel probably has some seasick pills you can take, and you might not even need them. Who knows? You might do just fine; you'll be so excited about seeing the whales, you won't even think about being sick."

Turns out the restaurant did have quesadillas, and they weren't half bad. Despite his earlier claims of being famished, Clemsen uncharacteristically didn't eat all that much. *All that discussion about being seasick probably had something to do with it, too,* thought Suzanne.

51

"Jeez, I'm really excited about seeing the Sanctuary and the whales," Clemsen said, as he pushed aside his plate. "I know it's too late in the day to go out now, but let's go down to the docks and see the whale watch boats, okay?"

They walked down to the docks and could see that most of the slips were still empty, not having returned yet from the Sanctuary. There were two boats tied up at the dock space rented by Cap'n John Whale Watches. Cap'n John had a total of four boats, two of them out today at the Sanctuary. "Well, it's still pretty early in the season, and it's *cold,* especially on the water. I hope you brought warm, waterproof clothing," Suzanne said, as she more closely inspected one of the docked whale watch boats.

"Jeez, you sound like a commercial for Eddie Bauer's or something," quipped Clemsen, "I got enough clothes to stay warm."

The whale watch boats were indeed professional vessels, outfitted to ensure passenger comfort and security. *No wonder they were expensive to acquire and maintain,* thought Suzanne. She wasn't sure how fast the vessels could travel, but they offered a variety of amenities, including a closed cabin in the vessel's mid-section, where passengers could get a hotdog or hamburger from the grill and a drink to wash it down. Even though the whale watch operators did their best to inform passengers ahead of departure of the necessity to dress appropriately, it was always amazing to Suzanne how many people seemed to think the trip would be just a little sail around a big, calm pond. She had actually seen women climb (with some difficulty) onto these boats wearing high heels.

"Aren't these boats wonderful?" Suzanne exclaimed, "I really hope we see lots of whales tomorrow."

"Yeah, they're pretty neat, Suze, I'm looking forward to this trip to the Sanctuary tomorrow. When's the first trip scheduled to leave?" It was the first time Bud had called her by a nickname. She silently tucked this away for private savoring later. "Somewhere around nine A.M., I think. We can check the schedule at that kiosk at the end of the dock."

"Cool. Say, by the way, do you know if there's like a Quick Copy place near here? I gotta make a copy of some files and return them to the precinct back in D.C."

"Yeah, I think there's a Quick Copy in the little strip mall on Harbor Street here in town. I think it's next to the Krispy Kreme doughnut shop," replied Suzanne.

"How fortunate; I could use a doughnut or two," Clemsen replied. "Wouldn't you just love to have ten percent of the Krispy Kreme franchise? 'Course, I'd probably eat all the profits."

They found the kiosk at the end of the dock and determined that the Cap'n John's boat was scheduled to leave at 7:00 A.M. "Whew, brutal, man," exclaimed Clemsen. "Well, keep in mind it takes about two hours to get to the Sanctuary from here," Suzanne reminded him.

"I can make it if you wake me up early tomorrow," Clemsen said. He was getting excited now at the prospect of actually leaving the harbor aboard a Cap'n John's whale watch vessel and moving through the cold northern Atlantic toward the Sanctuary and the elusive northern right whale. "Okay, we can do this; it'll be great!"

"We better get our tickets for the trip now, and then get to the Quick Copy so you can copy your files and get them mailed back to the precinct. Nothing like a relaxed vacation, huh, Bud? Before we settle in for the evening, I want to call Dr. Baio at the Sanctuary office before he heads back to Provincetown," Suzanne said. "I want to get any ideas he may have about houses in Provincetown or Truro."

They got their tickets for the 7:00 A.M. trip, and then drove back to the Pilgrim Plantation Motel, where Bud could grab the files he wanted to copy and Suzanne could call Dr. Baio.

"Dr. Baio, it's Suzanne Douglas. Sorry to bother you, but I wanted to catch you before you left the Sanctuary office and headed back down to P'town. I have an unrelated-to-whales question I wanted to get your thoughts on."

"Always to the point, aren't you, Suzanne? What's on your mind?" Dr. Baio responded.

"Well, for one thing, Bud and I are going out tomorrow morning early on one of the Cap'n John's boats, and since we won't be back until around two o'clock or so, I wanted to be sure to catch up to you before you left town."

"What's the question, Suzanne?"

"I wanted to get your thoughts on realtors familiar with the P'town and Truro areas who might be able to give me some guidance on possible houses in those areas."

"So you're thinking about buying a house on the outer Cape? I know of a couple of good realtors in P'town who I'm sure would be happy to show you what's available. I'll be back in P'town on Thursday; why don't we have that lunch at the Moonakis Café and talk some more, okay?"

"Sounds great, Dr. Baio, I'll see you at the Moonakis for lunch on Thursday, and thanks."

Lunch plans for Thursday made, Suzanne said to Clemsen, "Okay, let's get those files copied and mailed back to D.C."

They drove to the small mall on Harbor Street and found the Quick Copy store. As Clemsen was opening the files and reports to be copied, Suzanne said to him, "Are these the files from the Kennard case? Bud, I know you've got your suspicions about who the killer might be; give me a hint. I've got some thoughts, too."

"Oh, yeah? Like who do you think did it?"

"Oh, I have no idea, really. Could I take a look at your file

54

notes and reports? Is that snooping where civilians shouldn't be snooping?"

"It's definitely snooping where you shouldn't be snooping," Clemsen replied, "and I could get in a lot of trouble if I let you look at these files."

"Gotcha, Detective, civilian backing off here," Suzanne smiled. Suzanne wandered casually out the door of the Quick Copy store, and said to Clemsen, "You ready for a couple of doughnuts? My favorites are glazed and glazed with chocolate frosting."

"Mmm, and the caramel-frosted ones, too. Let me finish up copying these files, and I'll join you."

As Suzanne was heading toward the Krispy Kreme counter, she was thinking to herself, *I want to see the notes in the files; see if there's any comments about Jodie. But guess I can't let Bud know I'm snooping. How did this innocent little trip to the Cape get so complicated? I should really concentrate on looking for houses and talking to Dr. Baio. Hope I remember how to find the Moonakis Café.*

Clemsen finished the copying and joined Suzanne next door in the Krispy Kreme store. "Boy, it sure smells good in here; I could eat a dozen!" he exclaimed. They held their orders down to two apiece, however, and ate them quickly, as they made their way to the nearest post office to mail one set of files to the precinct back home.

"Well, that's done; what a pain in the ass," remarked Clemsen when they had dropped the thick envelope through the "next-day delivery" slot at the counter.

"Have you ever noticed, "Suzanne said, "how the day seems to zoom by when you've got twelve thousand little 'must do' things to get done, and when you finally finish them all, you realize the day is gone already? I mean, it seems like we just had breakfast, and here it is, already four o'clock. It's almost happy hour."

"Close enough for me," Clemsen said, "let's go back down to the docks and see if any of the boats have come back in. There's bound to be a bar close by."

They wandered back over to the harbor and saw that indeed, there were a couple of whale watch boats now docked in their assigned spaces. Passengers had mostly off-loaded and headed for their cars or the nearest restaurant or bar. Clemsen almost immediately regained his childlike enthusiasm and walked up and down the docks, drinking in the smells of the ocean and excitement of the passengers.

"Anybody look a little green around the gills?" Suzanne asked of the naturalist/interpreter as she got off the vessel. She looked familiar, but Suzanne couldn't immediately place a name with the face. "It was pretty rough out there; we had a few people lose their breakfast, but all in all, it wasn't too bad. We did see three or four right whales, though; that was the most exciting part," the interpreter said. The interpreter looked to Suzanne to be not more than twenty years old. *I could never do this. Wonder if they saw any calves,* she thought, knowing that any such sighting would be cause for even more excitement and speculation about a possible recovery in this cetacean species' overall population. She wished, as she was sure many others did, that there was something she could do. But the northern right whale in particular was so elusive, its migratory patterns and behavior activities so poorly known and understood, that doing anything much to help was more often than not, an exercise in frustration.

As she turned away from the last of the whale watch boats, Suzanne asked of Clemsen, "Ready for a drink? I haven't had a cranberry cooler in about a million years; local delicacy, you know." They found their way to the Dockside Dinghy, where Suzanne felt like she owned the place. Clemsen quickly opened the menu and ordered a lobster roll and a cranberry cooler.

"Umm, this is good, what's in it?" Clemsen asked.

"Lobster, a little mayo, lemon juice, and spices," Suzanne knowingly responded.

"No, dufus, the drink, the *drink*," Clemsen chuckled in response.

"Haven't the foggiest, darlin'," came back the not-very-good Southern drawl. "All I know is that they'll put you on your backside in a hurry. Like so much else in life, it's good to pace yourself with these things. Enjoy."

By now, it was close to 8:00 P.M., and the sky had turned to night. Having had several cranberry coolers, Suzanne, at least, was feeling no pain and ready to call it a night. They were going to have to get up by 5:00 A.M. or so to make it to the docks in time for their early whale watch. Clemsen also, seemed a little uncharacteristically mellow.

"Whadda say we call it a day, and get some sleep before the wake-up call comes at 5:00 A.M.?" Suzanne said, as she headed for Harbor Street.

"Sounds good to me; believe it or not, I'm stuffed; couldn't eat another lobster roll if my life depended on it," Clemsen said. They slowly and carefully walked back to the motel, said goodnight, and went quietly into their adjacent rooms.

Suzanne undressed quickly, brushed her teeth and fell into bed. She was sound asleep within minutes. Clemsen also got undressed, brushed his teeth, and fell into bed, assuming the position (on his back) that Suzanne referred to as the "beached whale" position, from which soft moans could be heard emanating from his throat. He had eaten too much. An inauspicious beginning to the next eighteen or so hours.

Sleep came easily and quickly to both; 5:00 A.M. just came too soon.

Four
Thar She Blows

Even at 5:00 A.M., Suzanne could tell it was going to be a beautiful, if choppy day on the water. It hadn't taken any wake-up call to rouse Clemsen; he was dressed and ready to go at 5:30. They quickly made their way down to the docks and found the Cap'n John whale watch vessel still quiet in her dock space; not many people had arrived and boarded yet.

"Do you want any breakfast or coffee before we get on board?" Suzanne quietly offered.

"Nah, I'm still full of lobster rolls. Let's get on this baby," Clemsen responded brightly.

"You take some seasick pills?" She was beginning to sound like somebody's mom.

Clemsen ignored the question and started up the ramp. "I want to go all around this tub and stake out the best spot for seeing the whales and also the best seat on the inside." *Spoken like a true whale watch rookie, who doesn't yet understand that once underway, there won't be any "assigned" seats or saved spots on the railing for this trip,* thought Suzanne. Clemsen's unfamiliarity and childlike enthusiasm were endearing traits, and she felt that much closer to him because of those traits. She followed him up the ramp, watching his butt move slowly and easily in front of her. There was something about a man's ass that was surely the sexiest part of his anatomy. Even the ugly men of the world still had better asses than women in general. Although she understood why women had bigger hips than men, she still thought it was patently unfair that she always had more trouble getting into pants and getting her shirt to tuck in and lay flat against her skin and never cause a visible outline of her panties. *Life was so unfair,* she thought and sighed.

Finally, at 7:00 A.M. sharp, the boat blew its horn and started to chug out of the harbor and on to the open sea. Almost immediately, the naturalist/interpreter, perched on top of the vessel with high-powered binoculars in hand, stood near the microphone and broadcast her information about the Sanctuary and the marine mammals they were likely to see this time of year. Once she started talking, Suzanne recognized the naturalist/interpreter was Karen Clapham, from the Sanctuary staff. Clemsen was not paying much attention; he busied himself moving from one side of the vessel to the other, trying to find the perfect viewing spot. "Bud, relax. It's going to take about two hours to get to the Sanctuary, and you may not see the right whales. They're pretty scarce, and we can't get too close to them anyway," Suzanne reminded him.

"How come?" Clemsen asked.

"Well, there are both distance and approach rules for any vessels in these waters. So even if we spot a right whale, we can't get too close, or maneuver the vessel in such a way that it causes the whale to change its movements or direction in any way," Suzanne explained. "I'm sure the interpreter will explain this also, as we get closer to the Sanctuary."

So on they went. The ocean was pretty choppy, but the sky was brilliant. Suzanne was supremely content and happy; this was where she was supposed to be, back near the only sanctuary she had ever really cared about. Clemsen seemed happy, too; he was still the child about to see his first great whale. As Suzanne leaned on the vessel's railing, her face to the wind, she idly thought about how to get to Bud's investigation reports. Maybe this evening, she could distract him with some menial little trip to the drugstore or something, and she could sneak a look at his file notes to see what comments he might have made about Jodie.

Just then, Clemsen came out of the cabin to the railing where Suzanne was lost in her private reveries. "Hey, stranger, you feeling okay?" she asked.

"Yeah, I'm glad I took those seasick pills ahead of time, though," he said. Maybe it was the magic of the moment; she didn't know for sure, but for the first time, Clemsen put his arm around her and pulled her tight to his side. It felt wonderful, and Suzanne was sure she would remember this moment always. More than wonderful, it felt right.

"Hey, look at that! Is that a whale?" Clemsen shouted. It was difficult to see much of anything in the choppy water, but Suzanne thought she saw a large black body, moving slowly near the surface. Clemsen was really wound up now, moving quickly up and down the vessel's railing and pointing excitedly. "Is that northern right whale? Did we just see one of the most endangered marine mammals in the world?" He was almost beside himself.

"If it was a northern right, then we just saw *the* most endangered whale in the world," Suzanne answered. They continued straining to get another glimpse of the large black body, but it was very difficult, and they could not. Clemsen was moving from the left side of the boat to the right side, trying not to miss seeing anything.

"Know why they're called 'right' whales?" Suzanne quizzed Clemsen.

"No, how come?" responded Clemsen, not taking his eyes off the ocean.

"Because back in the days of commercial whaling, they were considered the 'right' whale to harpoon, because they are slow moving and, once harpooned, tend to float near the surface, making recovery easier than other whales."

"No kidding. I guess that explains why they're so endangered huh?" Clemsen had now turned his attention to Suzanne. "Added to the fact that apparently the species does not reproduce very often, so there are not many calves born in a season," she added.

"Man, it's a tough life if you're a whale, huh? I can see why the government feels the need to protect these critters by passing rules and regulations and stuff. And I can sure see why the Sanctuary staff needs more enforcement officers. Too bad they can't put a fence around the sanctuary to protect the whales and stuff from thoughtless boaters."

"You kind of hit the nail on the head about putting a fence around the sanctuary," Suzanne said, "it's been maybe the biggest problem of the Sanctuary Program, the lack of public knowledge and support because you can't really see what's being protected. It's all under the water's surface. That's why both enforcement and education are such important parts of the Sanctuary Program."

"Yeah, I hear ya," Clemsen said. He seemed lost in thought as he gazed out at the ocean.

They didn't see any more right whales that afternoon; they did see a couple of white-sided dolphins and numerous seabirds, the names of which neither Clemsen nor Suzanne knew for sure. As the afternoon wore on, both of them were glad when the whale watch vessel turned around and headed back to Scituate. It was close to 1:00 by the time they got back to the harbor. *Boy, I must be getting old, or out of shape,* thought Suzanne, *I'm really exhausted.*

"You know what, Bud? I've got a raging headache; I think I'd like to go back to the motel and lie down for a while. Would you mind getting some aspirin for me at that drugstore in town; I'm sure I forgot to pack any. What a jerk, huh?"

"No problem, Suze. You just relax and I'll get some aspirin for ya, okay?"

Almost as soon as Clemsen left for the drugstore, Suzanne pulled out the investigation reports and started looking for any notes made after his interview of Jodie. She found the interview notes quickly and found the comments Clemsen had made concerning Jodie's whereabouts at the time of Justin Kennard's murder. The detective had noted the need to pin down a little more specifically where Jodie Cranson was during the hour she said she had been on her lunch break. Apparently, Jodie had not been very forthcoming with that information. There were notations about the need for follow-up inquiries.

Aha, thought Suzanne, *this must have been the point when Bud got taken off the case.* She quickly put the interview notes back as she had found them and returned to her room and laid down. Although her head was pounding, she felt better. Clemsen returned shortly with the aspirin and poured a glass of water for Suzanne. "Boy, the combination of bright sun and the rough sea can really knock you out," said Suzanne, as she sat up to take her aspirin. "I feel like I could sleep for another two or three hours easy."

"Go ahead," said Clemsen, "you're on vacation, you know. I wouldn't mind taking a little snooze myself."

As he laid down on the bed next to her, Suzanne had momentary feelings of guilt, as she thought about Doug, but only because she thought she was *supposed* to feel guilty. She hadn't done anything to feel guilty about—yet. And she didn't really care that much; Doug didn't really matter that much to her anymore, anyway. They both fell into that most delicious of treats: the afternoon nap; it lasted for a couple of hours. And Suzanne felt so comfortable and comforted being close to Bud. *They may be stolen moments,* she thought, *but they're* my *moments and no one can take them away from me.* By the time they "kind of" awakened, it was close to 4:00 P.M.

I suppose I should call Doug, Suzanne thought, as she arose slowly from the bed. *Oh man, oh man oh man; I could sleep all night, no problem.* She felt like she was in a heavy, heavy fog, and it weighed a ton, pulling her back down to the bed. It took a monumental effort on her part, but she finally got up and splashed some water on her face. Now somewhat revived, she wandered out of the bathroom and quietly said to Clemsen, "How you feeling, partner?"

Clemsen looked over at her and said, "Great, just great. Those seasick pills really work."

"So do the aspirin," Suzanne responded, "better living through chemistry, huh?"

"You watch a lot of TV or something?" Clemsen joked. Suzanne smiled at Clemsen's unknowing reference to the fact that she *did* watch a lot of TV, more than she should, that was for sure.

"You know, Bud? I think I'll let you go out on the whale watch alone tomorrow. I've got to meet Dr. Baio and talk about the availability of houses in the P'town or Truro areas. He's agreed to meet me for lunch at the Moonakis Café over in town, so I'll take the rental car while you're out on the whale watch, okay? I should be back by the time you get done with looking at whales."

"Okay with me," Clemsen replied, "I wanna talk with the interpreter person anyway about enforcement needs in the Sanctuary. So I'll meet you back here probably around three or four P.M., right?"

"Sounds good to me," Suzanne said, "in time for cranberry coolers, okay?"

"No repeat of the last time, right, Suze?" Clemsen looked at her with some concern.

"Right, Bud, no repeats."

Suzanne breathed a deep sigh of relief; now all she had to do was find the Moonakis Café and call home to Doug. *Sure, like it's nothing. It's not like I'm a born juggler or something. What in the hell am I going to say to Doug? I thought life was supposed to get easier when you're over fifty,* she thought.

Finding the Moonakis Café wasn't as tricky as she thought it might be; Scituate was, after all, a small town. And when she got there, Dr. Baio was just pulling up in his old Jeep.

"Hi, Charlie Baio," Suzanne shouted as she drove into the small gravel parking lot next to the restaurant. They shared a warm, old friends, it's-been-too-long embrace and went together into the café. Charlie never failed to amaze Suzanne, and she imagined everyone else that knew him had similar impressions and feelings. Suzanne figured he was pushing sixty; yet he looked the same as when she had first met Charlie in the small offices of the Center for Cetacean Research, some fifteen years ago, to talk about the nomination of Stellwagen Bank as a potential national marine sanctuary. Charlie had helped the rookie Sanctuary Program employee with the nomination document, and mapping the coordinates for the proposed boundary, as well as alternative configurations. Charlie's real passion in life was doing whatever he could to lessen the detrimental impacts of fishing activities to cetaceans who somewhat routinely became entangled in fishing gear by directing and helping with disentanglement activities. When not out on the water, he was active in guiding the center's efforts to get the word out to the varied user public, and to commercial and recreational fishermen in particular, about the necessity of care in the proximity to whales who shared the same waters. The activities of Charlie and the Center were a natural fit with those of the new Sanctuary, as it initiated programs to heighten public knowledge and support for the Sanctuary's environment.

"So, Charlie," Suzanne started.

"Let's order lunch first," Charlie broke in, "I'm starving."

"Good idea, I'm hungry, too. What's good here?"

"Almost everything; stay away from the fried clams, though. Not their best effort," Charlie chuckled.

If anyone should know good fried clams from bad ones, he should, Suzanne thought.

"Okay, I'll have a tuna sandwich on rye toast," she said to the waitress.

"Me, too," said Charlie, and the waitress disappeared into the kitchen after quickly leaving two ice teas on the table.

Lunch orders settled, Charlie said, "Boy, it's good to see you; how've you been and how are things in D.C.?"

"I sure do miss being up here, I can tell you that, Charlie, I think my heart is always on the Cape. That's why I'm interested in looking at houses in P'town or maybe Truro. I thought you might have some good realtor contacts, since you know *everybody* in P'town."

Charlie smiled and responded, "It's true, I do know everybody in Provincetown and most everybody in Truro. And baby, just 'cause I love ya, I'm going to let you in on a true insider's secret. There's a great realtor in town, Marti Benjamin, who's getting ready to list a lovely little place on Commercial Street that I think you might like a lot."

Suzanne's eyes got big and she moved her chair close to Charlie's. "Really, Charlie? Where on Commercial Street? How much does the owner want for it? God, this is so exciting." *Could it possibly be this easy?* Suzanne wondered to herself.

"That's the good part, Suzanne, it's the house two doors away from our offices. Close to the harbor, and the center of town. The owners are retiring to a nursing home in Wellfleet, I think. Don't know what they want for it. It'd be great to have you as a neighbor; you could maybe help with our research efforts and outreach," Charlie concluded. They finished their lunch and caught up on old times. Charlie concluded by telling Suzanne that he'd be back in Provincetown on Wednesday and would put Suzanne in touch with Marti Benjamin, also of P'town.

Her head swimming with the speed and thrill of these distinct possibilities, Suzanne drove back to the harbor to await Bud's whale watch vessel return from the sanctuary. She could hardly wait to tell Bud how what she viewed as "destiny" was about to fall into her lap. Finally, *finally,* at about 2:00 P.M., she saw the Cap'n John boat come into view and back slowly into its reserved boat slip. Even from his perch on the upper deck of the vessel, Clemsen could see the grin on Suzanne's face, as she waved excitedly to him. He, too, had some exciting news to share. Bud had spent a fair amount of the trip time talking with Karen Clapham, the naturalist/interpreter aboard the Cap'n John boat about the Sanctuary's need for enforcement officers on its staff. She had invited him to come back to the Sanctuary office, where they could discuss in detail the qualifications and training necessary for the position. Both Suzanne and Bud were eager to share their happy news with each other. Little did they realize how fully their lives were about to change forever.

As he got off the boat, it was as if the two had not seen each other in a year or more, and they embraced with such fervor and intensity that some of the passengers stopped to stare at what appeared to be the reunion of two lovers. She didn't care about the stares, even those of Karen Clapham, who certainly knew Suzanne was married, and this guy was not her husband. Even so, it didn't matter. Here, it didn't matter. It was part of the magic of New England and whales and the Cape in particular. It just didn't matter.

They got back to the motel to change clothes, and Clemsen announced he was hungry, hungry for some French fries and a cheeseburger. Over the late lunch, Suzanne decided to tell Bud that she had to talk to her husband, Doug. She didn't really know what to tell Clemsen; nothing really "over the line" had occurred between them, but it might well. In fact, it probably would, truth be told. They had only been here a few days, and yet in some ways, it seemed like they had always been here. Suzanne didn't really know how Bud felt about their relationship, and in some ways, she didn't want to bring it up. The feelings she was experiencing for Bud were forcing her to examine those she either had or no longer had for her husband. She knew she had to confront those feelings honestly and come clean with Doug; did she really want to continue their marriage or bring it to an end with as little pain and discomfort as possible? Suzanne didn't know how she ever thought this could somehow be neatly avoided, like no one would ever know these feelings and activities occurred. With heavy sighs, she finally said to Clemsen, "I have to talk to Doug, and we have to make some decisions about our future, and whether it's going to be one spent together or one spent apart. Man, I didn't want to have things come to this, and I sure as hell didn't want to involve you, Bud, but I'm afraid it's going to. I'm sorry for getting you dragged into this; I should have dealt with all of this long before I came up here with you. I hope you can forgive me, Bud."

With that unresolved and unfinished discussion lying on the table between them, there seemed to be not much else to do but to change the subject and talk about houses and possible employment by the Stellwagen Bank Sanctuary staff. After all, Doug wasn't there, and these heavy decisions couldn't be made over the phone. Suzanne sighed, and turned toward the ocean. *In many ways,* she thought, *these decisions would be easier if Doug were here, and not Bud.* But she just didn't feel "warm and fuzzy" anymore about Doug. They had shared almost ten years together, and although she greatly admired

Doug and relished his devotion, she couldn't honestly say she held great passion for him. She made plane reservations for the return flight to Washington on the following Tuesday. She then returned to the table, where Clemsen was wolfing down his cheeseburger and fries; he certainly had risen above any queasiness he might have experienced while on the ocean. Yeah, Bud was a natural on a boat. He'd probably be a great enforcement officer for the Sanctuary.

The next morning, they went out again to look for right whales at the Sanctuary. Although they didn't see any, they and the other passengers got an unexpected surprise. Breaking the water's surface just inside the Sanctuary were several black bodies whose shapes and behavior characteristics were unmistakable: humpbacks.

"Wow," exclaimed, Bud, "what are those? They're not northern right whales, are they?"

"No they're humpbacks!" exclaimed Suzanne. "They're not supposed to show up this early in the season. But who knows? Maybe something in the water temperatures or currents or the food supply made them change their migratory timing. Pretty exciting, huh?" *This is good,* thought Suzanne, *it'll give Bud the opportunity to see the behavior patterns of humpbacks and how they differ from right whales.* Suzanne went up top of the vessel, and she and Karen both counted probably six humpbacks, and they stayed around for the entire afternoon they were in the Sanctuary. It was easy to forget the northern right whales, as rare a sighting as they were, in the presence of seemingly playful and exuberant humpbacks.

By the time they got back to the harbor, both were exhilarated and exhausted. Clemsen, although tired from shifting from one side of the whale watch vessel to the other, was clearly excited (as well as little windburned) at having seen his first humpbacks. By the time they got off the Cap'n John #2, Clemsen was already talking to anyone who listened; "Aren't they magnificent? We should do everything possible to protect them."

Yeah, he's going to be a great Sanctuary enforcement officer, Suzanne thought.

So Bud and Suzanne went from the boat to walking around the harbor; both talking about their excitement *du jour*: Bud was enthralled with the appearance of humpbacks so early in the season and Suzanne was almost giddy about the distinct possibility of a house in Provincetown. "So, Charlie's going to put me in touch with Marti Benjamin, the realtor, when he gets back to Provincetown on Wednesday. The house Charlie is talking about is only two houses away from his research center and close to the Provincetown harbor. God, this is so exciting, Bud; I might actually be able to afford it. 'Course, I have to deal with Doug somehow. That's going to be a bummer."

As promised, Charlie had called Marti Benjamin as soon as he got back to Provincetown, and Ms. Benjamin got in touch with Suzanne at the motel in Scituate. Not like she was anxious or anything; she knew the house would sell quickly once listed. It was just that everyone, including Marti, had such admiration for Charlie, that an endorsement from him almost certainly gave the prospective buyer an inside track.

"Ms. Douglas? This is Marti Benjamin, Outer Cape Realty. Understand you're interested in some property in Provincetown. Charlie Baio called and said you were looking. What'd you have in mind?"

The speed and lack of warmth, for want of a better word, in Ms. Benjamin's opening questions put Suzanne off a bit. She figured maybe Benjamin had had a tough day or something. She hesitated a bit in answering. "Well, yeah, I am interested in finding something in the P'town or Truro area. Preferably on the water." She realized how stupid she must have sounded, but something in Benjamin's brusque and quick opening remarks probably caused Suzanne to "drawl" a bit more than usual.

"You're not from around here, are you?" Marti continued.

"I guess that's obvious; I grew up in Virginia. But I've spent a lot of time on the Cape both as child with my parents and more recently, in connection with my job," Suzanne answered.

"And that job might be?" Marti asked abruptly.

"I'm with the National Marine Sanctuary Program, part of NOAA, within the Department of Commerce," Suzanne replied.

"A fed, huh? I got little use for Feds. They make it next to impossible for working folks like me to make a living. It's a good thing you're a friend of Charlie's; he's okay. If he says you're okay, we'll talk. He may be thinking about the small house a couple of doors from his whale research center. The owners are old and sickly; they're moving to a nursing home in Wellfleet. It's a two-bedroom cottage, in pretty good shape, about fifty years old. Doesn't need much work; you could move in as is. Asking price $500,000. You interested?"

Suzanne had to catch her breath at the asking price before responding, "How firm is the price?"

"Up for discussion, sweetie. When are you gonna be in Provincetown? This thing will probably be listed by Wednesday or Thursday. Expect it'll move pretty fast."

"I can be there by late morning, Thursday," Suzanne heard herself answer. She had no idea how she was going to pay for this thing, but it sure sounded like the right house and the place to be. *Man, this is no way to buy a house,* she thought. *Or maybe it's the* only *way to buy a house.* Suzanne agreed to meet Marti at the house at 55 Commercial Street, Thursday morning, at 10:00 A.M. She was shaking when she hung up the phone.

70

"Bud, I'm going to drive down to Provincetown early Thursday morning to look at that house Charlie Baio told me about near his research center. The realtor called me at the motel here and gave me some information about it; it sounds perfect, but I have no idea if I can afford it. Want to come along and see Provincetown?"

Clemsen smiled at Suzanne; he could tell this was her dream. Although he wanted to be with her more than most anything, he also really wanted to take Karen Clapham up on her offer to discuss more fully a Sanctuary enforcement officer position in Sciutuate. "Thanks, Suze, but I think I'll stay here and talk to Karen about Sanctuary enforcement. I can tell we both got our dreams working here, and I'm not gonna get in the way of yours. Why don't we hook up back here when you're done with the realtor, and we can figure out what's next. I have to get back to D.C. by early next week, and I guess you do, too, right?"

"Yeah, you're right. I've got to figure out what to do about Doug, and what to do about early retirement from NOAA. Man, I don't want to leave here, but there's unfinished business at home." She turned to her notebooks, primarily to check on personal resources, and to start getting her thoughts together about Doug and the future of their marriage. *Life is still getting much too complicated,* she thought, *entirely too complicated. I can't deal with all these carefully timed orchestrated decisions. Sure hope nobody makes an offer on that house on Wednesday.*

"Hi, hon, it's me. I'm just checking in to tell you I miss you and we're seeing some *great* whales, and a whole pod of early humpbacks right here in the Sanctuary, can you believe it? They're not supposed to be here this early; they're probably a month or more ahead of schedule." Her rapid account of the past ten days left even Doug fairly breathless. Truth was, she did kind of miss him; Doug was a good husband with a

71

myriad of flaws, most of which only endeared him to her further. *Who among us has no flaws,* Suzanne thought, *and it keeps life interesting in any event.* Nonetheless, it was Doug's near obsession with trying to please everyone that had pushed her to find personal fulfillment elsewhere: like researching and studying the whales of New England, and doing what she could to educate the public about what they could do to help make life a little easier for these "denizens of the deep."

"So, what's going on at home?" she asked. They made idle conversation for a few minutes; Doug making his usual comments about his sales rep job and the "assholes" he had to deal with on a daily basis, which included both the support staff in the company he worked for and the clients he called on daily who never seemed to appreciate how invaluable his attention to their needs was. *Ah, the life of a regional sales representative. You never get the respect and appreciation you deserve,* she thought. *In retrospect,* she thought, *you should have gotten more of both.*

Suzanne did not say anything to Doug about the house she was going to look it Provincetown. She figured the timing was not good; it would all come to light within a couple of weeks, anyway, when she envisioned herself signing the sheaf of papers necessary to gaining ownership of the modest little cottage facing the ocean and the clean New England air, and supporting the persons lucky enough to reside in such a paradise.

Suzanne was up early Thursday morning after a night of not being able to sleep at all. Like she always did at home, she went to the window (in this case) of the motel room and peered out even before she went into the bathroom to dress for the day. Although it was still dark, she could tell the weather was not going to be as idyllic as it had been the past several days. *Typical New England,* she thought, as she got out of the shower, dried her hair and applied make up. She dressed quickly, and pulled together the papers she had assembled last night and thought she might need for reference today when she met with Marti Benjamin. Within an hour and a half of getting up Suzanne was on the road and heading out toward the Outer Cape. *This was the best part of the day for travel,* she thought, as she pulled out onto State Route Three, south of Boston, and headed for the Bourne Bridge which crossed over the Cape Cod Canal (a marvel brought about by those friendly folks at the Army Corps of Engineers), and where the road changed to Route Six and one found oneself actually on the Cape, finally. *At last,* she thought, *at last. I'm home at last.* As she crossed over onto the Cape, Suzanne thought about how the Canal, connecting Buzzards Bay to Cape Cod Bay, saved boat captains, commercial and recreational alike, the considerable time and expense of having to traverse the entire periphery of the Cape to get from one Bay to the other. *I guess the Corps does do some good work,* Suzanne thought, as she pulled into a gas station/convenience store, to fill both her gas tank and personal tank with gasoline and coffee and cranberry muffin, respectively. She wasn't really hungry, but supporting the local economy seemed the right thing to do.

The morning sun was just beginning to provide faint illumination, and Suzanne pressed the little rental car on, shifting onto Route 6A, which more closely hugged the Cape Cod Bay shoreline. She passed through West Barnstable, East Dennis and Eastham, where the road turned sharply north and headed directly toward the "clenched fist" of Provincetown. She was now on that portion of the Cape where not only the road but the land itself became much more narrow; she could begin to see where the sand from the shoreline had blown onto the road. As she passed Wellfleet, Suzanne thought about the elderly couple who were moving into a rest home there and silently thanked them for making this house available to her. *Yeah, available,* she thought, *for a mere four hundred thousand or so.* They probably had no idea how important this house was to her. God, she hoped no one had already put a contract on the place.

She slowed down and stopped to look at Truro, which was smaller than she had remembered and utterly charming, as the realtors would describe it. Good place for writers and isolationists, those among us who want to be alone. *Stephen King would like it here,* she thought, realizing that Mr. King was probably situated in an area even more isolated and further to the north. "Up to Banga, or somewhere like that," Suzanne muttered in her best imitation "Down East" accent. It was about 9:00 A.M. when she reached Provincetown, and when her stomach started to knot up. Marti Benjamin's reputation, especially among federal employees, was legendary. Rumor had it that Ms. Benjamin "ate feds for breakfast," and based upon her conversation thus far with the "monster from P'town," Suzanne had no good reason to doubt the rumors.

Marti Benjamin had directed Suzanne to meet her at 10:00 A.M. at the Fisherman's Café on Shank Painter Road in Provincetown. Although she didn't know exactly where Shank Painter Road was, she figured it couldn't be too tough to find; she would just ask some local in the small town. As it turned out, the café was just around the corner from the P'town police station, and everybody seemed to know of it and where it was. The café was definitely a local hangout for fishermen and town merchants alike. Suzanne found it with no trouble, and quickly parked the car and went inside to await Ms. Benjamin's arrival. It was almost 11:00 A.M. and Suzanne was on her third cup of coffee when the object of her dread finally arrived. From the minute she first saw her, Suzanne could easily understand why people were leery of Marti Benjamin. With no apology for being almost an hour late (Suzanne figured it was carefully calculated to further put her off), Ms. Benjamin sauntered in the café like she owned the place and sat down at the table across from her. Physically, she was not a big person. She was sturdy in build and looked like she didn't get her appearance from a gym; she had earned it through hard living. The most striking feature about Marti Benjamin was the black eye patch covering her right eye socket. *No wonder she intimidates people,* Suzanne thought. From preliminary inquiries to her co-workers about Marti Benjamin, Suzanne knew Marti Benjamin had spent many years as a commercial fisherman, and this foray into real estate was a relatively recent change in lifestyle. This morning, she wore blue jeans, a more-or-less clean work shirt and sturdy work boots. She could just as easily been dressed for running a fishing boat out to the Sanctuary for a full day of gill netting for any variety of fin fish. She did not know for sure, nor did it matter one way or the other, but Suzanne had also been told by Charlie Baio that Marti Benjamin was a lesbian, or as Charlie referred to her, a "dyke." Being a dyke didn't seem to matter much to anyone; it just added to the mystique.

The two women exchanged perfunctory pleasantries, and Marti ordered some coffee. Cutting right to the chase, Marti said, "We got two offers on the house yesterday, but it ain't under contract yet. Still want to go see it?"

"Yes, I want to see it," Suzanne responded, trying not to sound overly enthusiastic. Suzanne tried not to look at Marti's eye patch, but it was almost impossible to avoid doing so. She was dying to know how the dyke had lost her eye. Maybe sensing Suzanne's curiosity Marti offered a brief explanation on their short drive over to Commercial Street. "Nothin' very dramatic; I got caught by some flying fishin' gear. Hurt like hell, I can tell ya. Was about then I decided to get outta fishin'. Too dangerous."

By the end of the explanation, they had arrived at 55 Commercial Street, and it was to Suzanne at least, the perfect house, but she tried not to show it. In realtors' terms it was a "darling" (another word for small) little bungalow with shingled roof and shuttered windows that opened out to the Provincetown harbor. It was steps away from the harbor itself, where she could see all the daily activities of the staff and volunteers at the Cetacean Research Center. And a short walk in the opposite direction led to the center of town, with all its cute (also meaning small) tourist shops and restaurants and bakeries. That was one of the things she liked about New England coastal towns: everything seemed to be accomplished in miniature. The house was, indeed, exactly what Suzanne had hoped for and fantasized about for so long. It had two bedrooms, a remarkably well-appointed kitchen and a very comfortable living room overlooking the harbor. And no lawn to labor over; just pretty little window boxes filled in the summer with petunias.

"So what kind of shape is the plumbing in? Any major repairs needed?" Suzanne inquired.

"Nah, like I said, this place is in good shape and you could move in right away if the contract is accepted by the sellers. They've been offered $410,000 and $420,000; you wanna kick it up to $430,000?" Marti said. Suzanne could tell this could get into a bidding war and that she wouldn't be in the war for very long. Using what she hoped was her most forceful delivery, she responded to the realtor, "Ms. Benjamin, I am prepared to offer $440,000, but that's the limit."

"See what I can do, sweetie. I'll make the pitch to the sellers agent," Marti said. She couldn't help it; but Marti made her uncomfortable. Any kind of discussion or dealing with her made Suzanne feel like she was waiting for the other shoe to drop.

"Good. I've got some errands to run up in town; you can reach me at Charlie's offices late this afternoon or evening; you got his phone number?" Suzanne said as she rose to leave this wonderful house and get to her rental car. Once again, she was shaking, and she hoped that the realtor didn't see it. She thought back to her weekend sojourn in Seattle about a million years ago, and how she had escaped into the safety of a taxicab and rushed off to the anonymity of her hotel, in an effort to escape having to confront Pete and explain why she was walking around downtown Seattle near his office. She was shaking then, too; the knot now residing in her stomach had the same uncomfortable feeling.

She walked up, strolled really, to the center of Provincetown. She didn't really have any errands to run; she just wanted to reacquaint herself with the small-town friendliness and utter charm that was Provincetown. And frankly, she wanted both to get away from Marti and to allow her time to present the offer to the sellers' agent. *This is good,* she thought, *the bakery is still here and doing a great business. Guess people will always need somewhere to get a good cup of coffee and freshly baked scone or loaf of bread. And people are still finding inspiration to paint their interpretations of local vistas.* There were four or five easels set up around the periphery of the harbor, some facing the water, some facing the town behind. And there was one facing the somewhat stylized statue rendition of a humpback whale planted squarely at the center of the head of the harbor. *Wonder if any of these artists have ever seen the real thing out in the water,* Suzanne thought to herself. Probably not, since transporting all those paints and easels would make the trip not very feasible, she concluded.

All in all, this town was still a neat place to be, and to maybe find some meaning again to her life. Suzanne finished strolling along the primary roads, checking out the local shops and real-estate storefronts, with pictures in their windows of houses available for sale or rent. The house on Commercial Street was not pictured in any of the store fronts she looked at; *probably an inside deal,* she thought. But based on the asking prices of the houses she saw pictured, the price of the Commercial Street house was certainly in the ballpark with the others. Man, she hoped the owners would accept her offer; the house was the perfect answer to her needs and dreams. Maybe I'll even take up painting, she thought, as she ended up back at the bakery, where she got some coffee and a cranberry (what else?) scone.

When she got back to Marti's small office at Outer Cape Realty, the one-eyed wonder met her with the unbelievably happy news: the owners had accepted Suzanne's offer. To the chagrin of Marti, it turned out that the elderly couple were big supporters of the Stellwagen Bank Sanctuary, and were thus very inclined to sell the house to the federal employee who had been so instrumental in getting the site designated. *Nothing wrong with their mental faculties,* Suzanne thought to herself. *Now how am I going to come up with the down payment?*

Timing is everything in life. This was confirmed beyond any further question when Suzanne called Doug again to let him know about her flight arrival time on next Tuesday, and in the course of their brief conversation, Doug told her that her application for early retirement had been approved. This meant retirement money would be paid to her in a lump sum, and she would have the money available for down payment with a considerable amount to spare. And she was pretty sure she could get Charlie to hire her as a research/public outreach assistant, thus assuring her of a reasonable income from a job that she felt she was born to: making life better for whales and other marine mammals. Suzanne felt the knot in her stomach loosen its grip, even though she was incredibly excited. Everything was moving fast, and it at least looked like it was all falling into place. While still in Marti's office, she wrote with trembling hands a check for fifteen percent of the purchase price and handed it over to Marti. "For once, I can say it's been a pleasure doin' business with a Fed," she gushed, or as close to gushing as Marti ever got.

She had to consciously pay attention to her speed driving back to Scituate; the last thing she needed was a speeding ticket. *Can't afford any foolish expenditures,* she thought. Suzanne pulled into the motel parking lot around 6:00 in the evening, and found Clemsen waiting for her. "Bud, I got it, I got the house! God, I can hardly believe this is real; I don't know where to start. There's so much to do and it's all happening so fast," Suzanne excitedly relayed to him.

"That's great, Suze," Bud exclaimed, "you should hear how my talk with Karen Clapham went. I think the Sanctuary wants to hire me as an enforcement officer. I'd get to wear a uniform and everything!"

"What about your job with the D.C. Police Department? Aren't you putting the cart before the horse a little bit here?" Suzanne replied.

"Well, to tell you the truth, I didn't leave on vacation from the Police Department under the best of circumstances. I was kinda forced to take some time off. My boss thought I'd gotten too obsessed with the Kennard murder case. I wasn't obsessed, just wanted to find the killer and wrap that thing up," he said. "I mean, I can't stand knowing the murderer is walking around scot free, know what I mean?" Bud was really getting worked up in talking about the real circumstances of his being on "vacation."

Suzanne thought maybe this might be a good time to let Bud discover by himself what she had known for several months, but couldn't tell him outright without breaking her promise to Jodie. How to work it into conversation, though, that was the thing. She decided to take the indirect route. "So, Bud, about what time did your reports say the murder occurred? I mean, could all the Sanctuary Program employees you guys questioned account for their time?" She attempted to appear nonchalant.

"Well, the murder occurred sometime in the afternoon, and yeah, everybody seems to be covered in terms of their whereabouts at the time. 'Cept maybe for Jodie Cranson. She was pretty vague about where she was. I gotta look at my notes, but seems like she said she was at lunch, but couldn't say for sure where she was. It was a pretty long lunch hour, I can tell ya that."

Ah, the perfect time to interject what I know about Jodie's late lunch hour, Suzanne thought. "You know, Bud, I'm pretty sure that Jodie was having a very late lunch at her desk that afternoon. Seems funny, since she was always talking about the need to lose weight; I mean, that's a lot of lunch for one day, don't you think?" There, the truth was laid at Bud's feet. It was up to him to do something with it.

Five

Sounding

"Are you kiddin' me?" Bud exclaimed. He immediately got to the phone and called the D.C. Police Department. "Let me talk to Parker," she heard him say excitedly. "Parker, it's Clemsen. I know, I know; I'm on vacation. I'm up near Cape Cod; yeah, it's great. Listen, I don't know where you are on the Kennard thing, but I think I got a break in the case. Go pick up Jodie Cranson. Seems she was lying about her whereabouts during the early afternoon the day of the murder. Seems she had a late lunch at her desk; sort of double-dipping, so to speak. I think she's your killer. Motive? Hell, I don't know. I've been talking to one of her coworkers at NOAA, and she's been giving me some read on Cranson's personality. Seems Cranson had a thing for this Kennard guy and he blew her off. Oldest motive in the book, although a little extreme, right? Don't know how I missed it."

When Bud had finished talking to Parker, he turned to Suzanne and said, "You went into the files, didn't ya?" For an instant, she thought he was really going to deck her, but within just a few seconds, it was like Bud just realized what Suzanne had done: she had solved the case. The Kennard case was brought to closure. "And you're going to get the credit for it," Suzanne said, as she stood in front of him. "Your reputation is salvaged, darling. Oh, Bud, I'm so happy for you." They grinned at each other simultaneously and fell into a warm and now-familiar hug.

"Did you know," asked Karen Clapham, "that whales sometimes exhibit a behavior known as 'sounding', which is their way of locating other members of their family, or pod, by deep diving and, we think, emitting distinctive noises that not only identify a particular whale, but also carry for miles and miles under water?" Karen had taught Clemsen quite a lot during his interview with her back at the Sanctuary office. As Bud filled Suzanne in on the details of his interview, she began to think about how Karen had found her meaning for life through the Sanctuary; she knew so much about so many things. She was happy for Bud, if this Sanctuary enforcement officer position worked out. She let herself fantasize about she and Bud working together for the Stellwagen Bank Sanctuary, she for the Cetacean Research Center in Provincetown, and he at the Sanctuary office in Scituate. 'Course, they wouldn't be together all the time, and that might be okay, too. As much as she liked Bud, it had been moving too fast for her; maybe a couple of hours between them would be a good thing. Besides, she had things to resolve at home. She was aware of the fact that folks who worked with her at the Sanctuary Program office in Washington thought she was a little "flighty" and never took things too seriously. So maybe it was time to go home and try to get some long-standing issues resolved once and for all. Only then could she get on with her life.

Speaking of things moving too fast, she and Bud had only a couple of days left before they both needed to get back to Washington. They made one more trip out to the Sanctuary, where again Suzanne felt like it was so right to be with Bud here, on the water, holding onto each other tightly as the Cap'n John #2 rocked through the waves and the salt water sprayed their faces. They saw no more northern right whales, but they did briefly see white-sided dolphins and lots of sea birds.

Tuesday came too soon. Suzanne had packed up her suitcase and Bud also had pulled his stuff together. *The trip back from Scituate to Boston was markedly different in tone,* Suzanne thought. A mere twelve days ago, they were both filled with high expectations and high hopes. In a way, each of them had gotten almost exactly what was hoped for. There was no reason for unhappiness; Bud was probably going to quit his job with the police department and take the job with the Stellwagen Bank Sanctuary, and she had found the house of her dreams. It was just that both of them silently realized that this two-week vacation had brought about profound changes in their lives. She didn't know about Clemsen, but she had a lot of things to clear up at home.

Getting boarded on their flight back to Washington didn't seem as burdensome and time-consuming as the process had been for the flight up from D.C. National to Boston. *Maybe we're getting used to it,* thought Suzanne. *Sorry state of affairs. But I guess that's the way the world is now; we can't undo what has been done. We can rebuild the demolished buildings, and we can punish those responsible for the acts of terrorism, but can we rebuild peoples' spirits? Oh, stop philosophizing and start rebuilding,* Suzanne thought. *Yeah, and you're going to get a great start on rebuilding spirit by maybe telling Doug that you're now in love with this police detective, and calling it quits on this marriage of more than twenty years.* She didn't now what to do. That familiar little knot in her stomach was back.

The flight itself was uneventful, except for the outward public displays of affection, or PDA's as a girlfriend from her very remote work environment had referred to them, that Bud engaged in for most of trip. Personally, she thought they were kind of neat and reassuring, as long as they didn't cross certain bounds of decency. *God you sound just like your mother,* Suzanne thought. Still, Mom had been correct on this point: Certain behavior between consenting adults should be confined to the privacy of the home.

"So, Bud, the early retirement will let me come up with the down payment on the house in P'town. Even though I'll have to pay taxes on the "income," I still should have enough to make the down payment and first month's mortgage payment.

"And just to recap here," Bud said, "when we get back to D.C. I'm puttin' in for retirement myself, now that the Kennard case is solved. And I'll be on my way back to Scituate. Karen's put me on to some cheap housing in the area, so all I gotta do is hold one of them, whatdaya call it, 'estate sales', and start packing. Pretty friggin' cool, huh?"

"Pretty friggin' cool," Suzanne muttered.

The plane landed in Washington, and Suzanne and Bud made their way to the baggage claim area on the lower level of the terminal, where they waited with what seemed to Suzanne to be hundreds of people, all pushing and shoving to get to their own luggage. *I won't miss this,* Suzanne thought. She had been a little concerned that Doug might show up at the airport to give her a lift home, but then remembered that Doug had mentioned that he had to get to his company's headquarters for an early evening sales meeting. So, all there was left to do was to say goodbye to Bud and to hope that he would bring up the future in discussion.

It seemed really odd being back to their full-time existences; everything was the same, and nothing was the same. "Well, partner," he said, "I guess it's time to head back to the barn, huh?"

"Uh, yeah, I guess so. I sure had a good time showing you around the Sanctuary office and Scituate, Bud, I just had a really good time being up there with you. When do you think you're going to resign from the D.C. Police Department?" she asked.

"Don't know for sure yet. Could be end of next week, if the paperwork gets through the system and approved, and I can get my act together enough to have a very successful yard sale; I'll be able to pack up and move to little ole Scituate," Bud explained.

"That's a lot of if's," Suzanne said, "are you pretty sure about moving up to Sciuate?"

"Yeah, I'm pretty sure; I know I could handle Sanctuary enforcement duties. What about you, Suze; are you coming back?" Clemsen asked.

"Oh, I'm definitely coming back to the Cape, to Provincetown. I have this house now; it's just what I wanted. I guess the only question is whether or not Doug is coming with me," Suzanne responded. She was feeling the beginnings of some significant self-doubt. And this trip was supposed to be about finding her own independence and self-awareness. *In spite of everything, not much has changed,* she thought.

They got separate cabs to their destinations: Clemsen to his apartment, Suzanne to hers (and Doug's). Since she had spent more than half the day traveling home from work, her day was considered a full day of work, and she would be getting a full day's per diem for travel to Scituate, MA (God, there were times she hated the "government way of doing things." This was one of them.)

By the time she arrived home in Washington, it was close to dusk. As she hauled her bags up the stairs to their apartment building, she was hoping that Doug would be home by now, and would come out to help her. He wasn't. *Guess he's still at work,* she thought, as she struggled to get the last of her stuff into the second-floor apartment. She felt a great tiredness and fatigue as she finally finished and sank into the familiar and well-worn sofa. *God, I'm tired,* she thought to herself; *I'm so tired.* She sat there for about an hour, before she made herself get up and start to unpack. She just couldn't move at all for a while; she was thinking about the northern right whale and the precarious status of its population, about how hard its fight for survival was, the difficulty of its annual migratory journey, finding sufficient food, all of it. There must be some way to get more people to care and to take preservation actions on its behalf. She also thought about the humpback whales, and why they had shown up in the Sanctuary at least two months early. *I'm so tired,* she thought, *there must be some innovative way to get people's attention.* As Scarlett said in *Gone With The Wind, "I'll think about that tomorrow,"* or *something like that. Trouble is, there may not be many tomorrows left for the right whale.*

It was close to 8:00 P.M. when Doug got home to the apartment. *He was, as they say, a sight for sore eyes,* Suzanne thought, *and I've really missed seeing you; you're so warm and familiar, kind of like the old sofa. How can I even think about leaving this? He's a good man. Maybe I can get him to at least think about moving up to the Cape with me. People on the Cape need hardware, too; maybe Doug could be happy in Provincetown. He doesn't even have to care about whales; he could just be a really good regional sales rep, covering southern New England and providing hardware, electrical and plumbing supplies to apartment and condominium buildings. I could make him happy here, I know I could,* she thought.

"Welcome home, sweetie," Doug said as he put down his work files and gave Suzanne a hug and kiss on the cheek. "I sure missed you; it's kind of lonely when you go on these business trips. I don't eat good, and I don't sleep good, either." She smiled at him and inquired about anything new in the neighborhood. "Not much; Barney sure missed you, though. He hasn't eaten much during the past week." She looked down at their now-happy, tail-wagging golden retriever, who always filled her heart with happiness even when his full-feathered tail swept things off the coffee table and he left muddy paw prints all over the rugs.

"So, honey, I've got some great news: I found the *perfect* house for us in P'town. It's right on the harbor and short walking distance to town; you've got to see it. I know you'll love it. And my early retirement money will cover the down payment and the first month's mortgage payment. The owners have accepted my, I mean our, offer, and the place is in move-in condition. What do you think? I mean, could you live on the Outer Cape? People there are just like people here; some of them live in apartment buildings which need periodic repair, and well, you could be the prime source of supply for those repairs." She finally had to come up for air, even though she was so excited she could hardly contain herself. "And there's more. If we move to Provincetown, Dr. Baio has offered me a job doing research and education for his Center for Cetacean Research. The house is only a few doors away from the Center; it's perfect. I mean, it's perfect for both of us. I know you'd find a lot of customers, and I'm assured a steady income that will supplement my retirement. I've already got some ideas about education and outreach efforts to reach the many user publics in and around the Cape and the Stellwagen Bank Sanctuary. This could be really great, honey; we'd be working in the fields we both love, and we'd be together. There'd be no more travel. We'd be home. C'mon, honey, what do you think?"

"And did you have *any* thought about discussing this with me before you put in a contract on a friggin' house?" Doug said. There was a pause in the one-way conversation before he continued. "I want to know more about what you and Detective Clemsen did while you were away on this business trip," he finally said. It was almost as if he was afraid to hear the truth. "Are you and Clemsen involved now? C'mon, Suzanne;

we always promised each other the truth, if nothing else. So let's have it."

Suzanne thought about the truth, and how it would hurt Doug, or so she thought. So she decided to not provide *all* the truth, just some of it. "Doug, you're right, as usual," she said, "I did get kind of involved with Detective Clemsen but it's not what you might think. I was just so caught up with the thrill of being on the Cape, and at the Sanctuary, and finding the house. Showing Bud around Scituate and getting him on the whale watches so he could see the whales; it was all just so exciting for me. You know how I am. I love getting people excited about the Sanctuary Program, and about how much it means to educate people about what they can do to help these endangered species. But nothing sexual happened between the detective and me, I promise, hon. And that's the truth."

"Well, in the interest of the truth, I have something to tell you," Doug said. "Maybe nothing happened between you and the detective—what's his name, Bud—but some things happened here while you were gone, and I'm sorry if this hurts you, but there's someone else, and that's the truth. I'm tired of being alone and tired of the quick phone calls, and tired of frozen dinners alone in front of the TV, and *hell*, I'm just tired of being a part-time husband. Nothing's happened yet, and I didn't go looking for it, but I'll tell you, Suzanne, a wonderful, caring woman has entered my life and she has made me very happy. I thought I at least owed you a face-to face explanation before anything else happened."

Suzanne was stunned; she never thought Doug would look elsewhere. She didn't know what to say, but she couldn't help starting to cry. She had always said, or thought to herself, "I hate bad endings." Now she was faced with one she didn't create. Or did she? Through the tears and sobs, she had to admit that maybe she had created this breakup of what she had thought was strong relationship. One she had, admittedly, taken for granted for a long time. Finally, Suzanne responded to the exploded bombshell Doug had dropped at her feet. "I never thought this would happen, Doug, how can you do this to me, to us?" It was all she could get out before sobbing overtook her, and she crumpled to the floor. Doug looked at her with almost disbelief, but said nothing.

Momentarily, Suzanne overcame her loss of composure and stood up. In addition to being really hurt, she was mad as hell for Doug's indiscretion. "You know, we've been married for a lot of years; we've been through a lot together. I can't believe you want to just throw it all away, Doug. I guess it's good thing we never had kids; it'd be really awful to put kids through this nightmare. Doug, please, can't we work this out and make a new and real commitment to better communication? I've always loved you; I still love you. Please, can't we try again? Don't you, don't we owe it to our marriage to give it another chance?" She realized she was coming very close to begging, but it didn't matter. She just couldn't lose Doug; she just couldn't. The thought of being alone was more than she could bear. *Yeah, I'm really independent,* she thought; *I can do it all by myself. God, I am such a basket case, I'm hopeless.* Suzanne looked hopefully to Doug and waited for some reaction.

"I'll think about it. I'm going out for a while. Why don't you think about what you've done, and why I'm so annoyed with you. God, it's no wonder I'm getting involved with someone who doesn't make life into a godamn show starring herself. Other people are affected by your actions, Suzanne. You seem to constantly forget that," Doug finally said. With that, any further discussion came to an abrupt end, and he left the apartment. Suzanne sat motionless on the end of their bed, not knowing what to do next. The apartment was very quiet and totally dark, with the exception of one light on in the living room. With a heavy sigh, she got up slowly and went to the bathroom. As always, she glanced in the mirror over the sink. *God, I look terrible*, she thought. Some women, mostly actresses, I think, *never* look bad when they cry and sob in the movies; they never get all red and puffy around the eyes, and you never see them with snot dripping from their noses. She couldn't stand looking at herself in the mirror any longer; it just made her lose any control she was starting to regain. She ran a cold, damp washcloth over her face and returned to the bedroom. She felt so lost here with Doug; he probably did also for his own reasons.

Suzanne knew she had to start thinking about what to do next. She had to make a plan. She had this wonderful house in Provincetown; she had hoped Doug would move there with her, but she realized that she had made a mistake by not discussing this monumental venture with him. He was right about that; their communication, in truth, have never been very good. Although she was incredibly tired, she could not fall asleep. She started thinking about all the friends she had on Cape Cod, and in Scituate. So much of her life had been tied to the marine sanctuary at Stellwagen Bank; so many of the people she had come to know and work with on that huge project, which had taken over ten years to designate and establish, had become such close friends. They were family, and always would be; she knew that now. Even though she was technically now retired from the National Marine Sanctuary Program, she had this incredible opportunity to work for the Cetacean Research Center and Dr. Baio, and continue through his non-profit organization, to provide both research and outreach to the Sanctuary's many and varied user publics. All the pieces were in place; all she had to do was "carpe diem" and show some independence for once in her sorry, self-absorbed life. *What's going to happen with Barney?* she wondered, *he's such a loyal and trusting friend, and I love him so much. If Doug's not moving to the Cape with me, I guess it makes sense for Barney to stay here with him.* The extended and heavy planning finally took over and she drifted into sleep.

As always happened when Doug wasn't in the bed with her, Suzanne slept only in short intervals; she awoke several times during the night. When morning became insistent and she awakened for the last time from her broken sleep, she realized Doug had not been in the bed at all during the night. Her immediate thought was that he must have come home late and was asleep on the sofa in the living room. She padded out there, past Barney, sound asleep on his back with back legs propped up against the wall. She had to smile at his total comfort and relaxation; *What a great dog, how can I leave him here? Doug doesn't love him as much as I do,* she thought. *Maybe I can find a way to take him with me.* Doug wasn't on the sofa in the living room; he wasn't anywhere in the apartment. *Well, now what?* she thought. She looked out the apartment window and could see that his car wasn't in the parking lot, either.

That son-of-a-bitch is sleeping with someone else right under my nose, she thought. *I hate him; how could he do this to me?* Glancing at the clock it the kitchen, she realized it was close to 7:00 A.M., and more or less time to get the household going. In the normal sequence of morning routines, she would have turned on the coffee maker, and let Barney out to pee while she prepared his morning meal, while Doug walked down the driveway to get the paper. But today, Doug wasn't here, the paper was still at the end of the driveway, and she was starting the day in a bad mood. *I gotta get out of here,* she thought; *I can't live like this. And Doug is definitely not going with me to the Cape.* "But Barney is, that's for sure. I'll find a way," she muttered quietly to herself.

Meanwhile, Detective Clemsen slowly pulled himself out of bed, and contemplated his immediate future. Sanctuary enforcement officer. He could do it, he knew, but did he really want to live in New England? And how much of his final decisions, retirement from the police department, and move to Scituate were tied to Suzanne? *A ton of it,* he thought, as he stepped into the shower, lathered up with the soap-on-a-rope hanging on the faucet head and sighed with pleasure at the hot water streaming down his back. I can do this; it's a new beginning, and if Suze is there, so much the better, he said to himself as he dried off and lathered up again for a shave. "Guess I'll go on into the precinct, and see what the final is on the Kennard murder," he muttered to himself.

When he saw Detective Parker back at the precinct, Clemsen grabbed his hand and pulled him close. "Hey, fish breath, you finally got a case closed, huh? Congratulations, Parker, I knew you could do it. I wanna hear all about it. What happened when you picked up Cranson? Did she fall apart?"

"Oh man," Parker said, "let me tell you, she fell like a house of cards, Bud. Your tip about the late lunch at her desk really blew a hole in her alibi; she had no excuses. Man, thanks again for the help; we were really at a standstill on that case, it was going nowhere, man. You said you got your information from one of her co-workers at NOAA, who was that?" Parker asked.

"Suzanne Douglas," responded Clemsen. "She told me quite a lot about Cranson and her obsession with power games and maintaining control over everyone she worked with. She also had this thing about losing weight; apparently always talking about how she would be *perfect* if she could just lose about ten or fifteen pounds. Women. Go figure, huh?" Clemsen had to chuckle at the outrageous "logic" of this power-obsessed, overfed control freak who seemed to be able to control everyone and everything in her world except her own appetite. "Boy, ya talk about your state of denial," Clemsen surmised. "I guess in the end it was her undoin', huh?" The two detectives were swapping notes and stories when the Lieutenant came into their work area.

"Well, well, look what the cat dragged in," Lieutenant Shaw smirked. "Have a nice 'vacation', Detective? I see where you didn't completely divorce yourself from the Kennard case, did ya? Guess you just got lucky, in more ways than one. So when are you reporting back in for duty? I trust you can obey orders now, right, Clemsen?"

Clemsen remained seated and responded to the Lieutenant, "I'm gonna be obeying a whole new set of orders now, boss; I'm puttin' in for retirement and signin' on with a new precinct in a new department, boss. I'm gonna be answering to much larger authorities than there are in this hell-hole." Detective Parker, now standing, looked at Clemsen with surprise.

"You gotta be kidding, Bud, right?"

"Nah, I'm for real, pal; I've had it with this chicken-shit department; I'm gonna be an enforcement officer for the Marine Sanctuary office in Scituate, Massachusetts." And thus the commitment was made by Clemsen to move north to New England. "Guess you know why I call you 'fish breath' now, Bud; working with all those big fishes in the Sanctuary, you can't help but get the fish smell all over you, huh?" Parker teased.

"There're not big fishes, Daniel; they're mammals. I know it's hard to believe, but it's true. They're big slow-moving mammals that can hold their breath for a really long time under water."

"Nah, I don't believe it. You're not for real, Bud. They can't be mammals; they're *fish!*"

"You can't believe how many people think the same way you do, pal. I think it's one of the problems in getting people to support the Sanctuary Program; they just don't get it," Clemsen said by way of quick explanation to his friend. *You're sounding like Karen up in Scituate,* Clemsen thought; *guess it's rubbin' off on me. Can't wait to get my retirement approved and get back up there.*

"You forget, Clemsen, I'm the one that's gotta sign off on your retirement, and the Chief, too. All the way up the chain of command to the Commissioner," Lieutenant Shaw said. "So don't go packin' your bags just yet, Detective."

"Oh, yeah?" Clemsen got to his feet and faced the Lieutenant. "Listen, you mother, all you assholes ain't gonna stop me from getting the hell out of here." There was split second of silence and no one said anything. Then it got very noisy. Other guys from the precinct gathered around the small cubicle and shouted support for Bud. In thinking back on the morning, Bud would tell you "they had to clear the decks" before it was all over. The thin blue line was broken. *So much for family,* he thought, once the dust had settled on the aftermath of that morning.

It was much quieter across town at Suzanne and Doug's apartment. Doug wandered in later that morning and announced the expected news: he was not moving to Cape Cod. The statement was short and to-the-point. He didn't feel he owed Suzanne any further explanation. Another crying jag ensued, but at least this one was shorter in duration. Suzanne had come to the realization last night that Doug was lost, and she didn't want him anyway; not if he was in love with someone else. There was no fixing the relationship they once had. As painful as it was, she had to face the future.

I should have expected this, she thought *Well, on to a better life. It's just getting through this one with minimal damage, that's all.* Glancing at the clock, she sighed heavily and started to get dressed. *It's so damn dreary here,* she thought. *This is why captured animals don't do well in zoos; they can't adapt to living in a box. I can't live in this box anymore. Especially alone in a box. 'Course, I've never lived free, either, and I am a social animal. Moving to Cape Cod would give me the op-*

portunity to live free and still maintain my social nature. She went to the window and breathed deeply as she gazed out at the uninspiring parking lot below. *Sure doesn't smell like the ocean; not at all like Cape Cod, either. Time to get on with it,* she knew. Just then, Barney trotted slowly into the bedroom and did his long, bowing stretch before coming up close to her face and planting his warm, raspy tongue near her ear, several times. *Goldens are so great; they never ever question anything you do, they just want reciprocated affection.* Which Suzanne gave immediately by scratching his head and softly tugging on his ears. People say Goldens are dumb as rocks, but highly trainable, although Suzanne had her doubts about that dismissive assessment; she was convinced that Barney understood exactly what she said and often what she felt, too. "Think you'd like to live in Provincetown, Barney?" The dog cocked his head as if to say, "What's Provincetown? Are you going to be there, too?" She smiled and gave him a big hug. "Yeah, we'll be fine up there. You'll meet lots of other dogs, and maybe you'll even get to go on a boat, if Charlie says it's okay. And maybe you'll get to see whales, whatdaya think, Barney?" At this, Barney gave his trademark little growly whine and swished his magnificent tail faster. "And people think you don't get it; what do *they* know, huh boy?"

Barney always made her feel better about things; even unfaithful husbands. *Like Jimmy Carter, I at least have only lusted in my heart. 'Course, it was just a matter of time, I suppose. Wonder how Bud's getting on at the police precinct. Hope they give him his due credit for solving the Kennard case. Hope Jodie gets her due, too,* she thought. *I'm so glad to be rid of her so-called friendship.* "Who needs friends like that, huh, Barn?" *You know, people in New England are much more honest and straightforward; they don't play games and deceive,* she thought. "Oh, c'mon, Suzanne, people are people everywhere. P'towners are just as likely to lie and deceive as

95

they are here in D.C., you just gotta be careful about who you trust, that's all." Barney seemed to agree, as he turned around and flopped happily into a warm and fluffy pile near Suzanne's feet. She finished showering and dressing and was heading into the kitchen when the phone rang.

"Hey, Suzanne, Charlie Baio here. You need to get your butt up here as soon as you can, babe. We got some stranded pilot whales on the beach; we could use your help."

"Where are they? How many?" she asked. The usual questions, with the usual lack of definitive answers. Even though Charlie Baio and others with the Cetacean Research Center had been assisting with the stranding network for several years, no one seemed to know why the whales sometimes beached themselves and made little or no attempt to get back to the ocean. *Well, now I have a need to go up there right away,* she thought. "What do you need me to do, Charlie?" she asked.

"Handle the media interest and the educational efforts of the Center, of course. You know, use your patented passion in getting both the press and the public to care about the plight of these poor whales. And later on, we need you to assist with researching the number and condition of beached whales," Charlie continued.

"Gotcha," she replied. "I want to bring my dog up there to live with me. Do you think he could go on your boat sometime?"

"No damn dog is gonna pee or take a dump on my research vessel," Charlie answered.

"That's not what I meant, Charlie. What I mean was . . ."

"I know, I know, sweetie. If your dog doesn't get sick, he's welcome aboard. What kind of dog is it, anyway?" Charlie asked.

"He's a golden retriever; his name is Barney," Suzanne finished.

"You never miss a shot, do ya? How soon do you think you could get up here?" Charlie pushed.

Suzanne knew she had said this once before to someone else important in her life; who was it? Oh, yeah; it was Bud. "I'm on my way," she repeated to Dr. Baio, smiling in recollection as she said it.

"Good. I or someone from the Center will meet you at the airport. It'll be great to see you, and to get to work on these strandings," Charlie said and hung up.

Whew, Suzanne thought, after talking to Charlie. *I got a lot to do before I get out of here. If I take Barney with me, I'd be better off renting a car and driving up, rather than subject him to airline travel. Better call Charlie back and let him know he doesn't need to meet me at the airport. Let's see, things are more or less resolved here. Doug's not coming with me, so there's no reason why I can't get underway almost immediately.*

She started to pack, but realized quickly that she couldn't pack everything she owned. *This is not like a week-long business trip; this is forever,* she thought. How the hell do you pack forever? Pack for a week or so, take those things that are most important to you, and buy the rest as you need them up there. That old knot in her stomach was back, and the first thing she threw in the suitcase was the antacid medicine. *Talk about priorities,* she thought, *sad commentary.* The second thing she packed were extra leashes for Barney, a supply of his favorite kibble, and his old bed. Beyond that, Suzanne turned to her own two-week supply of clothes, shoes and toiletries. It didn't take long; she was done in about an hour. Next thing to do was call a cab and get to the nearest car rental agency, get the car and come back to pick up Barney and go. Easy, right? The last thing she wanted was another confrontation with Doug, if the son-of-a-bitch came back to the apartment. As past experiences had demonstrated, she didn't do well with goodbye scenes. She left a note for Doug and said goodbye forever. It was much easier to say goodbye in a note than face-to-face.

So earlier than she had thought, actually, Suzanne had Barney loaded in the back seat and she was on the road north. *You are such a coward,* she thought to herself as she headed onto the interstate. It wasn't until she had reached Delaware that she started to worry about where she was going to spend the night, with the dog and all. Although she didn't have any list of places with her that took pets, she was reasonably sure she could find a motel that would be happy (for an additional fee) to take Barney in for the night. Pretty sure. After all, she figured, motels wanted to make money and keep their rooms filled. Sure enough, she found a motel in northern Delaware that was more than willing to accommodate Barney for the night, if she could promise he was well-behaved (defined as no barking and no relieving himself where he shouldn't). "No problem there," Suzanne assured the night manager; Barney's primary interests in life are eating and sleeping; he'll be the perfect guest. The manager showed her an open grassy lot behind the motel where Barney could "take care of business." So an uneventful close to her first day of real independence came after she ordered room service dinner, and like her brief sojourn in Seattle, she ate the meal dispassionately, as though it was an assignment. Except now instead of feeling cheap and used, she felt a little scared and very alone. Ah, how life tends to repeat itself; especially if you don't learn from past mistakes. She fed Barney and took him out to the assigned grassy lot, where he did his business, gratefully she thought, and settled in for the night. As did Suzanne. Sleep came easily, in spite of her conscious feelings of being totally alone and not knowing exactly how to get to where she was headed. *Gotta call Charlie in the morning,* she thought, as sleep finally overtook her.

Barney woke her up around 7:00 A.M., and she adapted

quickly to her interim surroundings, threw on some clothes and took him out back to pee. "Boy, I'm glad you're not a puppy anymore, and your needs are minimal and easily satisifed," she said to Barney, as she scooped his dog food into the bowl and placed it before him back in the motel room. He ate in a hurry, as if he knew something different was going to take place. As Suzanne packed up the few things she had used yesterday and last night, she said to Barney, "You ready for a road trip, Barn?" In response to the added incentive of a biscuit, she leashed him, and took him out back for a last minute pee and dump. Bodily functions taken care of, she loaded him in the back seat and tossed her small suitcase in the trunk. Well, she was ready. "Time to hit the road, Barn," and they were off.

From Delaware, Suzanne figured it was at least an eight- or nine-hour drive to Provincetown. "Hope you're comfy, Barn; we got a long way to go," she said as she checked her rearview mirror. Barney was curled up on his bed and already dozing off. *What a great traveler; what a great dog,* she thought, and turned her attention to the road ahead. She got through the rest of Delaware with no trouble, and pushed on into New Jersey and the unending New Jersey turnpike. Fortunately, there were plenty of rest stops, and she and Barney took full advantage of these. There was not much worth noting about the New Jersey turnpike, except maybe for the constantly occurring toll booths. During one of their stops, while Barney was having a snack, water and pee, Suzanne took out the map and figured she had about five hours to go; she had better call the Center and let them know she was driving up, and that no one needed to meet her at the airport.

"Hello, Charlie? This is Suzanne. I'm calling you from somewhere near the end of the Jersey turnpike. I should be there in about four to five hours. What's the count on the pilot whales?"

"We counted at least twenty-seven, four of which were able to get back into the water. The rest are probably not going to make it, even though we've got tons of volunteers trying to keep them wet," Charlie summarized.

As Charlie related the current status of the beached whales, Suzanne focused her thoughts on pilot whales in general. She really didn't know too much about them; they were not 'great whales', in fact a good deal smaller than humpbacks or northern rights. Also, they were 'toothed' whales, unlike the larger species, which took in their food through baleen, and expelled unwanted water through the same baleen, while retaining food particles behind, inside the cavernous whales' mouths. She drove into New York and Connecticut, and stopped to let Barney (and herself) out for a "walk-around" break and pit stop. "One more state to go, Barn; we're getting there," she comforted the dog. It was close to 5:00 P.M., so they remained at the rest stop long enough to have a quick bite to eat, and Barney had his evening meal. During his "walk-around", Barney took care of business at the designated "pet walking field" behind the sandwich shop which enjoyed a constant and constantly changing stream of consumers. *You really see all walks of life here; everything is reduced to a common denominator,* Suzanne thought to herself as she downed the egg-salad sandwich, bag of potato chips and soda meal purchased at the deli counter. "Actually, Barn, there is one extra, small state between us and Massachusetts. It's Rhode Island, probably the smallest state in the whole country. So it won't take us long to get through it." As Barney looked at her attentively and with some concern, she reached over and gave the dog a big hug, while kissing the top of his head. "It's alright, pal; we're gonna be alright."

Barney settled immediately into his bed in the back seat and dozed off with that contented look that Suzanne adored. She never got tired of watching him. *It takes so little to please him,* she thought, as she pulled out onto Interstate 95 and headed toward New Haven, Connecticut. Staying on I-95 allowed Suzanne to hug the coast, and catch views of Long Island Sound, and she found her thoughts wandering to some of the history of this area. The shore was punctuated with many ports that had seen the rise and fall of shipping activity over time; New London, Mystic, Narrangansett, Newport, and on up the New England coast, to New Bedford. Mystic, in particular, was famous for its shipbuilding industry. In more recent times, there was even a movie made about Mystic. 'Course, the movie was not about the town's storied shipbuilding heritage, it was about its wildly popular pizza. It had taken on a life of its own, and was nationally known as "Mystic pizza."

"I know you'd like some of that pizza, but we're not going to stop in Mystic, Barn; we've got important business in P'town," Suzanne said carefully to Barney. Like he could really understand.

They hugged the shoreline until they got through New London, where the interstate veered away from the coast and took them in a northeasterly direction in a direct path toward Providence, Rhode Island. *Interstates are both a blessing and a curse;* Suzanne thought, they get you where you may need to be, but they're such a bloody aggravation. And you can't depend on them to stay the same, either; they're always changing them, with the addition of some overpass or detour; you have to pay attention. Providence was an old and somewhat dirty town, or at least that was Suzanne's impression. Or maybe "thru traffic" was always routed through the older, less showy parts of the city. In any event, they pushed on, staying on the interstate until they could feed onto yet another interstate which headed them south toward the Cape. By now, it was close to 8:00 P.M., and Barney was awake. "Yeah me too, Barn," she said as she pulled into a gas station and rest stop near Wellfleet. When both had taken care of urgent business,

Suzanne fed Barney and gazed out toward the ocean, even though it was completely dark now. It sure smelled good, though. *There's nothing like the smell of the ocean,* she thought to herself. "And guess what? We're almost home, Barn. Man, am I going to sleep well tonight; ready to push on, partner?" Barney wagged his glorious tail and jumped back in the car.

Six

Cleaning Up

It was nearly 9:00 P.M. when they finally pulled into Provincetown. Marti Benjamin had told her that a key to the house would be (where else?) under the door mat at the front door, and it was. *One thing about fishers,* she thought, *they were honest, at least.* She opened the door slowly, taking in fully the smell and feel of her new home. Barney also took his time smelling everything, and checking out the "newness" of all the furniture and knickknacks that had been left there. Mrs. Brady (Angela) had also left the bedding and towels, as well as all the dishware and pots and pans and table linens. She and Mr. Brady weren't going to need any of it at the nursing home, where their lives would be totally controlled and accounted for. *Guess that these are the benefits bestowed on someone who was primarily responsible for getting the Stellwagen Bank National Marine Sanctuary designated,* she thought with a small smile to herself. In addition, the phone was still connected, so she gave Charlie a call to let him know she had made it.

"Charlie, hi; it's me. I'm just calling to let you know we're here, we made it. I'm sorry it's so late. We just got into the house, and I'm really beat. If it's okay with you, Barney and I are going to bed. I'll call you in the morning okay?"

It was a good thing Suzanne dialed the correct number, 'cause Charlie never got a word in before she had finished, was half asleep, and had already hung up.

"Okay with me, Suzanne, Good night," was all Charlie got out before the conversation was ended.

"Whew; I'm beat, Barney. Let's take you for quick out, and we'll unpack tomorrow." When she finally settled in to bed, she silently thanked Mrs. Brady for the clean sheets and down comforter and immediately fell asleep. Barney, as always, curled up on the rug close to the bed and let out a long, contented sigh. It was almost 8:30 A.M. before she woke up, and she only woke up because of Barney's endearing habit of standing by her side of the bed and laying his head close to her face and breathing on her. 'Course, if this failed to wake her, he would resort to executing some well placed licks on her face and ears. This always worked.

"Okay, okay, I know, buddy. You need to go out, right? Let's go, Barney," and she took him outside and let him poke around the small yard until he found the perfect spot. Then it was quickly back inside, where Suzanne prepared his morning meal, and got dressed. While Barney was still eating, she called Charlie.

"Well, Dr. Baio, what's it look like this morning? I should be there in about twenty minutes or so. Can I bring anything?"

"Just yourself, Suzanne. Looks like we got ten successfully back into the water; the rest are lost, I'm afraid. Mason and a couple of volunteers from the Sanctuary are coming down to help with cleanup. And I expect there'll be some media interest in this, probably this afternoon sometime," Charlie said. *Good;* Suzanne thought, *Mason can easily answer any questions about pilot whales.*

"Okay, great; I'll see you in a few minutes," Suzanne said. *Hmm, Mason,* she thought. *Mason's a tall drink of cold water and I'm parched dry. Oh, give it up, Suzanne; give it up! Mason's totally devoted to his work and he's probably ten years or more younger than you, anyway. Still . . . he looks great in his typical black pants and black shirt. Wonder if there's any way to get to him.* She poured some fresh water for Barney, left a biscuit, and got in the car and left for the Center.

"Hey, Dr. Charlie," she yelled as she pulled into the Center's small parking area. "I'm here at last. Are you set up for the reporters? I think I saw a few headed this way as I drove in."

"Yeah, I think we're ready. There have been a bunch of phone calls, too," Baio replied.

"When's Mason getting here? I hope he can answer questions about pilot whales; they're not my strongest suit," she said.

"He's here. Got here a few minutes ago," Charlie said.

"And the beached pilots?" Suzanne asked, as she headed for the beach.

"On the part of the beach closest to the Center," Charlie answered.

She was trying to appear professional and committed to the task at hand, but Suzanne couldn't conceal the pain she felt at the sight of the dead whales lined up along the beach area next to the Center. There just was no logical reason for the whales to have beached themselves. Oh, there were plenty of theories, including inner ear infections throwing off the whales' sense of balance and direction and the affected whales leading the others to their demise. Whatever the cause of the odd behavior, Suzanne mourned the apparently needless loss of the cetaceans. She knew it was a sign of weakness, but it was all she could do not to cry over the loss.

She found Mason also at the beach, towering over some of the pilots, hands on hips and looking confounded. "They just do this every once in a while; there's no really good explanation for the behavior," he muttered. Mason looked as good as ever, still wearing black and sporting a neatly trimmed mustache and goatee. With his fair complexion, he was striking in appearance, although Suzanne was sure he never thought about how he looked to others. *Little does he know,* she thought; *it's part of his unused charm. He needs someone to share his passion for doing what could be done to save cetaceans of all sizes, a true soul mate. Wonder if he's ever given himself to anyone? What a gift he would be.*

"So, Mason, how are you? Thanks for coming down to help out with these pilots. Charlie asked me to come up and help with the cleanup, too. Do you know how we're going to dispose of the carcasses? I mean, I assume they'll be necropsied first," Suzanne realized she was talking very quickly, and tried to slow the pace by taking a deep breath and letting it out slowly.

Mason smiled and gave her warm hug. "It's great to see you again, Suzanne," Mason said, "I'm glad you're here to help."

"And I'm glad you're here to answer questions about pilot whales," she replied, "they're just not my strong suit, you know?" She smiled warmly up at Mason, hoping he'd notice her lean and attractive figure. (Hey, when you've got it, you don't have to flaunt it; just show it off to its best advantage. That was her philosophy, anyway.)

"So when's the press conference scheduled?" she asked.

"Around one P.M., I think. Charlie tells me there've been calls from most of the local papers and TV stations, and also a couple of guys from Boston are coming down to cover the story," Mason answered.

"Who's coming down from Sanctuary staff?" she inquired.

"Um, I think Karen and a couple of others," Mason responded. She wondered if Bud was going to be among the "others." There being no need for further discussion, Mason, Charlie, Suzanne, and two Center staffers got to work on the smelly and difficult task of necropsy activities on the one hundred or so pilot whales. It took all day, and Suzanne was exhausted. Around 1:30 P.M. the informal "press briefing" took place, with Charlie and Mason fielding the questions from the six or seven reporters that had converged on the Center.

About the time they finally finished, Karen and three staffers from the Sanctuary arrived. Bud was with them, wearing a Sanctuary enforcement officer uniform and looking very official. Even though she reeked from the day's work, Suzanne went right away over to Bud and without embracing him (as she wanted to), said, "I've always been a sucker for a man in uniform; hey, Bud, it's great to you see you." In response to her teasing, Bud looked around from where he was standing over the whales, and greeted her with a warm smile and handshake. Suzanne glanced at her watch and said to no one in particular, "Oh, I've go to get home and let Barney out. He's been cooped up in the cottage all day. Guess I could use a shower, too."

Remembering his manners, Bud inquired "Hey, Suze, I almost forgot. How's the new house? Are you all moved in? I could maybe give you some help if you need it. I'd be happy to paint or hang pictures; just let me know."

"Thanks, Bud. I think I'm all set. How about the place Karen found for you in Scituate; how's that working out?"

"Oh, Suze, it's really neat. Karen found me a small little cottage-type house really close to the Sanctuary office. And it's furnished and everything, even though Karen insisted on putting in some extra stuff, so she can duck in there and do some extra work for the Sanctuary, you know, computers and stuff."

Just then, Karen joined in the conversation, and seemed to be listening closely to every word. Suzanne attempted to steer the conversation away from the Sanctuary office locale, and next asked Bud about the success or failure of his estate sale in D.C., and how things had gone with police Lieutenant Shaw.

"Oh, the estate sale thing was pretty good; I got a lot of extra money for my furniture and stuff. The thing with Lieutenant Shaw went pretty much like I thought it would, but that asshole had to sign off on my resignation, and the commissioner, too. Lemme tell you, there was a real good fight in the precinct before Shaw had to give in and sign off on retirement papers. But my buddies there in the precinct came to my defense. We really got it on before it was all over. Even Detective Parker got in a couple of good punches," Bud went on. He was really getting into relating the story of his departure from the D.C. Police Department; it was kind of like Bud's moment of fame and glory.

"But aren't you glad you made the right decision, and moved up here to Scituate?" Karen interjected, steering the focus of conversation back to life at the Sanctuary office (and herself, Suzanne thought). Karen then went on to dominate the conversation with discussion of her ideas about Sanctuary outreach and education activities. *Bitch,* Suzanne thought to herself, as she began to think there was more going on here than development of Sanctuary programs.

"Yeah, I'm happy to be here, and helping protect the Sanctuary's whales," Bud said. "I know we can make a difference for those critters." Karen beamed and stood close to Bud.

"Well, I really gotta get back to give Barney some outside time. I'll see you guys later, Okay?" Suzanne said as she collected her waterproof coat and headed for the car.

"Okay, Suze, see ya," Bud answered as he turned to say something to Karen.

She got in the car and resisted the urge to floor it out of the small Center parking area. *That bitch,* she thought to herself, as she got back onto the narrow road leading back to "downtown" Provincetown. "Who does she think she is, anyway?" she muttered. "She acts like she owns him, and he's really mine." Even as she muttered this, Suzanne knew how inane her so-called logic was. No one "owned" Bud, although someone conceivably could own his attention and heart. Was he not, she reasoned, his own man?

She pulled into the small parking space in front of her house, and dashed inside to find a thrilled-to-see-you Barney who greeted her like she'd been gone for weeks. Dogs are so amazing; not only were they *always* happy to see you, but they had the most phenomenal bladders! Not that Barney wasn't grateful to get outside immediately. Pressing matters taken care of, Suzanne leashed Barney and took him for a walk around the immediate neighborhood. That's another amazing thing about great-looking dogs, they provide a great opportunity to meet new people. By the time they got back to the house, five or six people had stopped to greet Barney and to introduce themselves. While Barney loved the attention, Suzanne had the opportunity to tell people she had just moved into the Brady cottage, and that she was working for Dr. Baio at the Center. She got plenty of recommendations about places to eat, and where to shop for groceries, and opinions about the Brady's health, as well as their choice of retirement homes. Suzanne had to smile; people were the same everywhere, for which she was enormously grateful.

Inside the cottage, she fixed Barney's evening meal, and took a much-needed shower. As she washed away the day's stinky activities, she started to think about getting some food into the house for herself. "Guess we have to get this place organized and stocked with provisions," she said to Barney. Another advantage (she guessed) of having a great dog is that they keep you so distracted that you don't really have time to dwell on the unpleasant personalities and situations which seem to keep cropping up in our complex lives. The hot shower definitely made her feel reinvigorated, and she quickly made a short list of necessities, and found the nearest grocery store. Nonetheless, as she unloaded the contents of two small bags of staples, including your basic supply of rocky road ice cream, Suzanne felt herself falling back into self-destructive patterns of thought and deed. Just like in D.C., she flipped on the TV and sank into the sofa with a large bowl of her favorite flavor. The local news was mostly boring, even though there was a short piece covering that afternoon's press coverage of the pilot whale stranding and the subsequent clean-up efforts by staff and volunteers from the Cetacean Research Center and Stellwagen Bank Sanctuary. There was extended coverage of Mason's statements at the briefing, and of his clean-up efforts on the beach; it seemed as though the local reporter (or maybe it was the camera-woman) was as taken with Mason as she was. *Maybe there's something in the water,* Suzanne thought; Mason always seemed to have a bunch of women hanging around him. It made her think about the old Tom Rush song, "Ladies Love Outlaws", where the outlaw always had a string of willing women who patiently took their place in line, waiting for their turn for a roll in the hay. What was it about the outlaw that made him so irresistible, anyway? *He probably wasn't even all that good looking,* she thought. Maybe it was just the immovable fact that he was just unavailable, except for those momentary encounters, which satisfied his physical needs and the lingering fantasies of all those pathetic women. 'Course, she wasn't even sure Mason ever had physical needs. *That's ridiculous, all men have physical needs,* Suzanne thought. Maybe he's got one or two women that you don't know about, or maybe he's gay, she wondered. "Or maybe you just don't appeal to him," she muttered. "Nah, that's just not possible."

The news over, she flipped the TV to some mindless sitcom and got up to scoop out yet another bowl of ice cream. She was actually just getting into the sitcom when the phone rang. Startled, she wondered who on earth could have gotten her phone number already; since the phone company had just hooked her up yesterday. "Now who can *that* be?" she muttered to Barney, as she got to the phone in the kitchen.

She recognized the voice immediately. It was Mason, and she suddenly lost all interest in the bowl of ice cream. "Hey, Suzanne, I'm glad I reached you. I have to head back to Scituate tonight, and I wanted to thank you again for all your help this afternoon. I'm sorry we didn't have much of a chance to talk; things were pretty intense, huh? I hope you got a hot shower and something to eat," Mason said.

"Oh, yeah; I feel much better after that hot shower. I probably smell better, too," she laughed. "And I got to the local grocery store, so I've got plenty of food laid in," she added, as she watched the ice cream melting in its little bowl in front of the TV.

"Suzanne, this isn't any of my business, but I assume you knew about Karen and Bud; they're more or less living together in that house that Karen found for Bud near the Sanctuary office," Mason said. Suzanne began to suspect that this was the main reason he called her; not necessarily to catch up with each other's lives, but to confirm in his own mind the relationship between Suzanne and Bud. She was glad Mason had not come over to the house; she was feeling particularly unattractive at the moment, and it was easier to maintain some control over her emotions while communicating by telephone.

"Yeah, I knew it," she said. "Bud and I came up here together, mostly 'cause I was looking for houses and Bud wanted to go on a whale watch. Both of us had pretty good luck. I'd say," she continued. " 'Course, I didn't expect Bud would get hooked up with Karen; but good for him, huh? I mean, they're probably a good match, don't you think? They have a lot in common, right?"

"Is your husband going to join you up here; what's his name . . . Doug?" Mason asked.

111

"Mason, that's another story. Nah, I'm up here perma-nently and I'm up here alone; does that answer your ques-tion?" she responded in quick answer, indicating to Mason she didn't really want to talk about it. "Charlie's offered me a job at the Center, so I'll be starting that right away," she con-cluded.

"I'm really sorry to hear that, Suzanne. Guess I thought that you and Doug had a pretty solid relationship," Mason said.

"Well, they say all good things come to an end, don't they? To tell the truth, our relationship was not all that good; we had our serious differences."

"Are you in one of those 'opposites attract' relation-ships?" asked Mason.

"Nah, you know what Mason? I really don't want to talk about this," she answered.

"Yeah, well, like I said, it's none of my business, and I've really got to get going. It was great to see you again, Suzanne; hope it won't be so long before next time. Good luck with the house," Mason said, concluding the conversation.

And before she knew it, the conversation was over, and she had hung up the phone. From the kitchen, she could see that the ice cream was completely melted.

Seven
Safe Harbor

Mason loaded his car with the two Sanctuary volunteers and headed back to Scituate. Karen had her own car, so she loaded considerable gear and Clemsen, and the two also headed back to Scituate. Clemsen was sorry that he hadn't had the opportunity to talk with Suzanne alone; he couldn't help but feel a little guilty about all of it. He knew she was obsessed with him. At first, it was flattering; but toward the end, it got to be kind of embarrassing. They drove in silence for almost an hour.

Finally, Karen said, "Hey, Bud, you seem lost in your thoughts. Care to share any of them?"

All Clemsen said was, "She didn't deserve this."

And for once, Karen decided not to probe any further, and changed the subject. "So, you did a really good job today, with the clean-up and everything. You going back to the office to check on vessel traffic in the Sanctuary?" she asked.

"Yeah, I really should check on activities in the Sanctuary, especially since I wasn't able to get out there today," Clemsen responded.

"What do you want to do about dinner tonight?" Karen pushed.

Man, it's beginning to sound a lot like we're married or something. I didn't sign on for this. I feel like I'm being tied down, Clemsen thought to himself as they drove on in silence. He decided that he should really have a heart-to-heart talk with Karen, but not right now. *Wait until they get back to Scituate,* he thought, *maybe tonight or tomorrow morning.* Man, he was tired; he didn't even want to think about this stuff.

Meanwhile, Suzanne was thinking, too, about *her* relationship with Karen. It was kind of ironic and somewhat uncomfortable that she and Karen would be working together on many of the same issues and projects. And to think that when she had first met Karen, she had actually kind of liked her. *Just goes to show,* she thought, *you can never trust anyone, at least other women. So they're living together, according to Mason. How cozy. And obviously, everyone at the Sanctuary office knows what's going on. How can I ever go back into that office again?*

Well, I hope he's happy, she thought, as she slammed some books down on the coffee table with such force that even placid Barney got up quickly from his nap and skulked away to the back bedroom. He had seen this behavior before, but not often. It always seemed to involve yelling and screaming and throwing things. Best to make yourself scarce until things returned to normal. About twenty minutes later, Suzanne realized that Barney had taken flight and was hiding, and she went to the back bedroom to comfort him. "I'm sorry, Barn, I really am. Didn't mean to upset you; it's okay, Barn, it's okay. Good dog," as she petted and hugged the big, lovable best friend. Barney gazed trustingly at her, and the tail immediately started thumping against the floor. "Ah, you know I'd never do anything to frighten you, you big lug," she smiled and gave him a big rub along his back.

The next day being Sunday, she slept in. Somewhere near eleven, she got dressed and walked into town to get a paper. *Guess I should sign up for home delivery,* she thought to herself, as she glanced at the front page's headlines. She was still scanning the front page when the aroma of fresh-baked bread

114

and croissants brought her to a quick stop at the P'town Bakery, which was doing a brisk business. She didn't even mind waiting in the long line to buy two loaves of the still-warm-from-the-oven Portuguese bread; it was delicious. Clearly, this was the place to go on Sunday mornings. Late Sunday mornings. She walked home, slowly tearing off pieces of the bread while taking note of the rest of town and the cottages that were her neighbors. Her favorite part of small-town newspapers was that section which described events and small-town catastrophes and triumphs that gave the town its character and charm. *Mrs. Evans' cat treed for hours, fire department to the rescue; Provincetown senior takes top honors in regional spelling bee.* I feel like I'm walking through a Normal Rockwell painting, Suzanne thought to herself. No, correction. *You are part of a Norman Rockwell painting.* I mean, think about it: Walking home from a bakery on a Sunday morning, with two freshly baked loaves of bread and the newspaper. No, to be a perfect Norman Rockwell scene, you'd have to have to be walking home *from church* with the freshly baked loaves of bread and the newspaper she muttered to herself, always the perfectionist.

What a great little town, she thought, as she opened the front (unlocked) door to the cottage and quickly surveyed the front room. *Got to get some new curtains,* she thought; *these are pretty horrible.* Barney got up from wherever he'd been napping, and greeted her with his customary nose-in-her-crotch and tail wagging. She often wondered about the purpose of this gesture; was it to be sure this was his beloved master, or was it the more basic search for intriguing smells? One of life's unending mysteries. She put what was left of the bread away, took the newspaper and plopped down on sofa to start thinking about tomorrow and reporting to work at the research center. The really good news about this job is the five-minute commute to the office. Even in "rush hour" traffic (ha), or in inclement weather when she had to drive, the trip was never more than five to ten minutes. And to think I used to fight the "inside the beltway" metropolitan D.C. traffic every workday morning. Back then, even when the weather was good and the traffic not too overwhelming, it took me at least an hour or more to get from home to that miserable, cube-sterile office where people rarely talked to each other, unless it was to delay the edict to report to some stupid staff meeting. "Fortunately, I've got you to talk to, huh, Barn?"

"*And*, she muttered, to top it all off, every day is 'casual Friday' here; I can wear jeans all the time if I want to." Finished with the paper, she pulled out the review material she had about the Center, and promptly fell into an early Sunday afternoon nap, the best kind. About two hours later, Suzanne was awakened in the usual way: Barney letting her know in no uncertain terms he had to go out. "Boy, with you around, who needs an alarm clock? I'm sure glad I brought you with me." Still, she put "alarm clock" on her mental list of things to acquire. "Actually, I better make a list; 'cause I'll forget for sure," she said to no one. Included on the list was a fence for the yard, so Barney could spend the day outside. And a doggy door, so he could come and go in and out of the house, as he pleased. The list sure is centered on Barey's needs, she noted; but then, who better to have all of his needs met?

Late lunch (or early dinner, who could tell anymore) consisted of a thick slab of Portuguese bread generously slathered with butter and heated in the microwave oven that Mrs. Brady had been kind enough to leave, and a large bowl of rocky road. *Boy, your eating habits are going to catch up with you quickly,* she thought. *You're not eighteen anymore, you know.* She found a favorite old movie on TV and settled in for the evening. Before the end of the movie, she had nodded off. Barney's quiet whining signaling his need to go out awakened her and she finally opened the back door so he could relieve himself and return to his comfortable old rug next to Suzanne's bed. She rinsed off the bowl, changed into the same oversized t-shirt she used to sleep in with Doug, and fell into bed.

Monday morning, the first day of her new life. She got up, let Barney out, and to solve the immediate problem of his wandering off to who knows where, tied him to a pole with a very long leash, and brought his kibble and water bowls out to the yard. She took a quick shower and got dressed. *Hope Barney will be okay if I leave him outside for the day; I'll check on him at lunch time,* she thought to herself. "I can always bring him back inside then; he'll be fine," she tried to assure herself. It was a beautiful morning, and the walk to the Center was a joy. You can't say that about most walks to work. She stopped at a newspaper stand and picked up the morning edition and walked into her new office at 6:30 A.M.

"Hi, you must be Suzanne Douglas, right?" came the bright, cheery greeting from Natalie Watson. "We're so glad you're here; did you have a good trip up? Charlie tells me you brought your dog with you; where is he? Or is it a she? You know, you're more than welcome to bring him to the office with you. I assume he's friendly," Natalie gushed.

Wow, and they say New Englanders are quiet and reserved. "Hi, Natalie, thanks for the greeting. I'm really glad to be here, too. I can't wait to get started on the burning issues of the Center. Where do you want me to sit?"

"How about over there by the window overlooking the harbor, is that okay? We're pretty cramped in here, so we tend to share just about everything, including desks and space in the refrigerator," Natalie pointed her in the direction of a well-used desk near the back of the Center's small building. *Wow,* Suzanne thought, *it may be small, but it's more window space than I got at that crummy government office back in*

D.C. She put her files and newspaper down on the desk by the window.

"Coffee?" she started to ask, when Dr. Baio came into the Center and answered her question with "is available at the deli in town or, for a slightly less exorbitant fee, here from the community coffeemaker, but you have to contribute to the monthly coffee fund, and agree to cleanup the pot and make more coffee anytime you finish the pot," Charlie explained. "We're very democratic here; everyone takes turns making the coffee and cleaning up the kitchen area. Suzanne, it's great to have you here, welcome aboard. Oh, the one thing we all share is phone duty. Natalie will show you around and talk to you about some of the current issues we're working on. We can talk later; I've got to get together with the local fat cats to explain why it's important for them to give us tons of money. My favorite part of the job, and there's always more of it to do," Charlie chuckled. "Kind of an unending source of pleasure, huh? Maybe in the future, you could help out with fund-raising, but first things first: coffee, right?" Charlie winked and hurried up to the second floor where the coffeemaker was already perking, thanks to Natalie.

"What time do you usually get here?" Suzanne asked Natalie. "Must be the middle of the night, or they've got a cot set up for you somewhere and you never actually see the outside of this building," Suzanne joked.

"Sometimes it does seem that way," Natalie replied, "but I love it here, and I guess I feel like I'm helping to make a difference, you know?"

"Yeah, I know what you mean. I used to feel that way about the Sanctuary Program job I had with the government, but toward the end, the emphasis of the Program shifted to maintaining the status quo, and not expanding the number of marine sanctuaries," Suzanne said. She knew there was a lot more she could say about what she thought was the lack of vision currently being demonsrated by the higher-up's at NOAA, but what was the point? As much as Natalie might agree and commiserate, it wouldn't change anything. So maybe she had just picked exactly the right time to leave NOAA; maybe fifteen years was enough. Enough anywhere. Anyone who's as disenchanted as I am with the direction being taken by a once-visionary program *should* get out, while there's still new and innovative ways to protect those special and unique areas of the ocean. Maybe those ways are found by working outside the government, by finding and nurturing a large (and vocal) public consitutency.

About then, the phone rang—and it was only 7:30 A.M. "I can get that," Suzanne said. She grabbed the phone on her desk and greeted the caller with "CRC; good morning. No, I don't thnk he's in yet, but I'll check for you. Please hold on for a second."

Suzanne asked when Jason White would be in, and Natalie answered, "Probably not until after ten o'clock or so; he's tending to a sick harbor porpoise, I think." Suzanne relayed this information to the caller and soon hung up.

"You know, we don't usually answer the phone that way," Natalie said.

"What do you mean?" Suzanne responded. "Wasn't I friendly enough?"

"Oh, no; it's not that at all. It's just that 'CRC' sounds like a government branch or something for a larger 'Department of Conservation'," Natalie explained.

"Well, I *was* a government bureaucrat for over fifteen years, don't forget. Guess I got used to thinking and speaking in acronyms. I'll answer more fully in the future, Natalie," she said.

"Oh, don't get me wrong, Suzanne; it's just that we like to make sure that folks who call this office know immediately and exactly who they've called," Natalie answered in an almost apologetic tone. "No big deal, anyway," she concluded.

The phone rang again and Suzanne was quick to answer. 'Good morning, Cetacean Research Center," she said cheerily, as Natalie smiled and gave her a thumbs up.

"Suzanne, is that you?" asked Mason. 'So you've just started and they've got you answering phones. Hey, is Charlie there? I need to talk to him about those necropsy results on the beached pilot whales."

Suzanne took a deep breath and responded, "Sure, Mason. I think he's still here; he's got to meet with some potential corporate donors late this afternoon, and I think he's working on his presentation," she said. She couldn't believe how flustered just talking to Mason on the phone made her feel. Kinda like she used to feel when good old Pete used to call, or even Doug, back in the old days. She connected Mason to Charlie's extension and exhaled, audibly.

"You okay?" Natalie asked. "You looked a little flushed. That Mason sure is easy on the eyes, isn't he?"

Boy, we *are* working in close quarters, Suzanne thought; I have to be careful of even *sighing* aloud here.

"Yeah, he is; there's something about a tall, lean bearded man dressed in black," Suzanne joked, "Is he taken, I wonder?"

"I don't think so, but I think he's seeing someone," Natalie replied.

"Boy, I don't know when he finds the time; Mason seems so devoted to his work," Suzanne observed.

Just then, Charlie came bounding down the stairs and said, "Mason's coming down early this afternoon to go over some of the necropsy results from last week. I have to meet with a couple of corporate types here at one or two o'clock. Gotta keep the doors open and us in coffee, you know?" he joked. "Suzanne and Nat, can you go over the necropsy tests with Mason for me? Get one of the volunteers to cover the phones. I should be done about four o'clock or so, okay? We can get some supper at McGinty's if you want," Charlie concluded.

"Sure, no problem, Charlie," Natalie said, with Suzanne nodding in agreement.

"Anything to get me off these phones, right Natalie?" joked Suzanne when Charlie had left the room to get coffee, "and since I did such a bang-up job this morning, huh?" *Wow,* she thought, *an afternoon with Mason; wonder how much I remember about necropsy techniques (other than the mess and stink).*

"Well, here are the necropsy test files on the beached pilot whales," Natalie said as she placed them on Suzanne's desk. She pulled up a chair and started going through the files with Suzanne reading through a second set of files. After several minutes, Natalie observed, "Looks to me like there was a definite ear infection in at least some of these guys that may well have caused a loss in equilibrium and maybe in sense of direction. It's happened before, but not very often, thank goodness." They continued to swap notes and observations about the fate of the pilot whales for the next hour or so, when Natalie stood up, stretched and said, "I could really use some coffee; can I bring you a cup?"

"Yeah, thanks, Suzanne. I take mine black."

"Me, too, Nat. We call it high test," Suzanne replied with a laugh. *I think I'm gonna like this woman,* she thought to herself as she climbed to the second floor and found the coffeemaker and clean mugs hanging on hooks near the sink. By the time they had finished going through the files, Suzanne began to get the feeling that the pilot whales were a very close-knit family, or pod, and followed their leader and appeared to act as one unit. So if their lead whale became disoriented and lost his sense of direction, the others simply followed wherever he went, in this case, up onto the beach near the Center. She wondered if this phenomenon happened to other cetacean species as well.

"This has happened to other whales, too," Natalie said, as though she had read Suzanne's thoughts.

"How did you . . ." Suzanne started to ask.

"Because those are logical questions when you encounter this occurrence. I've read about pygmy whales, even humpbacks, getting into the same predicament. I guess it's easy enough to figure out why whales get ear infections, but why the disorientation causes them to beach themselves and resist going back into the ocean . . . it beats me," Natalie concluded. Suzanne made a mental note to learn as much as she could about beaching behavior; *there have to be answers,* she thought.

Just then, they heard Mason's car pull into the small gravel parking lot in front of the Center. He was carrying yet another set of files, and was still dressed in black. Suzanne and Nat exchanged quiet giggles as he entered the front office. *God, you'd think we were thirteen-year-olds or something,* Suzanne thought.

"Hey, Mason, how was the trip down from Scituate?" Natalie asked.

"Pretty quick this morning; traffic was light. It only took about two-and-a-half hours to get here. 'Course, I left Scituate at six A.M. There wasn't much to get in my way," Mason joked.

"Coffee?" Suzanne offered.

"Sure, take mine black," Mason responded.

"And here I thought Nat and I were the only ones to take their coffee 'high test,' " Suzanne said. The two young women couldn't resist a shared giggle. Nat went upstairs to get another cup of coffee, and Mason sat down at Suzanne's desk.

"Well, it sure is good to see you here, Suzanne; I'm glad you're going to be working with Charlie. How's the house working out? Are you all settled in yet? I'm actually going to be here overnight before I head back to Scituate; can I give you any help with anything at the house? I understand it's like walking distance from here; maybe I could see the place before I leave tomorrow," Mason asked.

Suzanne's head was swimming. She was trying hard not to read anything into Mason's offers of assistance, although she'd like to. "Gosh, I can't really think of anyting in particular, Mason, although I'm sure there's plenty of things that need to be done. I just haven't had time to get organized enough to prioritize. So far, the only things that are glaring needs at the house are new curtains and a fence around the yard and a doggy door for Barney," she rattled off.

"Sounds to me like you're pretty organized already,' Mason said. "How about when we're finished here, we can go over to your place and take a 'glarin needs' inventory," he asked.

"That'd be great, Mason, but I think Charlie has offered supper at McGinty's for me and Natalie when he's finished with his presentation to some corporate donors here at the Center. I'm sure he'd love it if you could join us," Suzanne answered. She silently wished Mason wasn't attached to another woman; it would make things a lot easier. *Oh, give it up, Suzanne; you are hopeless. Not everyone thinks you're irresistible, you know.*

"Hey, lobster chowder at McGinty's would be great; maybe I'll have time to stick around for supper. I'll try, anyway. I haven't found any place in Scituate or nearby that knows how to make good lobster chowder. *Another good reason to be in P'town, that and the Portuguese bread.* Mason returned to work on the necropsy files, with Nat and Suzanne hovering about his desk and making small talk. *I hope he stays for dinner, and I hope he can come see my house afterwards,* Suzanne thought.

"Well, I think we can safely conclude that there were ear infections which caused imbalance and loss of orientation, even though there are some inconsistencies in the data," Mason finally said after poring through the remaining necropsy files. He stood up from the desk and stretched. "Man, I'm whipped; didn't think I'd be so exhausted. Guess I'm getting a little old for this stuff," he quipped.

"You've got a long way to go to catch up with Charlie," Nat said. "That guy is flat amazing; he seems to never stop," Nat continued, and Suzanne nodded in agreement. "Guess there's no such thing as retirement from this job," she observed.

"The one thing you *can* count on in this job is the need for a good supper at the end of the day. Ready for McGinty's?" Mason asked.

"Boy, I sure am," piped in Natalie, "let's go."

"We're with you pal," Suzanne said as she rose and put on her jacket. They piled into Mason's car and were quickly delivered to McGinty's, where the aromas of great food and promise of ever-strengthening friendships filled the atmosphere. As tired as she knew they all were, the food and close-knit bonds among them seemed to reinvigorate everyone, as they swapped stories and shared experiences, both of on the water and in the office. And the lobster chowder did not disappoint; it was as wonderful as always.

"Just as I suspected," Mason finally said to Charlie, "the vast majority of pilots suffered from ear infections, which caused the disorientation and subsequent beaching."

We knew this already, Suzanne thought, but she said nothing. Charlie responded, "So you mentioned some inconsistencies in the data, Mason. What were they?"

"Well, I spent last night and most of this afternoon going over the necropsy files, and as idiotic as it sounds, it looks like the data were entered incorrectly in several places. I can show you where when we get back to the Center," Mason answered.

"It's getting pretty late," Charlie observed. "Can you stick around tomorrow? I'm through with the donor presentations; we could rectify the data entries in the morning, okay? Or maybe Suzanne and Nat can help clean up the records. The last thing potential donors want to hear about is messy files, you know?"

"Yeah, that *does* tend to dampen the enthusiasm for donors to empty their pockets," Suzanne said.

"Sure, I guess I could stay another day down here, Charlie. I'd like to get these files cleaned up, too," Mason responded.

"Good, we'll see you in the morning, Mason. You got somewhere to bunk tonight? You can stay at my place, if you want," Charlie offered.

"That'd be great, Charlie, I'll take you up on that," Mason said, as he stood up from the table. With that, everyone in the group also stood and headed for the door. Suzanne and Natalie both thanked Charlie for the meal, as they headed for Mason's car.

"Boy, that was a great meal, huh?" said Suzanne as she climbed into the back seat. "I feel completely sated and totally mellowed out," she added.

"Me, too," echoed Natalie, as the two flopped together like two fat and happy sea lions. As he started the car, Mason concurred: "You're not kidding; that was by far the best lobster chowder I've ever had. Makes me kind of sad to leave Provincetown."

Then don't, Suzanne thought.

Mason dropped Nat and Suzanne at the Center, where Nat picked up her car and left for home. "Well, we're down to two," Suzanne said.

"Yeah, I thought she'd *never* leave," Mason joked. As they

were only a couple of houses away from Suzanne's place, Mason parked the car and the two walked the gravel path to 55 Commercial Street, where they found Barney curled up and sleeping on the front door mat. "Not known for his watch dog abilities," Suzanne whispered, as she stopped over to gently rouse her faithful friend. Barney slowly rose and muzzled Suzanne; he then investigated Mason with his usual friendly sniffing and tail-wagging.

"Wow, this is some great house, and it's so close to the Center," exclaimed Mason.

"Yeah, I got really lucky on this house. Turns out the former owners are big fans of the Stellwagen Bank Sanctuary, and they accepted my bid even though it wasn't the highest offer they got," Suzanne explained as they went inside, followed by Barney. Once inside, Mason, too, seemed to "breathe in" the scent of the wonderful little house on the edge of the harbor.

"Man, this place is great," he said, "How many rooms you got upstairs?"

"Two bedrooms and a bath," Suzanne answered. "One of the bedrooms I'm going to make into a study, where I can solve the mystery of whale stranding," she smiled, as Mason followed her upstairs. "You know? I think that when whales become disoriented due to ear infections or whatever, the other whales will follow the lead whale up onto the beach *because* they're members of the family; they kind of have to. At least that's my theory," Suzanne smiled slowly, indicating her serious demeanor.

"Gee, I didn't know you could solve mysteries like that in a quiet study," Mason teased. "I thought you had to be out there observing whale behavior," he said, motioning to the harbor through the window.

"Very funny, *Dr.* Weisner. I'll be out there, believe me, observing and making some educated guesses. But I really think the answer to the mystery of beaching lies in the family relationships."

When they returned downstairs, Suzanne changed the subject and asked, "So, Mason; Nat tells me you're seeing someone. Serious?"

Mason looked like someone unaccustomed to personal questions, and he fidgeted a little.

"I mean, I know it's none of my business," Suzanne said.

"No, it's okay. Until now, I hadn't really thought about it being serious or not," Mason finally anwered. "Yeah, I guess it is, or at least as serious as I've ever been." He sat down on the sofa and started scratching and petting Barney, who had made himself very available for the activity.

Without meaning to probe too much, Suzanne asked, "Anyone I know?"

"I kind of doubt it. She went to several of your public meetings during the early designation stages for the Sanctuary. I know Jenny made an oral statement supporting the Sanctuary at the public meeting in Gloucester. That's where I met her," Mason explained.

"Jenny, hmm; I'm trying to remember. Oh, yeah, I think I remember her now. It was Jennifer Mason, right? God, Mason, just think: it's good thing that you're the man and she's the woman and you're not marrying her. Then you'd be Mason Mason. How weird is that?"

"Yeah," Mason said, "I guess I'd have to keep my own name, for the sake of confusion."

"So, are you?" Suzanne asked. "You know; are you and Jenny getting married?"

"Sometimes, Suzanne, you are so confusing," Mason scowled.

"Yeah, I know!" Suzanne said, "confused and confusing."

They sat and talked for another hour or so; finally, Suzanne couldn't stand it any longer. She had spent the last several minutes visualizing Mason without any clothes, and boy, he looked good.

"So when *are* you getting married, Mason?" She had to know.

"Well, I haven't asked her yet, but I was thinking sometime late next spring," Mason responded.

For reasons that make no sense at all, Suzanne felt like a knife had been driven through her heart. Her shock must have showed, because Mason asked her if she was okay. Even though she said she was fine, she had never in her life felt so alone.

"I could use some water," she said. Mason got up, went to the kitchen and poured some ice water from the refrigerator into her favorite coffee mug, the one that had 'Stellwagen Bank National Marine Sanctuary' printed on it. It was already chipped, because she used it for everything, from morning to night. Truth was, it hardly ever got washed. *Should have bought more than one,* she thought.

"Well, I guess preliminary congratulations are in order," she said after draining the cup of water.

"Thanks, I guess they are, although Jenny hasn't said 'yes' yet. Don't put the cart before the horse," Mason smiled.

"What if she says 'no'?" Suzanne asked.

"Are you kidding? Who could resist this?" Mason countered, smiling.

Not me, she thought; *not me.*

"Well, she'll say yes, I'm sure. I mean, you guys have so much in common. I wonder if we could start a special fan club composed of couples that were brought together by the Stellwagen Bank National Marine Sanctuary. Think of the promotional items we could develop that would be great fundraisers," Suzanne said excitedly. Her creative juices were really flowing now.

"Promotional item development: that's definitely your

area, Suzanne," Mason said; "I'm sure I could be of no help at all." Suzanne was already thinking of ways and items to get the public enthusiastically supportive of the Sanctuary Program, and of the Stellwagen Bank Sanctuary in particular. Hopefully, the support would be accompanied by donations. *And why not? All the world loves a love story, right? We could focus on couples that were brought together at the public scoping sessions or the public information meetings. Couples like Mason and Jenny at the Gloucester public information meeting. After presenting an endearing piece on their backgrounds and interest in the Stellwagen Bank Sanctuary, we could market black turtlenecks and jeans, coupled with preppy little pink sweaters and color-coordinated short skirts and headbands. And in the promotional pieces on Mason and Jenny, they would each be holding a Stellwagen Bank National Marine Sanctuary coffee cup. Okay, maybe the clothing items are not feasible; they wouldn't fit everybody. But a coffee cup does. Ah, the possiibilities are endless.*

Snapping her back from her way-down-the-road reveries, Mason stood up and said, "I've got to go, Suzanne. Charlie's putting me up for the night, and I've got to leave for Scituate pretty early in the morning. Thanks for the quick tour of your new place, and all your help with the necropsies; you're just great."

"So let me know when and where you've registered your silver pattern," Suzanne teased. "Seriously, Mason, I'm really very happy for you both. I'm just sorry you missed your chance with me." She felt like she had just released the most beautiful fish back into the ocean. And she again had that familiar feeling of loss and solitude. Even Barney whimpered a little when Mason left. "It's just you and me again, huh, boy?" she said as she turned off the outside lights, and climbed into bed. *I'm exhausted,* she thought, as she snuggled under the down comforter. She didn't need any ice cream to finish off her day. Mason had done that for her.

*   *   *

She always slept well in Angela's bed. Like Mason, she had to get up early and get to the office. She didn't think about the fact that her routine here wasn't really all that different from that back in Silver Spring; the main difference (and it was a big one) was she did not have to drive to work and fight the commuter traffic. Sigh. At least she was doing her part to save what was left of the clean air over this part of New England. So, despite the keen sense of loss and loneliness, Suzanne slept soundly and without break until 6:30 the next morning.

When she got to the office, Natalie was already there and eager to ask lots of questions about Mason and how things had gone the night before.

"So, Suzanne," she started. "Tell all. Is Mason getting married to the little cutie we've seen him hanging around with so much lately? Honest to God, if I'd only had the chance . . ."

"Chance to what, Nat? Get in line? You've got to admit, Mason's the best catch on the East Coast. Believe me, I wish I could've had a shot at him, too, but you know what, Nat? Mason and I had a long talk about Jenny, and it's pretty apparent to me that he's really happy and really in love. Turns out he met her at one of the public information meetings we conducted in Gloucester on the proposed sanctuary at Stellwagen Bank. You know what else, though? He hasn't even asked her yet," Suzanne said.

"God, you mean there's still a chance?" Natalie's eyes widened.

"Nah, I don't think so, Nat. I think Mason's 'signed, sealed, and almost delivered,' and happy about it. Sorry. Is the coffee made yet? I'm really hungry this morning; think I'll dash up to the bakery and get some sweet rolls. You want some?" Suzanne asked.

"How can you think about eating right now? I'm so depressed, I couldn't get more than one or two down, but thanks," Natalie responded. "I did bring some fresh pineapple in; it's upstairs in the fridge," she added.

"Yum, sounds great. I'll be back in a flash," Suzanne said, as she threw on her jacket and headed for the door.

As usual, the P'town Bakery was crowded, even at 6:45 A.M. *Pizza and hot cross buns: they are always a profitable venture*, she thought as she took her place in line. *But I'm glad the two smells don't have to compete with each other.* In her former life, when she was kind of sour about almost everything, she would have characterized the folks working in the bakery as "disgustingly cheerful," but that was then and this was the new life, and she now regarded the bakery help as bright, happy, and competent. She picked out six hot cross buns, and the young woman at the counter carefully placed them in a cardboard box and tied it with a red string. The mood at the bakery was contagious, and Suzanne found herself whistling as she walked quickly back to the Center with her fresh-baked prize. *Can't remember the last time I whistled,* she thought as she opened the door to the Center and placed the hot-cross buns on Natalie's desk. Natalie had brought coffee and the sliced pineapple down from upstairs, so all was right in the world.

"I brought some extra buns in case Dr. Baio wants some," Suzanne explained.

"He hasn't come in yet, but he should be here soon. It's already almost seven-thirty, usually he's here by seven," Natalie said, as she enthusiastically got into the first of the buns. Even removed from the bakery, the scent of cinnamon and sugar filled the Center's front room. Coupled with the cut-up pineapple and fresh brewed coffee, it was almost intoxicating.

"Hey, what's this? A coffee klatch in the office?" exclaimed Charlie as he came in the front door of the Center. "Somebody's been to the bakery; it sure smells good. Did you bring me some?" asked Charlie, as he hung his coat on one of the series of pegs behind the front door.

"Yeah, Charlie, there's hot cross buns, fresh pineapple and coffee, all the comforts of home," offered Natalie.

"You know," Charlie admonished, "this *is* an office, not a kitchen at home. Eat quickly, so no one walks in and sees you two acting in such an unprofessional manner."

"Yeah, I wouldn't want to have to share this with someone," Natalie said. Charlie went upstairs and got more coffee, and the three of them discussed the day's agenda, with a small bit of gossip thrown in for spice. Idle gossip was something Charlie did not spend a lot of time on, but once in a while, even he couldn't resist a particularly juicy comment or two about something or someone that deserved special attention.

"Maybe we should consider moving the coffeemaker downstairs," Charlie chuckled, as he returned with his third cup.

"Ah, but then the front office would start to look like someone's kitchen," Suzanne laughed between bites, "very unprofessional."

"To say nothing of running the risk of having to share hot cross buns with the public," Natalie said, as she finished off her second bun.

"So, anyway, I hear Mason's getting married to someone named Jenny; anyone have information or details?" Charlie asked.

"I spent some time talking to Mason yesterday. He tells me he hasn't even asked her yet," Suznane offered.

132

"Yeah, I was hoping I could change his mind," Natalie sighed.

"Nope, I really don't think so. I mean, look at Mason: he's great looking; he's got a good job; both of them are doing things they love; what more could she ask for? She'll say 'yes', whenever Mason gets around to asking her," Suzanne said.

Natalie sighed in resignation. "Don't worry, Nat; there's plenty of fish in the ocean, right?" Charlie said in a consoling manner.

"Not if you listen to the local commercial fishermen," piped in Suzanne.

"Yeah, you're right; they're always bitching about something. Truth is, they just plain overfish the resources. The resources don't have any time to recover. And the only thing the fishermen can blame is the federal government for imposing more restrictions and shorter seasons on their operations," Charlie continued.

"Good thing the Sanctuary doesn't impose any new regulations on fishing activity, huh?" Suzanne said. "Sometimes I think that's the only reason the Sanctuary got through the final designation steps," she added.

"That and the efforts of Congressman Studds," Charlie finished. Having wrapped up the discussion on the unreasonable nature of the local fishermen and how the Sanctuary *really* got designated, Charlie popped another pineapple chunk into his mouth, took his coffee mug and moved upstairs.

"God, I thought he'd *never* leave," Suzanne said jokingly. "I have some fundraising ideas I wanted to get your thoughts on. I got these ideas while I was talking to Mason. I thought the ideas would be a natural campaign to get the public really interested and supportive of the Sanctuary," she said to Natalie.

Suddenly, the intercom button on Suzanne's desk buzzed. "I heard that," Charlie barked. "Let's not forget who you're working for now, okay? The Center could use some aggressive fundraising too, you know," Charlie continued.

"Charlie, this idea could work for the Center, too; why don't you come on back downstairs, and I'll fill you in on what I'm thinking," Suzanne replied.

When he got downstairs, Suzanne and Natalie were already talking about the concept of highlighting couples who had been brought together by the Stellwagen Bank Sanctuary. Natalie thought it was a great idea (even if she and Mason were not such a couple). Charlie could immediately see how this "love story" theme could also be applied to the Cetacean Research Center, since he, too, was a romantic.

"Great idea, Suzanne; we can tie great passions for each other to great passions for the work being done at the Center. I like it! It's a natural connection; one people can really relate to," Charlie said.

"And hopefully, people will relate to the passion by donating much-needed funding for the Center, as well as for the Sanctuary," Suzanne concluded.

"The Center puts out a periodic publication, and so does the Sanctuary. However often the publications are issued, there could be a small feature on one or more couples who share their passion for each other and their passion for the work of the Center and that of the Sanctuary," Natalie added. "I could do the photography; it's my hobby, you know," she finished.

"And of course, there would be a tasteful understated spot in each publication for the reading public to offer contributions to further the *glorious* work of the Sanctuary and the Center," Suzanne stood up and took a bow.

Just then the phone rang, and Natalie and Suzanne resumed their more mundane duties. Charlie grinned, gave a thumbs-up to both, and returned upstairs. At lunch time, Suzanne walked home to her cottage, grabbed the sandwich she had prepared the night before, put Barney on a leash, and returned to the Center.

"So, here he is, Nat; you said it would be alright if I brought Barney to the Center once in a while," Suzanne said as she unleashed Barney and let him loose in the front office.

"Oh, he's beautiful!" exclaimed Natalie. She reached down and gave Barney a vigorous rub along his back. "How old is he?" she asked.

"Almost six-and-a-half, but he sure doesn't act it," Suzanne answered.

"Why, you're just hitting your stride, huh, boy?" Natalie said softly to Barney. Barney seemed to like this attention (so what else was new?), and he nuzzled Natalie, wagging his tail vigorously.

"Yeah, I figure he's got another five or six years in him. I hope he's always this healthy and responsive," Suzanne opined as she rubbed his nose and under his chin.

Suzanne sat at her desk and unwrapped her sandwich. After taking a bite, she said to Natalie, "I forget; are there sodas upstairs in the fridge?"

"Yep, help yourself. Just remember to replace what you use, okay?" Natalie was totally entranced with Barney, who for the time being, had focused his total attention on Suzanne's sandwich: "God, the way he acts, you'd think he hadn't been fed in a month," Natalie said.

"Emphasis on *acting*," Suzanne said. "He had his breakfast this morning, and he doesn't get fed again until this evening. Don't be fooled by his big brown, pleading eyes, Nat," Suzanne answered loudly from upstairs.

"If you two are finished gossiping and playing with the dog, I suggest you get to work," Charlie commanded. "Suzanne, I'd like you to go over the necropsy data that Mason looked at when he was here, and make sure the final figures are consistent with the figures entered in the initial data gathered," Charlie said. "Nat, please man the phones until about three or so, then Suzanne can take over OK?" And to Suzanne, Charlie said, "I really like your fundraising ideas. Why don't you spend some time this evening putting some couples' names together, and you know, link them to their work here at the Center and at the Sanctuary."

So Suzanne passed the afternoon matching necropsy data to initial necropsy figures. She wondered if Charlie doubted Mason's work in any way, or if this was just a second set of eyes checking the same data. She knew Charlie had a great deal of respect for Mason, but figured it was possible that Charlie thought Mason was distracted, at least for the moment, by his upcoming nuptials. *Wonder why the're called "nuptials" anyway,* Suzanne thought to herself. *Stupid name. Oh, well, another one gone.*

By around 3:00, she had finished (right on schedule, she noted). As far as the results, she *had* noted two discrepancies between the initial findings and the final numbers noted by Mason. But she was sure it was just an honest mistake. She made a written notation of the mistakes, closed up the files and went downstairs to relieve Natalie on the phones.

Natalie was busy working on a crossword puzzle; the phones were quiet. So were Barney (napping) and Charlie (who knew for sure?). "Well, I guess there are no strandings, entanglements or other mishaps to report," Natalie said as she looked up from the crossword. "I think I'll get some more coffee, and check on Charlie; want some?" she asked.

"Coffee or Charlie?" Suaznne quipped in response. "No thanks; neither one."

The phones *were* very quiet, so much so that for a while Suzanne thought there must be something wrong with them. But truth was, she was happy for the quiet, as it gave her time to start thinking about her promotional ideas for the Center and the Sanctuary. By five o'clock she had roughed out some further ideas; all she needed now was to do some research on individual names of those who had been thrown together by their mutual passion for saving whales, and for the Sanctuary's educational and outreach programs.

"Well, I think I've got a good start on this promotional fundraising campaign; I'll flesh out this stuff at home tonight," she said, as she stood up, stretched and grabbed her jacket off the peg on the front door. "Have a good night, Nat; c'mon, Barney, let's go." Barney also stood up, stretched and walked over to Natalie and gave her a big "lean to" and tail wag. The only difference in their behaviors was Barney did not grab for a jacket; he didn't need one.

"Good night, Suzanne; see you in the morning. More pineapple tomorrow?" Natalie answered and asked.

"I'd love it," Suzanne replied as she headed for the front door with Barney.

Back at the cottage Suzanne first fed Barney and then checked her mailbox. She was surprised to see a legal-sized envelope from Doug crammed into her cottage-sized mailbox. She rushed inside, hoping that Doug had ditched his latest love interest, was begging forgiveness, and wanted desperately to be given another chance. She ripped the envelope open, but the contents were not at all what she had expected: they were divorce papers awaiting her signature. She sat down quickly, and tried to catch her breath. Although divorce had been a distinct possibility, given all that had happened, she never thought it would actually come to pass. She truthfully had not thought about the possiibility much at all. At this point, she was in that safe and secure denial mode. *Secure only until reality catches up and slaps you in the face,* she thought. *I don't even know if I really want to be divorced from Doug: apparently, he does.*

She slowly got up and wandered aimlessly to the windows facing the harbor. Nothing had changed and everything was changed. Well, wasn't this what she wanted, to be alone and on her own? She told herself, *You know the old saying: Suzanne, be careful what you wish for; you just might get it.* And now she had gotten what she'd wished for (at least secretly); what the hell was she going to do with it? She was about to become the single, friendless woman with the golden retriever living in the Bradys' old cottage and working for Charlie Baio. If she wasn't careful and didn't make some friends right away, she ran the risk of becoming known as the town oddity, even measured by Provincetown's standards.

Everything seemed to have fallen so easily into place for her: this house, the job at the Center, getting away cleanly from D.C. with the dog, the goodbye note (goodbye forever, as it now appeared). And now she didn't know what to do with herself. She felt numb. She had always had Doug. Somehow she just couldn't imagine living life without him. *Well, wasn't that what you always planned for, you dumb ass?* There was nothing left to do but cry. She seemed to be doing a lot of that lately. And once again, she had to face the reality that no one really cared about her problems, or felt sorry for her. If she thought she had problems, she had to fix them herself. And in the grand scheme of things, her problems didn't amount to squat; there are plenty of people in the world with problems the likes of which would put her to shame.

Okay, okay, okay, Suzanne thought, enough self-analysis. I've got to get on with the rest of my life. She looked again at the divorce papers she had tossed on the kitchen table. Maybe there was something else in the envelope. There wasn't, not even a personal note from Doug. The only places that bore the signs of personal attention were the various places where she was supposed to sign. These were marked in red ink, *I'll look at this later,* she thought. *Ignoring it won't make it disappear, you know.* "I know, I know," she muttered aloud. "Oh, great, now I'm starting to talk to myself. Isn't that the first sign of losing your mind?" she continued as she gazed out at the harbor. "Besides, there are lots of other things to think about, like dinner, right, Barney? And the evening news. Think I'll see what Brian Wililams has to say about the world." Barney looked up at her with his unquestioning gaze of adoration. *At least someone thinks I'm great,* she had to smile, as she reached down to stroke his head.

Brian Williams had plenty to say about the state of the world, and she would hear it re-stated two or three times during the present and subsequent presentations of *The Evening News.* By the time she went to bed, she could almost recite the broadcast *verbatim.* "At least it stops me from talking to myself," she muttered. No, it doesn't; I've got to stop watching so much TV, she thought, as she turned out the lights.

*   *   *

The next morning, Suzanne got to the office extra early, so early in fact, that she beat Natalie's arrival. She climbed upstairs with every intention of making coffee, and found that Charlie was also in early, already at his desk.

"Hey, good morning, boss; I think I got some the names of young lovers for you," she said, as she measured the coffee into the filter and filled the pot with water.

"That's great, Suzanne; I'll be downstairs in a few minutes. Is Nat in yet?" Charlie asked.

"She wasn't in when I got here. Hope she's not sick or something," Suzanne answered.

"She's not allowed to get sick; no one is," Charlie joked.

About that time, Natalie arrived at the office. "Sorry if I'm late," she explained, "The blankity-blank hair dryer conked out on me so I'm still kind of damp."

"But you're not sick, right? Charlie explained how no one on this staff is allowed to get sick, *ever.*" Suzanne feigned a very serious demeanor, as she started upstairs to get coffee. "Did you bring more pineapple?" she asked on her way up.

"Yeah, buddy; did you bring in any hot cross buns" Natalie asked.

"No, but I can go get some if you want," Suzanne replied on her way back downstairs.

"Oh, that's okay. I suppose I don't really need them; they're just so good, they're hard to resist," Natalie said. "Guess I'll have to suffer through with fruit and coffee," she grimaced.

"So, where are the hot cross buns?" Charlie asked as he bounded downstairs.

"Oh, for heaven's sake," exclaimed Suzanne. "Do you want me to go get some or not?"

"Forget it," they both said in unison, "don't need it!"

Taking a seat and sip of coffee, Charlie then asked, "So, Suzanne, what have you got for me?"

"Well, I came up with the names of people in love because of the Sanctuary last night. Looks like there are at least three couples we could develop focus pieces on in the Sanctuary newsletter, or in the Center's publication," Suzanne started.

"Let's hear 'em," Charlie said.

"You remember Mark Smythe and Melanie Yates, don't you? They were definitely brought together by the Stellwagen Bank Sanctuary. I did a little research into their backgrounds, and, well, they both worked for NOAA at the same time; Mark was employed by the Sanctuary Program and Melanie was an intern employed by NOAA's Policy Coordination Division, or PCD. I remember Mark more than I do Melanie, mostly because he worked in the same division I did, the Sanctuaries and Reserves Division, or SRD. But I also remember Mark because he was incredibly handsome and very much aware of that attribute. Being originally from somewhere in

England, he also had that British accent, which has always been a magnet for women. He had it all, that boy.

"As I remember, back in D.C. they dated each other for a while, but apparently, at some point, Mark dumped her. Melanie was also very pretty, in a cute sort of way, very perky and soft spoken. I didn't really get to know her very well until the dumping event took place, and Melanie needed a shoulder to cry on. She and I went to lunch a couple of times, just to get out of the office, you know? She was very young and naïve about guys, and I guess I offered her a willing ear to listen to her pain and confusion. Well, Melanie ended up moving to Boston, where she worked for the Director of the Commonwealth's 'coastal and ocean programs' department, or something like that. Meanwhile, in his effort to gain promotions within NOAA, Mark moved over to the National Marine Fisheries Service, and took an assignment in Gloucester. The next thing I remember hearing about the two was that they reconnected at the dedication ceremonies for the Stellwagen Bank Sanctuary in Plymouth, back in the summer of 1993. They were all over each other that day; what a couple! Now I understand they've bought a house in Rockport and are parents of two young boys."

Charie and Natalie both were rapt to Suzanne's descriptions of this cover-material couple.

"Wow; are there more love stories tied to the Sanctuary?" Natalie asked.

"Yeah, what else you got, Suzanne?" Charlie said.

"Well, I guess the most recent and most strongly tied to the Sanctuary are Mason and Jennifer Mason," Suzanne started. "Although with this couple, there are ties to the Center, as well."

"Now you're talkin'," piped in Charlie, who really wanted to hear about love connections tied to the Center. "Mason has done a lot for the Center, by applying his science backround and hands-on knowledge to improving the welfare of cetaceans that *we* come into contact with," Charlie went on.

"You know, I imagine some of those cetaceans are the same individuals seen in the Sanctuary. But you're right, Charlie; Mason is indispensable to both the Center *and* the Sanctuary," Suzanne continued.

"And what's the love connection with Jennifer Mason?" Natalie asked, even though she knew the answer.

"Well, I personally got to know Mason during my many, many trips to Cape Cod and the Gloucester areas during the designation process. He was a big help to me in identifying the user groups and their concerns about possible regulation of their activities, should the site become designated. And Jennifer was an early advocate for designation of the sanctuary; she testified at public information meetings in Gloucester, as well as in Boston and right there in Provincetown," Suzanne explained. "I guess there's something about a pretty young woman that can melt even the hardened hearts of commercial fishermen. She became one of our biggest allies during that period," Suzanne smiled knowingly. "She has the biggest brown eyes, and a very soft voice and demeanor; kind of endeared her to many of those rough-and-tumble fishermen," Suzanne continued.

"Well, she certainly endeared herself to Mason," chuckled Natalie. "I guess I was just in the wrong place at the wrong time, huh, Suzanne?"

Charlie looked with some confusion at Natalie, and seeing this, Suzanne said to Natalie: "Men. They're always the last to catch on."

The love stories concluded with Suzanne's description of the Sanctuary's Karen Clapham and Detective Charles "Bud" Clemsen. "This couple, as you no doubt know, is particularly close to me, or at least Bud Clemsen is particularly close to me," she said.

"Bud Clemsen is or was, a detective first grade with the D.C. Police Departent; he's recently retired. But while he was still with the police, he was the lead investigator in that murder case involving someone on the staff at the National Marine Sanctuary Program in D.C. And during the course of his interviews of Sanctuary Program staff and other employees of NOAA, he became kind of intrigued by my various descriptions of the whales and other marine life found at the Stellwagen Bank Sanctuary. Anyway, to make a long story short, Bud had some time off coming to him, and he wanted to see the whales at Stellwagen Bank. And I wanted to get back up to the Cape to look for houses, so we decided to travel together, so I could steer him in the right direction about whale watch boats, while giving him a crash course on what kinds of programs the Sanctuary had to offer.

"Needless to say, that's how Bud met Karen Clapham, the education/outreach program coordinator for the Sanctuary. And, of course, as you know, Karen also serves as a naturalist on the Cap'n John whale watchboats. I guess it was only natural the two got together. The next thing you know, Karen talked to Bud about the possibility of working at the Sanctuary as an enforcement officer, and today, he is one. Actually, he is the *only* one the Sanctuary staff has," Suzanne smiled.

"Did I detect a little bit of an emotional relationship between you and Bud?" Natalie asked.

"Yeah, as I said, Bud was, and still is, important to me. I value his friendship, but I'm happy that he and Karen are together now. They seem to have a lot in common, and I know Bud will be a great Sanctuary enforcement officer. I guess it's hard to get a man to give up the uniform, especially when he looks so good in it," she winked at Natalie.

"Well, a great set of couples-in-love stories," Charlie said.

"I can see how any of these pairs could be great fund raisers for either the Sanctuary or the Center. Suzanne, in all your spare time, do you think you could start developing pieces for the Sanctuary's and the Center's publications?" he asked.

"And I could take the photos, no problem," Natalie added.

"Sounds like we're in business," Suzanne folded up her notes, and rose to answer the phone. *Well, you've always said you wanted to be an author,* she thought to herself, although this type of writing wasn't exactly what she had in mind. *Well, gotta start somewhere, I guess.*

Eight
Settling In

On her way home that late afternoon, Suzanne stopped at the local hardware store to inquire about fencing for her yard. After prolonged haggling over the per-foot price of various fence designs, she finally settled on a pretty, rustic (and importantly) five-foot-high design that was in stock and could be installed within forty-eight hours. While she was there, Suzanne also inquired about "doggie doors." *This must be my lucky day,* she thought, as the hardware store manager referred her to a pet supply shop over on Bayside Street which could help out.

"Got a German Shepherd myself," the manager relayed, "and those doggie doors are indispensable. You know, with dogs, it's always 'out again-in again, in again-out again, out again-in again, in again-out again.' Never ends until they bed down for the night." This all sounded pointedly familiar to Suzanne; Barney was a very good dog, and he always let her know when he *really* had to go out, but he also played the 'out-again-in-again' game to the fullest advantage.

She found her way to the Happy Paws Pet Shoppe and was able to quickly zero in on a doggie door that she thought would work. The assistant manager stepped up behind her and asked if he could be of assistance.

"Hi, how big a dog do you have?" he asked. His name tag stated "Tim Collins," and Suzanne responded, "Oh, he's a golden retriever, about eighty pounds, I think."

"Great dog; used to have one myself," Tim smiled as he reached for a large-size doggie door. "I think this is probably the size you're going to need. Are you going to need any help installing it?"

"Nope; I'm pretty sure I can handle it," Suzanne said. "But can you deliver it? I've got a lot of stuff to get home tonight. There's no particular rush, but I would like to have it in by the weekend," she said, as she pulled out her wallet.

"We can bill you if that's easier," Tim offered.

"No, I'll just go ahead and pay now, okay? And here's my address so you know where to deliver it," she handed Tim a handwritten card with her name, address and phone number.

"Well, great, Ms. Douglas. We should be able to get this out to you day after tomorrow," Tim smiled and shook Suzanne's hand.

Whew, that was a successful trip, she thought as she walked home. Upon entering the small cottage, she was able to envision the handsome fencing surrounding the entirety of the house. She had decided to install the doggie door in the existing kitchen door at the back of the house. A tight fit, but it would work. "So long as you don't put on a lot of weight, Barney, okay?" Barney, looked at Suzanne somewhat quizzically, as if to say, "is there any food in this deal for me?"

"No, I'm afraid not, buddy; but you have other ways of getting food; you're not exactly starving, you know. Just be glad you're not living in some Asian country, where they eat dogs!" It was a good thing that Barney didn't really understand what Suzanne was talking about; he'd be out the door and down the road in a heartbeat.

"You got nothing to worry about, Barn. It's gonna be great here for both of us; you'll see."

She plopped the rest of her materials from work on the coffee table, went to the kitchen and fixed herself a drink. With a pad of paper and pens, she and Barney adjourned to the small back yard, where there was a smallish round table with three chairs around it. Since it was about time (at least according to Barney), Suzanne also brought out his dinner bowl accompanied by a larger bowl of fresh water. *Ah,* she thought, as she sat at the table, *all is right with the world.*

For an hour or so (until it started getting dark) Suzanne thought about and made notes on what she wanted to say about each of the three couples they had talked about that morning at the Center. Since she knew almost all of the young lovers (some better than others, but that was maybe another story), she first started scribbling down notes and insights on Mark Smythe and Melanie Yates.

There was discussion of where each person had come from and how they wound up working on the proposed Sanctuary. Tied in with this background were insights about the personal feelings of each on the worthiness of trying to identify and establish uniquely safe areas in the ocean for whales and other associated marine life to thrive. She remembered the time back in D.C. when Mark had once commented on a particularly cool jacket-and-skirt outfit she had on; said it was "a bit of all right," and had stood close to her and smiled as he said it. Even back then, she was grasping at "thin air straws." Just another lost opportunity, she had told herself at the time, although the truth was, of course, there never was any opportunity with Mark. He was *way* out of her league, and at least ten years her junior to boot. "You sure can pick 'em, Suzanne," she said to herself; "you are so pathetic," she sighed and continued with some additional thoughts on Melanie Yates. Melanie was a truly nice young woman with enormous soft brown eyes, and apparently quite bright, too. After leaving NOAA, she had moved to Boston and gone to work for the Director of the Commonwealth's Coastal and Ocean programs.

By the time she had finished with the "Mark-and-

147

Melanie" story, it was almost dark, and she and Barney went back inside the cottage. She ran off a copy of the material she had written, and got a fire started in the small fireplace. "Time to start thinking about dinner, I guess, huh, Barn?" she said softly under her breath. While dinner was heating up, she once again looked at the divorce papers from Doug. Sighing heavily, she decided she probably ought to consult with a lawyer before she signed off on the documents. Did she really want a divorce? Probably, but she wasn't at all sure about it. She mulled this over a bit while she and Barney ate dinner in front of the fire. "I'm going to find a really good divorce lawyer tomorrow," she said to herself, "and we'll see who comes out ahead in the end; after all, Doug's the one committing adultery, not me. I bet I can get a tidy settlement sum out of this, and I deserve it!" It was beginning to seem like she ended almost every day by making rather detailed lists of things to be done. It was a ridiculous habit, a little bit like playing Solitaire for hours on end, with no particular goal in sight. It was just a way to kill time, while she tried to think about what she should be focusing on. Nonetheless, she made her list for the next day, and decided to continue tomorrow evening with the Bud Clemsen and Karen Clapham story. Tonight, she just didn't have the fortitude or stomach to document what appeared to be true love. "That love was supposed to be mine," she grumbled.

"I can work on developing the stories of these others, if we get a decent reaction and return for both the Center's publication *and* the Sanctuary's monthly newsletter and magazine."

"Yep, that sounds like a good idea," Charlie said when she floated the idea with him the following morning at the Center. "Might as well see who in the world still believes in love, right?" Charlie chuckled, "I know *I* still do."

"And don't you ever lose it, Charlie; the world would be a

148

much sadder place if it didn't have your love and passion to sustain it," Suzanne said.

So with Natalie fussing around with her wide-angle lenses and panoramic view finders, she quickly got to a comfort zone of locations and lighting for the first "in-love-because-of-the-Sanctuary" couple, Mark and Melanie, and the pictures turned out great.

"Oh, I can hardly believe these; they look, I mean, we *look* so wonderful, Mark," gushed Melanie. "Are you going to take pictures of Mason and Jennifer, too?" asked Melanie; "they're the really gorgeous couple in the group, you know," Melanie continued.

"Oh, all these wonderful folks who fell in love because of the Sanctuary will be profiled and photographed, and their stories will be published in both the Sanctuary newsletter, and in the Center's quarterly magazine," Suzanne answered. "And don't worry; it'll work. People who love whales and other marine mammals will also love stories about people who share their love and passion for marine mammals.

"For now, we're going to run the story and pictures of Mark and Melanie in both the Sanctuary's and the Center's publications," Suzanne said. "And we'll see how good the response is, especially the response to our *subtle* plea for contributions. And you know there will be a great response; and both the Sanctuary and the Center will use those generous contributions to further the good work underway here."

So, that's where they started, and the stories were published in the Sanctuary publication, *The Ways of the Stellwagen Bank Whales*. Also published at more or less the same time were articles and pictures of Karen Clapham with Detective "Bud" Clemsen. Karen had been handling naturalist and public education activities; Bud was a huge help in carrying out whatever enforcement and patrol activities needed to be done for the Sanctuary Program. "With any luck at all, and some really hard work from both the Sanctuary staff and the equally intense employees at the Cetacean Research Center, we *could* make and institute some really forward-looking programs for all these wonderful small whales, larger whales, and also for the people who want to commit serious time and money and serious effort into both the present and the future of all Gulf of Maine marine inhabitants.

"Well, I'm game; how about you guys?" Suzanne continued.

Mason, Mark Smythe, and Suzanne, and the great Charlie Baio all had a look at the prelimary plans and seemed pleased with the prospects of getting these magnificient animals a safer, more nourishing environment. "Well, it sure sounds like a good deal all around, and I think if we can pool our resources, we can make it a great place for our friends, *The Leviathans,* and they will be more inclined to return to these waters year after year," Suzanne had said her piece, and hoped the others would see things the same way she did. There was, as it turned out, never a problem. Maybe it was the abnormally great weather they were having; maybe it was just the right combination of players and creative ideas all converging at the right time and place. In any event, all involved in this grand production seemed to think great benefits would be bestowed on both the Sanctuary and the Center.

"We'll keep our fingers crossed, and maybe something really great will come out of this little venture," Charlie said. "When can we expect to see these articles published, do you think?"

"I think we can get them both into the Sanctuary magazine and the Cetacean Research Magazine by next tmonth," exclaimed Natalie.

"Yea, good work, guys," Charlie beamed.

*   *   *

On Tuesday evening, true to his word, Tim Collins brought the doggie door Suzanne had picked directly to her house. Two additional guys also came from Happy Paws, bringing along the rustic fence Suzanne had selected.

"Oh, Mr. Collins, it's so great to see you again," Suzanne gushed. "About how long do you think this fence installation will take?"

"Aah, shouldn't take more than three, maybe four hours," Collins said, as he unloaded what seemed like a *lot* of wood pieces and various tools and other equipment in the small side yard to Suzanne's house.

"It's going to look beautiful; I can tell. Can I get you guys something to drink?" Suzanne asked.

"Not yet, ma'am; when we're done we'll take something, right?" Collins said. By seven P.M., two-thirds of the fence was installed; Collins rapped on the kitchen door. "Ms. Douglas? If it's okay with you, I think we'll quit for the evenin', and finish up tomorrow morning," Collins asked, as he wiped his sweaty face with an old towel from his back pocket.

"That's fine with me," Suzanne rpelied, "you guys do look kind of exhausted. Thanks for what you've done so far, and I guess I'll see you tomorrow morning, okay?"

"You got it, honey; we'll be back tomorrow around eight A.M.," answered one of the carpenter guys. "You should be all set up by tomorrow evening," Tim assured her.

"That's great, I can hardly wait to get everything installed and working; it'll look fantastic, I know!" Suzanne gushed again, ignoring the reference to 'honey' by one of the carpenters, although she would have loved to poke him in the face.

So the following early morning, Tim and his friends were at it again, and both the fence and the doggie door off the kitchen to the backyard were finished by late afternoon. The additions had really transformed the small Cape Cod cottage into an even grander cottage that obviously cherished its canine family member. It was, in Suzanne's mind, perfect.

"Thanks, you guys . . . I mean, *really* thanks. How much additional money do I owe you?"

"Ah, you don't owe anything more for the fence, and we already got your payment for the doggie door, so I guess we're just about even up." Tim and the other guys nodded in agreement.

"Well, the least I can do for you *hard* laborers is provide some icy cold Sam Adams. Wadda ya say?" Suzanne offered.

"Sounds great to me," Tim and the others said, as Suzanne cracked open three or four bottles and put them on the counter.

*   *   *

"If you think they're good enough, we can run similar stories about Mason and Jennifer in the following month's issues so they appear at the same time. 'Course, it all depends on how good the public reaction is to the first 'lovebirds' stories," Suzanne continued.

"It's good enough; let's run it. We still need a couple of pictures. And I guess we need permission from Mark and Melanie," Charlie concluded.

"I can handle the photos; do you want them taken on site?" Natalie asked.

"Of course; where else?" Charlie said.

"Okay, then; let's go. I'll call Mark and get him lined up with Melanie for some photos," Natalie added.

By late afternoon, Suzanne had reached Mark at the Sanctuary office, and he somewhat reluctantly agreed to a "short" story about himself and Melanie, and to one or more photographs of them, to be taken by Natalie on site. Natalie was delighted, of course, and suggested they take some photos both out on the pier and onboard the Center's research vessel.

"Oh, this will be great; the weather's just right, and I think I remember how to use this stupid camera!" Nat teased. Nervous chuckles all around, as Nat began to size up her intended photographic subjects, and what location or locations would bring out the best in both Mason and Melanie. "Wear your usual clothes for working with the bottlenoses; we're going to be showing people when and how the dolphins are fed here, what they eat and how much . . . you know, all the critical stuff. It'll be fun; everyone relates to the bottlenose dolphins; they're so much fun and they really do seem to respond to people's needs," Natalie continued, "and I'm writing some glowing material about you both that will accompany the gorgeous photos to be provided." Melanie blushed a little, and Mark seemed more enthusiastic than previously demonstrated. In the final agreed-upon arrangement of glowing words and great photos, it was quickly decided that some of the most beautiful shots should be taken near the holding pens where the recovering dolphins and porpoises could be medically treated and hopefully released to fend for themselves, and for their families.

"Yeah, I think this story lends itself well to both the Sanctuary Program magazine, *and* to the Cetacean Research Center. Both magazines could run at the same time, and we could get a pretty good feel about the public's reaction, and if people are moved enough by these stories of love, hard work and devotion to saving the lives of porpoises, dophins and larger cetaceans, both Sanctuary and the Cetacean Research Center's research programs, as well as their educational programs, could be greatly expanded and enhanced," Suzanne added. "I'll give Karen a call at the Sanctuary office, so she's involved in this project, too. She's got to be good with editing and placing people where they should be for the most effective shot Natalie could take, right?"

"Right," answered Karen quickly when Suzanne gave her a call the following morning to fill her in on the story plans and the ties to the Sanctuary and the Center. "I *am* good with people and placing them in the right places for catching great photos. I also do a pretty fair job of editing text," Karen went on. "Why don't you send me up what you've got so far, and I can start looking it over and making editorial changes and suggestions, okay?"

"Sounds good, Karen; I can fax this copy up to you, and maybe we can get together on say, Thursday, okay?" Suzanne asked. "I hope to God I'll be finished with the installation of dog gates and fences by Wednesday, so we can turn attention to the important task of fundraising for the Sanctuary and the Center."

"A noble plan, to be sure; let's get on it, partner!" Karen exclaimed. Suzanne was actually glad to have Karen helping out on this. To some extent, it kept her from being so preoccupied with Bud.

Two days later at the Center, Charlie asked Suzanne if she would like to accompany him out on the Center's research vessel. Of course she said yes; she was very much looking forward to getting a good look at the Atlantic White-sided Dolphins which frequented the Sanctuary this time of year. So off they went, two mornings later, aboard the *RV Ever Barbara,* with Suzanne anxiously looking off both sides of the sturdy little vessel for signs of White-Sided Dolphins. *What a great side benefit,* she thought to herself, the extra "field trips" with Charlie. They hadn't been out for more than two hours when Suzanne, standing in the crow's nest with her trusty binoculars, spotted a fairly small number of the Dolphins in question. The group (or more properly called, the pod) seemed to enjoy the attention being shown them, and stuck around close to

Charlie's boat pretty much all afternoon. They spent a good deal of time diving under the vessel and quickly resurfacing on the other side of the boat. It seemed quite a game for the dolphins, and it also allowed Suzanne and Charlie many opportunities to shoot some wonderful footage of these 4- to 6-foot-long black and white denizens of the deep.

"Oh, Charlie; they're so beautiful," Suzanne exclaimed.

"Yeah, they are something great, and we're going to try to get a pretty close head count on these guys, if we can," Charlie responded. "It may be impossible, but I've got this theory that Atlantic White-Sided Dolphins, like Humpback Whales, can be individually identified by their body and fin markings. They're all pretty distinctive in appearance; I'd like to see if we can start cataloguing them, like we've been doing with the humpbacks. Sound interesting?""Yeah, I'll say! Do we have the necessary photo equipment for this project?" Suzanne asked.

"Think we got everything we need," Charlie responded. "Maybe Nat can help, too; she's pretty good with a camera on moving targets."

"Hey, this will be fun; when can we get started?" asked Suzanne.

"Right away, I think," Charlie answered. "We'll check with Nat tomorrow at the office."

Nat was excited, too; and quickly arranged for one of the volunteers to cover the reception desk at the Center.

So two days later, off they all went, with eager anticipation that the identification plan of Charlie's would pay off beautifully. It didn't. But Nat got some beautiful photos, nonetheless.

"Damn, I don't know what I was thinking," Charlie humphed. "Well, guess it was just one of those things that seemed like a good idea at the time," comforted Nat. "We still got some great photos, and I'm real pleased I didn't lose the camera overboard, at least!"

"Yeah, I still think we can get some very useful photo images of Atlantic White-Sided Dolphins. There's a lot of comparison and contrast interest in the Atlantic White-Sided and the Pacific White-Sided. We could certainly do an in-depth review of both species; it would be quite useful to researchers trying to better understand dolphin families found throughout New England." Once again, Charlie demonstrated he was very resourcrful at planning other ways to pursue the same objectives, so he wasn't too distressed at having the first round of photos not displaying what Charlie thought would be a clear and smashing hit. "We'll get there; not to worry; let's get what we can and move on, guys, okay?"

Once docked and in the process of off-loading, Suzanne glanced again at the neatly painted lettering on the aft of Charlie's research vessel. She couldn't deny her curiosity and asked Natalie: "So who's Barbara? Is she Charlie's true love?"

"You didn't know? Barbara was Charlie's wife; she died of cancer almost five years ago. We don't talk about her much; I know Charlie's still grieving," Nat said quietly. "She was quite a brilliant scientist in her own right, you know," Nat continued briefly.

"What was her speciality?" Suzanne asked.

"Mostly near-shore invertebrates; you now, the flotsam and other things that whales live on," Nat responded.

"Whales and *other* critters, right?" Suzanne asked.

"Right; I really don't know much about that stuff," Nat answered.

"Me neither," Suzanne smiled.

Nine

Charlie Cool

"You're a pretty good spotter," Charlie observed next morning in the office, as Suzanne, Nat and Karen looked over the film from the trip. "You were the first one to see the White-Sided Dolphins," he continued.

"You inspire me," Suzanne said, as she bowed in a deep deferential motion and chuckled almost inaudibly.

As Nat put some of the film prints on the other desk in the front office, and in what must have been a giant leap back into the real and social realm, Charlie asked Suzanne, "Would you like to catch some dinner tonight? Believe it or not, there's a prettey good little French restaurant just outside of town," Charlie suggested.

Caught kind of off guard, Suzanne nonetheless quickly answered that she would love to have dinner, and asked what time would be good for him.

"Meet you there around eight, okay?" Charlie responded.

"Now let me get this straight," Suzanne said, "I don't have to catch my own dinner, do I?"

For what seemed like the first time in a long time, Charlie finally chuckled out loud. "Nope, you don't; I guarantee."

"Oh, great! I'm a sucker for those French pastries, washed down with a great little merlot," Suzanne exclaimed.

That evening, they pulled into the restaurant's parking

lot at about the same time—seven-fifty P.M. *This is a good sign,* Suzanne thought to herself, as she straightened her light cord skirt and crossed the gravel parking lot at a casual pace to the side entrance of the *Stuffed Flounder* from which drifted mixed and tantalizing aromas. *No wonder the fisheries are becoming depleted; they can't reproduce fast enough,* she thought quickly, noticing at the same time that the sun- and wind-tanned Charlie Baio looked *fabulous* in a pressed, clean white shirt and just barely faded blue jeans. She sucked in her tummy, and hoped she looked at least decent.

"So, this isn't really a French restaurant, is it?" she smiled broadly and asked Charlie as they were shown to a small table near the window facing the small inlet near the south end of Racing Point. "You can't fool me," she laughed.

"Maybe not, but they *do* have some great wines here," Charlie smiled in return. "I'm not one hundred percent certain about the pastries, though," he smiled.

So, is this a date or what? Suzanne thought to herself as they looked over the menu after they had been seated. She was beginning to hope it *was* a date, or at least the beginning of one. *Oh, come on you idiot, you can't do anything about new relationships 'til you break clean and final with Doug.*

In an unstated effort to not further deplete the diminishing numbers of flounders, they both decided on entrees of fresh, farm-raised catfish, seasoned with lemon-pepper, or (in Charlie's case) cajun spices. It seemed the more politically correct choice, and besides which, both choices sounded really good.

Which they were; Suzanne hadn't realized how hungry she was. Even Charlie noticed how quickly she finished.

"Hungry?" he asked, as he settled back in his chair and slowly finished his wine and refilled his glass, as well as Suzanne's.

Finally, he said, "As good as the wine list here is, there's another reason I asked you to have dinner with me tonight."

Oh, God, she thought. *I'm going to get fired. Too much fooling around in the front office with Nat; why isn't he firing* her? That damned stomach knot was back big time and she felt slightly queasy.

"That promotional photo shoot with Mason and Jennifer has really started to pay off, Suzanne," Charlie continued. "I'm not sure about the most recent figures, but we've had at least fifty or sixty 'check-attached' responses."

"Oh, that's great, Charlie; any word on the Sanctuary also receiving positive responses?"

"Yeah, them, too, from what I hear," he said, as the second glasses of wine neared empty. "What I'd like to talk to you about is shifting your responsibilities to focus more on fund-raising efforts. You've always been so good at talking to folks about the importance of the Sanctuary; you could also convince people with deep pockets about the importance of the Center's research. Interested?"

"Boy, am I!" *What a thrill this could be,* she thought.

"Good," Charlie continued. "You can fill in for me when schedules get impossible, as they often do. You'd be a really big help and keep me from going nuts!

"Deal, then, right, Suzanne?" he asked as he stretched across the table to reach and shake her hand. "With positive results, I'd like for you to become the Center's Director of Funding and Public Outreach Activities. How's that sound?" Charlie was now leaning forward in earnest on the table between them. *Funny,* she thought, *I never noticed his steel blue eyes before now. I bet he could talk the stripes off a zebra.*

For the moment, all she could think to say was, "Wow! When can I start?"

"We've got a meeting this Tuesday afternoon with some corporate investors from Boston; they're coming down to the

Center, though, to kind of look the operation over, so that makes it easier on us, right?" Charlie smiled.

"What exactly do you want me to do, Charlie?" Suzanne asked.

"What you're best at, kiddo. Convince them that the research we're doing is the most important that can be done for saving the future of the great whales and all of the smaller creatures sustaining them," he concluded. "And the ties with the Center and the Sanctuary's programs should also be illuminated and strengthened," he continued.

"Why, Dr. Baio, I do declare, you sound like a preacher yourself. Is that *all* you need me for?" Suzanne responded in her best imitation Southern drawl.

Chuckling, Charlie said, "You know, Scarlett, I just can't keep this stuff up forever; I've got to keep getting out there to the Bank."

"That's it, Charlie! What a great slogan for these investment types; and everyone else, too: 'The Bank: Invest in it and Watch it Grow!' " Suzanne was quite pleased with herself a this instant inspiration, and Charlie seemed to agree.

They finished dinner and negotiations, and parted with a hug. "See you tomorrow morning, right?" Charlie asked, as he pulled away in his car.

"Right, boss! See ya tomorrow!" Suzanne answered. She turned and headed to her car, with a feeling she couldn't quite describe. She was excited, to be sure, but also felt full of self-doubt: could she really do this? What the hell did she know about fund-raising? *Guess all I can do is talk about the Sanctuary and the importance of the Center's research efforts, and hope that people will respond the right way,* she thought. *Wish I hadn't eaten so fast; I could've watched Charlie all night . . . You know? Some people never learn,* she thought to herself, so she climbed into her car and slowly pulled out of the parking lot.

160

Barney whined his usual friendly greeting as she pulled in front of the cottage.

"Miss me, gorgeous? What have you been doing while I was gone all day? Make any friends with the local dogs? How about the local cats?"

At the mention of cats, Barney's ears pricked up, and he tilted his head to the right, as if to hear Suzanne better. She had to smile, and gave him a deep hug and rub along his back. "You are such a great dog; what would I do without you?" Barney followed her inside, and they both sought out the nearest soft place to recline and sleep or contemplate the next day.

The next morning, while brushing her teeth, Suzanne realized that her new job responsibilities would clearly involve working more closely with the Sanctuary staff, particularly Karen Clapham, their public outreach person. She liked Karen alright; however, she *did* move right in on Bud. *Showed poor manners. Ah, well, guess it was never going anywhere with Bud, anyway. And I don't care, either,* she thought as she spit and drank a large glass of cold water.

While walking to work, she started thinking about how she didn't have any *idea* of how to conduct a fundraising program; the stomach knot was back. Maybe Karen could help. Oh, joy, she thought. *Get over it, jerk; you're better than this.* Natalie was in a good mood this morning, still flushed with the high praise for her photographic efforts last week.

"So, are you thinking about goin' pro, with all those great shots, Nat? I'm really impressed," Suzanne continued with the praise.

Nat giggled and continued to blush, "Oh, gosh; I don't know." As soon as she sat down at her desk. Nat regained herself and said, "Oh, Suzanne, I almost forgot to tell you. You had a call early this morning from Karen Clapham, up to the Sanctuary."

I love the way New Englanders talk; this kid must be from Maine, or something. "I'll give her a ring; thanks, Nat," Suzanne answered.

"Is Karen Clapham there this morning? This is Suzanne Douglas, from the Cetacean Research office over in P'town. I understand Karen wanted to talk with me sometime today, if possible."

"Oh, yeah, hi, Suzanne, Karen's here and she does want to talk to you. Hang on, okay?"

"Hey, congratulations on the promotion; guess you and I will be working together some on stuff now, huh? I'm really happy for you, Suzanne," Karen gushed into the phone before she could even get in a "good morning."

"Yeah, Karen, I think you and I are going to be doing a lot of creative projects that will benefit both the Center's and the Sanctuary's interpretive and educational needs. In fact, I wanted to ask you if you've got some time to meet and kind of brainstorm. It could really help us both a lot, I think; waddaya say?"

"I say it sounds like a good idea to, as they say in D.C., do lunch; when's good for you?"

"How about tomorrow? I'd like to come down to P'town for a day, anyway. I can meet you at the Center around eleven o'clock or so; that okay with you?" Karen responded.

"Sounds good to me; I'll see you tomorrow, Karen. Take care, okay?" Suzanne gave a long, silent sigh as she hung up. She wasn't really looking forward to this. Truth be told, she thought, Karen kind of made her feel uncomfortable. *Boy, word sure gets around fast up here,* she thought. *Wonder who told her, anyway?*

As they settled in at the Lobster Shack, Suzanne initiated conversation quickly by asking, "So, how long have you and Charlie been working together?"

"Oh, gosh; I guess it started when I started going out on

162

the whale watches with Charlie. Must have been two or three years ago," Karen answered as she munched on her lobster roll. "Why do you ask?"

"Well, to tell you the truth, I'm a little bit worried about Charlie."

"Why's that?" Karen asked.

She couldn't help letting on a little more than she ever intended. "I think Charlie's a little more obsessed than he needs to be with being out on the Bank, trying to disentangle whales from fishing nets. He's not as young as those interns and researchers, you know; I worry about him."

"Well, I think he's going to be focused on population counts, for the immediate, anyway. Can't be too dangerous, don't you think?" Karen said.

"Yeah, I guess," Suzanne replied.

The two finished lunch and continued to talk about potential public information projects, and possible fund-raising gimmicks. *All in all,* Suzanne thought, *it was a worthwhile meeting.* In spite of herself, she couldn't help liking Karen; she had a lot to offer. She could see how Bud would like her.

As she left home, she also couldn't stop thinking about Charlie, and how rough it must be working to free a large, struggling whale from fishing gear. Unlike the young idealistic "whale-lovers" that clamored to Cape Cod and other shore research-and-rescue locations, Charlie certainly had no disillusions about the dangerous nature of the open ocean and its largest inhabitants. She hoped Charlie *was*, in fact, going to be focused only on population counts for the foreseeable future, at least. But in her heart, she knew otherwise; entanglements were just a matter of time. They were bound to happen. Didn't really matter what the protective statutes and regulations said, the reality was commercial and recreational fishing in the same areas that hungry great whales fed was almost certain to result in entanglement with fishing gear. Thinking about it made her shudder a little, and she felt maybe a little more the evening chill closing in.

True to his word, early Tuesday afternoon two men in suits (no less) showed up at the Center, ready to hear, she presumed, lots of good reasons why substantial investments in the Center's research activities should be made. Suzanne was very nervous, and tried hard not to show it, but Charlie was there to introduce her to Mr. Harrison and Mr. Bradley from the Boston Fleet Bank, as the Center's new fundraising and public information director. She was overwhelmed at the quickly pronounced title. *Lord, everything has happened so fast; my head is spinning!*

"Pleased to meet both of you," Suzanne smiled, as she shook hands with each man. "I'm afraid Dr. Baio may have inadvertently misled you into thinking that I am an expert on all the detailed research conducted here; I'm not. But I can and will introduce you to the skilled scientists working here with Charlie. I'm just good at keeping the records up to date," Suzanne said, as she showed the visitors into the laboratory. As they were shown around the small lab rooms, Charlie introduced the Center's two researchers, who cheerfully explained in sometimes foreign-sounding terms the varied focal points of the Center's inquiries. When one of them mentioned the importance of getting the results of their work to the many fishermen and other boaters, Suzanne couldn't help herself, and started making the connections between the Center and the Sanctuary. Within ten minutes, both Harrison and Bradley started asking questions about the Sanctuary's programs and how they were funded.

"Well, as you probably know, the National Marine Sanctuary Program is a Federally administered and operated program, but it's really different than what you might think because public participation and support are crucial to its survival," Suzanne responded. "The Program is largely funded by

Congressional appropriations, but of course, it's never enough, as the costs of establishing and maintaining Sanctuary programs continue to grow every year," she continued. Out of the corner of her eye, Suzanne could see that Charlie really wanted attention brought back to the Center's work. She quickly changed the focus of her discussion.

"One of the Center's most exciting and important research undertakings is attempting to learn a great deal more than is currently known about the highly endangered northern right whale. Did you know that it's thought by scientists that there are fewer than 350 of these giants left?" she asked, as she looked directly at the two bankers. "Stellwagen Bank, or Middle Bank, as many of the local fishermen call it, is unique to the East Coast, as its structure and makeup provide a varied and rich feeding ground for a wide variety of migratory cetacean species; and the Center's research is superior to any other regional or national effort. Its research also provides the basis of the Sanctuary's educational programs," Suzanne continued.

As Suzanne went on, both men from the Boston bank grew more and more interested, and finally Mr. Harrison asked, "How come there's so few of these big guys left, anyway?"

"Well, they don't breed that often, but more importantly, I guess, their feeding grounds are being overused by other activities, such as commercial and recreational fishing," Suzanne responded. "Plus, during the whaling era, this species was almost eliminated by commercial whalers, and it takes a really long time for a species like this to recover," she concluded.

As both of the visiting bankers seemed thoroughly convinced of the importance of the Center's research, and maybe particularly because they indicated that their organization would be favorably inclined to consider substantial funding to the Center, Charlie stood up and thanked them both for spending the afternoon with them. Suzanne, too, was happy that things had gone well (and that she had overcome her nervousness).

After the bankers had gotten into their car and pulled out of the parking lot, Charlie said to Suzanne, "Well, good job, Suzanne. I think the prospects for a favorable decision by Fleet Bank are looking real good. Thanks for your help."

Just then, one of the researchers from the lab came out to the conference room and said in a somewhat alarmed tone: "Hey, Charlie! Bud Clemsen just called from the Sanctuary. We got a whale entangled in some fishing gear out near the north end of the Sanctuary boundary, off Cape Ann."

"Crap," Charlie said. He immediately got Mason on the phone and the rest of the researchers assembled for a quick briefing. "Mason, I want you to get out to the Bank as fast as you can. Paul, Vinny and I will meet you in the zodiac, okay?" Charlie looked strained and worried.

Ten

To Save a Whale; to Break a Heart

"I'm going out there with you," Karen said as Mason got his gear together.

"Nope, don't think so, Karen; it's pretty dangerous out there in the zodiac," Mason replied, "and you're dealing in close proximity to a fifty-foot whale that's in distress."

Karen looked disgusted and threw up her arms at this unilateral assessment. She immediately called Suzanne, looking for assistance in changing Mason's mind. "I've got an idea," Suzanne said. "Why don't I just follow in the *Ever Barbara* carrying the zodiac, and you get the whole thing on video from the Sanctuary enforcement boat? That sound okay to you?"

"Makes sense to me," Karen replied, "I assume Charlie will be piloting the *Barbara* out to the Sanctuary, and you can take over once we get situated near the whale, and Charlie's out in the zodiac."

"Oh, yeah, of course Charlie will be piloting; guess I'm just excited and nervous. Did Mason say what kind of whale it is?" Suzanne asked.

"Not sure, but he thinks it's a northern right."

"Oh, God. No wonder Charlie looked so worried," Karen said. "Let's get to it."

Quickly, although it seemed like *finally* to Suzanne, the zodiac was outfitted and loaded onto the *Barbara,* and Sanctuary and Research Center personnel were on their way to the Sanctuary's northern end. The trip took about thirty minutes, but Suzanne was very worried they wouldn't make it in time. For the first time, she felt seasick, although she knew it was only nerves (and fear).

They got there, and it was just as Paul had predicted: the waters around a flailing, probably frightened, whale were wild and churning. Although she had heard of these situations before, Suzanne had never seen anything like it; it was terrifying. She was scared, and felt incredibly helpless; *I wish there was something I could do,* she thought. As she watched from the *Barbara,* the zodiac was lowered into the water, and Charlie, Vinny, and Paul started moving toward the struggling whale. The Sanctuary vessel was already stationed at the far side of the whale's location, and Suzanne could see Bud in the distance, helping to lower a second zodiac into the water. As he lowered himself into the zodiac, he looked as worried as Suzanne felt. Nonetheless, Bud did an impressive job maneuvering the zodiac, with Mason and two additional Sanctuary staff members aboard, toward the thrashing whale.

With high-powered binoculars raised to her eyes, Suzanne could see quite clearly that Charlie, Paul and Vinny had reached the "tail end" of the whale, which was plainly entwined in heavy nylon fishing line. Both Charlie and Mason had microphones attached around their necks, so there could hopefully be some communication between the boats.

"Charlie! Can you get a good look at what's going on at your end?" yelled Mason.

"Yep, tail's pretty tangled with fishing line; gonna try to cut him loose. What's it look like at the head?" Charlie's zodiac worked closer to the tail, and Charlie leaned out over the edge of the zodiac, while Paul and Vinny got hold of some of the fishing lines, using a long grappling hook. While Suzanne and Karen watched with great apprehension, Charlie leaned a

168

little further and cut two of the lines. He could see that the lines had cut through the whale's outer skin, deep enough in places to cause bleeding.

"This is a calf!" Charlie yelled to Mason. "Not more than twenty-five or thirty feet!"

"Holy jeez," Mason yelled back; "Any sign of the cow?"

"Yeah, I see her hangin' by just to the north; see her?"

As the rescue crew continued their slow work to free the young whale, and Mason started to loosen the fishing lines closest around the whale's head, the strangest thing happened. The whale became suddenly still, as if somehow he sensed he should; as if he knew these humans were actually trying to help. Thinking back on the incident Charlie and Mason both held an unspoken belief that in his own way, somehow the whale understood.

After what seemed like several hours, Charlie, Mason and the others aboard the zodiacs managed to disentangle the young cetacean, and he quickly made his way toward his mother.

"Whew, I think he's going to be okay," Mason said, as the two zodiacs drifted toward each other. "Did you get the same feeling I did when the whale just stopped moving and let us get closer to him?" Mason continued.

"Yeah, really weird, huh? Like the little booger knew we were trying to help him," Charlie replied, as he put his head down and took a deep breath. "I'm glad we don't have to do this too often. I'm beat; let's head home, pal." Mason nodded in agreement, and reached over to shake hands and give Charlie a congratulatory hug. But he was a little late, as Charlie had already slumped onto the zodiac's single bench, and Paul and Vinny quickly closed in on him to prop him up and offer water.

"You okay, boss?" Paul asked, as he held the cup of water close to Charlie's mouth. The two researchers and good friends of Charlie looked plenty worried. Mason pulled the Sanctuary zodiac close to Charlie and looked intently at Paul and Vinny and asked if there was anything he could do.

"Nah, Mason, I think he's just exhausted. We better get him back to shore," Paul responded. So both zodiacs now moved slowly in the same direction toward the Center. Mason had the feeling that this ordeal had taken more out of Charlie than he would ever admit to, and getting Charlie to slow down was not going to be easy.

Suzanne had watched the entire ordeal from the *Barbara*, and Karen used almost all the videotape in the Sanctuary's recorder; as the whale swam quickly toward the horizon and joined its mother, both witnesses to this nearly disastrous event felt themselves both emotionally and physically spent. In the aftermath, however, neither could express exactly the sequence of events or the actions of the rescuers. Both Karen and Suzanne agreed, however, that the previous four or five hours were a clear reminder of the magnitude of the inevitable conflict between whales and human fishing activities.

"See what I meant the other day about being worried about Charlie?" Suzanne said as they made their way back to the Center.

"Yeah, I think you're right," Karen replied.

It indeed, took Charlie a couple of weeks to recover from the whale rescue. He didn't seem to want to talk about it much, either. Toward the end of a relatively quiet day at the Center, when she noticed Charlie sitting at his desk, staring off into space beyond the Center's confines, she carefully approached him and quietly asked, "Do you think he made it, Charlie?" Momentarily startled, Charlie pushed back his chair and sighed, "God, I hope so, Suzanne. Those cuts from the fishing lines looked pretty deep. We can't afford to lose many more northern right whales."

Suzanne felt discouraged the rest of the afternoon. Was

there any way to stop these horrible entanglements? She just didn't know. *As if beachings weren't enough* . . . she sighed, as she collected her files and stuff to close up for the day.

As she walked home after work, Suzanne passed all the now-familiar sights and houses she had come to love, but even they aren't lifting her mood. Then she had a terrible thought: Barney. *Oh, God, poor Barney! He's been alone all day and he hasn't been fed or walked. In the rush to get out to the entangled whale, I forgot all about him! God, I hope he's okay,* she half muttered to herself as she quickened her pace toward Commercial Street. The first two things she saw as she rounded the corner to her cottage were the flag up on her mailbox and no Barney in the yard. She didn't even stop at the mailbox; she called for Barney. There was no response. Inside the house, there was still no response or sign of her beloved friend. *Don't panic: don't panic,* she tried to steady her thoughts as she looked hurriedly in all the usual places where Barney might be found. Nothing. Just at the point when she was about to call anyone she could think of, and realizing she didn't really know that many people at all in the first place, Suzanne found a hastily scribbled note that had been left on the kitchen table. It saved her sanity, and read; *Suzanne—I knew you were going to be out at the Sanctuary for a while, so I came over, fed and walked Barney, and took him home with me, okay? Hope you don't mind, he's a great dog! Call me when you get home! (Or he can spend the night here, if you want!) Natalie.* Suzanne smiled and let go a long sigh of relief. *I do have a few friends here, after all,* she thought, as she grabbed the phone to call Nat.

"Nat? Hi, it's Suzanne, and thank you, thank you, thank you! And I'm sure Barney thanks you, too! I must be the world's *worst* dog owner; with all the excitement going on about the entangled whale, I just completely forgot about time and getting home to Barney. Did he give you any trouble? I can't imagine he would have; goldens are not exactly known for their watchdog capabilities, you know?"

"Absolutely no apologies are needed, Suzanne. I was happy to pick him up and bring him here to our house; he sure is great company," Nat replied.

"Yeah, he is that. Nat, thank you so much; you're the greatest! Okay if I come over in about a half an hour to pick him up? I'll bring a pizza, okay?" Suzanne gushed. She was so grateful, both that Barney was all right, and that Natalie was such a good friend. Maybe things were going to be all right, after all. She quickly changed into some clean jeans and shirt, grabbed some money and her keys and headed out the front door of the cottage stopping to open the mailbox, she was surprised to see a large official-looking manila envelope stuffed in with the usual assortment of junk mail and bills. When she saw the return postmark of Washington, D.C. she caught her breath and thought, *Oh, no; it can't be. I'm just not going to look at this now.*

It was a short walk to the pizza carryout, and from there to Natalie's house. Even though the pizza smelled great, and she normally would have been dying to hurry up and get to Natalie's so they could dig into it, on this evening, at this time, she was not hungry. Actually, she was close to terrified. She mentally determined that she would not display this discomfort and fear to Natalie, as she turned up the walk to her house. After all, Natalie was a good friend; she certainly didn't need to be dragged into the grimy details of her relationship with Doug.

After only one light rap on the front door, Natalie opened the door wide, and Barney came slowly trotting outside. "Hey, Suzanne! I'm so glad you're okay, and that you came over!" Natalie exclaimed. Suzanne smiled broadly in relief, sank to her knees, and hugged Barney.

"Oh, Nat! I can't begin to thank you enough; I think I'd

lose my mind if I lost Barney. He's been everything to me lately; know what I mean?"

"Yeah, I now exactly what you mean, Suzanne, after all, he's your child! Now get in here with that pizza; I'm starving!" Nat exclaimed.

"Hope you like mushrooms, onions and green peppers," Suzanne said as she came inside and put the large box on the kitchen table.

"I heated up the oven in case we need to keep it warm for a while," Natalie offered, as she filled two glasses with diet Coke.

"I can't imagine that the thing will have a chance to cool off, you know?" Suzanne answered as she cut the large pie into eight generous slices and put two each on two plates. She then sat down and took a long drink of the diet Coke. After Natalie had happily chomped through both of her two slices, she came up for air with a satisfied grin and asked, "So, Suzanne, what's bothering you? You don't look happy at all, and you're not *eating*. That's not like you; what's going on?"

After a long sigh, Suzanne decided she couldn't wait until she got home to open the official-looking envelope from Washington, D.C. And besides, she needed to talk to someone. *Sorry, Nat; I guess you're the listening post,* she thought, and barged on ahead. 'Well, I got this envelope in the mail today and I'm pretty loathe to open it. I think it's divorce papers from Doug, back in D.C.," she relayed quietly.

With Natalie watching closely, Suzanne carefully opened the envelope. She was right. The divorce was final. She took a deep breath. She knew it would come to this, but maybe as it always was, it was hard to take in the reality without some reaction. Even though they were kind of new as close friends, Nat immediately got up from her seat and held her arms out to Suzanne.

"Suzanne, what is it? Is it what you thought? Is there anything I can do? I'm so sorry; God, I can only imagine how you feel," Nat said gently, as she wrapped her arms around Suzanne's shoulders.

Suzanne could feel her eyes getting moist and her chin beginning to tremble. She didn't want to lose control, even though it was useless to think that was possible. She let out a few muffled sobs, and Nat held on a little tighter. The two women held on to each other for a few minutes, and then Suzanne pulled away, whispering through tears, "Thanks, Nat; I really didn't mean to bring this pile of domestic woe to your door. Sorry. I don't know what ever made me think I could handle this without feeling or showing any pain. What a jerk, huh?"

"Nah, not at all. Do you want to talk about it? I'd be happy to listen; I'm not sure I can be any help, though," Nat offered.

"Oh, Nat; thanks so much. I can't unload on you; you're too good a friend, you know? I don't want to wreck our friendship over this stupid crap," Suzanne sniffled. In spite of the unpleasant news and the crying jag, she was feeling a little better, maybe a little stronger. "C'mon, the pizza's getting cold," and she managed a smile, and felt a little hunger coming back.

They finally finished, amid full mouths and laughter over silly things; even Barney got a slice of pizza for himself. It got to be 10:30 P.M. and Suzanne stood up, cleared the plates, and reached for Barney's leash and Nat's shoulders. "Thanks for taking care of my dog, and for being a good friend, Nat," she said, adding, "I'd appreciate it if you didn't mention the divorce stuff to anyone, okay?"

"Of course, Suzanne. If you need anything, or want to talk, let me know," Nat gave her a last hug and walked her to the door. As she walked down the sidewalk, Suzanne had a good feeling about her trust in Natalie. *I wonder if Nat's ever been married, or in a serious relationship,* she thought, as she wandered past the now-familiar cottages and storefronts that had become friendly landmarks to her, and increasingly made her feel like she was home. She glanced down at Barney with undying love and devotion; *what would she do without him?* She stooped and gave the big golden a long hug and rub behind the ears. That deep, familiar, contented growl greeted and comforted her, and she smiled all the way home. By the time she rounded the corner onto Commercial Street and unlatched the gate to her cottage, Suzanne was more than ready for bed. Barney was too, as he made his way quickly to his bed in the corner next to Suzanne's bed and lowered himself with a contented-sounding sigh. Almost instantly, his eyes closed, as Suzanne turned out the front lights and got into her pajamas. Even though she still had plenty of questions, life right now seemed pretty good except for having to deal with Doug and the divorce. Somehow, it all still seemed unreal.

When she got up the following morning, she reminded herself that there was really nothing left to do about the divorce: it was done; she was a single woman. So how come she didn't feel great about that? Wasn't that what she wanted? She wasn't so sure anymore. Doug had his faults, to be sure, but if she had felt lonely and alone in the past couple of weeks, she *really* felt alone now. *I'm not sure I like this, not sure at all,* she thought to herself, as she put out Barney's kibble and water bowls. Somewhat dejectedly, she telephoned the office around 8:30 A.M., because for the first time, she just didn't feel like going in to work. *This is not a good sign,* she thought, as she said to Natalie that she'd be a little late getting into the office.

"Hey, that's okay," Nat responded, "don't worry about it. You've had a couple of rough days, and besides, Charlie's not going to be in until late this afternoon. How about you? Are you okay?" Nat asked.

"Oh, thanks, Nat; has Charlie got another meeting scheduled with potential corporate donors?" Suzanne asked.

"No, I don't think so. Frankly, I think he's still bummed out about the right whale entanglement. You know, it just gets to be inevitable after a while. Every once in a while Charlie just kind of disappears for a while 'til he can get a grip on reality, I guess," Nat concluded.

"Yeah, I can relate; there seems to be a lot of that going around lately," Suzanne mumbled.

"Anything I can do to help?" Natalie asked.

"Nah; thanks Natalie; I just need a little time to clear my head; I'll see you tomorrow morning, okay?" Suzanne asked, and gently hung up the phone.

Suzanne spent the rest of the morning, and a good part of the afternoon wandering around the house (which now seemed quite small to her), and wondering if there was something, anything, she could or should do. *Life's so confusing, so frustrating,* she thought. *Just because I never did send those divorce papers back to him, I guess he presumed that was what I wanted to happen. I don't know; I just don't know what to do. Maybe moving up here was a big mistake; maybe he's pissed 'cause I took Barney.* The thoughts and recriminations circled around and around her head; by mid-afternoon, she had a massive headache and was extremely tired.

"Oh, Barney, what have I done? What should I do now?" At hearing his name mentioned, Barney lifted his head for his bed and gazed quizzically at Suzanne. The big sleepy golden got up and came over to Suzanne, wagging his tail and softly whining. As though he knew all was not right, he laid his chin in Suzanne's lap and patiently gazed at her with those huge soft brown eyes, waiting for her to assure him everything was going to be alright. "Oh, it'll be okay, Barn; I just don't know exactly what to do, do you?" she quietly wondered. Barney stood with his head in her lap and tail wagging slowly for a long time, while Suzanne tried to come to some rational decision. "Think I'll get some ice cream; it always makes me feel better, even if it doesn't solve the problem." So over her favorite rocky road ice cream, Suzanne finally picked up the telephone and dialed Doug's number. She knew he wouldn't be home; it was only about 3:00 P.M., so she left a voice message on his phone, saying she really wanted to talk to him, and to please call. She really did; and she really *didn't*; she just didn't know.

She wandered up to the extra bedroom/study area, where she sat at the old oak desk pushed up against the wall, gazing out over Race Point, at the northern tip of the Cape. It was getting darker, duskier, as the late afternoon sun disappeared behind an increasingly solid curtain of clouds. She could barely make out the horizon to the north, where she hoped in vain to see some signs of life; either marine mammals or late-day fishing vessels, working their way back to port. She could see nothing. With a heavy sigh, she turned to the files and reference materials she had relating to the beaching behavior of large and small cetaceans. There wasn't much to review that she didn't already know. There just wasn't any reasonable explanation for the behavior, other than the loss of balance or equilibrium, due to possible ear infection, followed by the "blind leading the blind" instincts demonstrated by pod members. Maybe it really *was* that simple, she thought; but how frequently do whales get ear infections, anyway? It was totally frustrating, because she didn't think uncharacteristic whale behavior could be that easily explained. *God, I don't know; just don't know anything anymore,* she thought.

After an hour or so, she again decided that she was not going to be able to solve this remaining mystery (although there were plenty of other mysteries to whale behavior, and, in fact, to human behavior, as well). *Damn, I feel so stupid,* she thought, as she closed the last notebook on the subject. *Well, hell, I'm not a damned scientist, anyway; I was an English major, and what good does that do me here?*

As she came downstairs, the phone rang. She picked up on the fourth ring, but apparently, the caller had given up; there was no response to her "hello?" She glanced at her watch; it was almost 7:00 P.M. "God, time flies when you're having fun, huh? Hell, even when you're not," she muttered to herself. "The least they could have done was leave a message," she said to herself. "Wonder if it was anyone important, or at least interesting. Guess I might as well clear up those files, and get some dinner together," she said to herself as she climbed back upstairs.

When she got back to the study, Suzanne could see that, at least for the moment, the sky had cleared and the last rays of sun were pouring down on the ocean surface. *God, is this the absolute best time of the day, or what?* she thought to herself as she gazed out across the calm ocean waters. *This is so beautiful; I never want to leave here.*

As she stared in a daydream without really looking at the water, motion there brought her eyes quickly back into focus. By squinting and by grabbing her binoculars, Suzanne could just barely make out the unmistakable movement of several large, gleaming, sleek black bodies making their way effortlessly northward. "Oh, Barney, maybe those are right whales, headed up to Canada," she said excitedly to her loyal companion, who had come into the room primarily to remind her that it was way past time for dinner. She ignored his little whines until she could no longer see the whales disappearing into the far distance; then she responded to him by saying, "Okay, boy, let's go get dinner." Barney gave a slight jump and quick dash to the door panting happily on the way. "They are so beautiful, so at one with their environment, you know?" she said to Barney on their way downstairs. He looked at her like she was asking some completely improbable question. In any event,

178

his interests were clearly focused on dinner, not the passage of those large, black monsters in the water.

As usual, Barney gulped down his dinner, as if he hadn't eaten in days. Suzanne smiled down at him, as he licked the bowl so clean it probably didn't even require washing. *So predictable,* she thought to herself, *and thank God for that.* "Want to go out, Barn?" she asked softly, and as if to confirm, Barney gave voice to a soft "whuff" and headed for the back door. By now, it was getting dark for real, and Suzanne knew there had to be more to learn from those volumes upstairs, so she grabbed a couple of trail mix bars (the kind with cocoa chips in them) and headed back upstairs. True to traditional patterns, the minute she got the light adjusted at the desk and comfortable in the chair, the phone in the kitchen rang.

"Suzanne? Hi, it's Doug; I'm returning your call from earlier," came the deep and familiar voice.

She couldn't think of anything to say. There was an awkward silence, and Doug said, "Suzanne? Are you there?"

"Yeah, I'm here. What do you want, Doug?" She was trying hard not to sound or act bitter, but it was difficult. *How did he get out first,* she thought. *I was supposed to be in control of this entire process.*

"Well, actually, I was going to call you as soon as I could get your phone number. It takes a while, you know, with new listings. Suzanne, listen. We both know this relationship isn't working very well. You're always traveling, and I'm up to my ears in work. We never really talk anymore, and we sure as hell never climb into bed together anymore. I'm tired of living like this, Suzanne, and I assume you are, too. Or maybe not; I don't know. I don't know anything about you anymore, except you have this thing about Cape Cod and whales. Well, I have a couple of things, too, you know? What I'm getting to is that you and I don't seem to have much in common, and I can't waste any more time hoping that things will work out. They never will, Suzanne. So I'm moving on; you can to."

"Gee, thanks Doug, I'm overwhelmed," was all she could come up with by way of a response. "What kind of things do *you* have, or should I ask, 'what's her name?' " Even though she couldn't resist getting in this final dig, Suzanne regretted it the moment the words came out of her mouth. As angry and hurt as she felt, she was really sorry things had to end this way. Choking back tears and the muffled sobs in her voice, she finally said, "I'm sorry, Doug, let's please just agree on parting as friends, okay?"

"Yeah, sure, Suzanne, I can do that. I wish you all the best of everything always. I'll send you my new address when I get settled in, and let's stay in touch, OK? I'll always love you, Suzanne. Take care of yourself." And the phone clicked its impersonal goodbye.

Suzanne put the phone receiver down very quietly and stood facing it for several minutes. Though she certainly had felt alone, afraid and even abandoned before, at this moment, she felt utterly and indescribably solitary. She never thought it would ever come to this. *I can't even imagine it would be this awful; God, I feel like just dying, or just escaping to some place where no one knows me, where no one knows anything about me. No, that wouldn't do any good; I've got to survive; I've got to thrive.* She sat on the edge of her bed and cried hard for over an hour.

When she finally forced herself to get up, she wandered slowly into the bathroom and stared at herself in the mirror over the sink. She was without a doubt, one of the world's *worst* criers: her face was red and puffy, and her eyes looked awful. In fact, all of her looked awful. "What a shitty day," she muttered. By now, it was pretty late; she wasn't hungry, so she let go of any further thoughts of fixing dinner. *What a divine way to lose weight,* she thought. *Just get your heart broken and stomped on; works every time.* As the evening passed on into night, she returned to the undemanding television and watched with disinterest a late repetition of local news. She used most of the time to change into bedclothes, brush her teeth, and let Barney out back to pee, and turn off the TV. Necessities accomplished, she coaxed him back into the cottage with a biscuit, and both settled into their respective beds with almost identical sighs. *Kindred souls,* she thought, as she pulled the covers up to her chin and tried to rid her mind of most of the day's events.

Eleven
Back to the Pod

The next morning, Suzanne pulled herself out of bed (even though she would have much preferred to stay under the covers all day) and made her way into the office. On the way, she began to think about how she needed to talk to Charlie; she just didn't think she could really be happy and effective here at the Center; but how was she going to tell him?

It was early when she got into the office, but Charlie was already there, and on his second cup of coffee.

"Good morning, sunshine," he said quietly, as Suzanne hung up her jacket. "How're you feeling? Nat told me to take it easy on you this morning, 'cause you got some personal problems to clear up, right?" He handed her a coffee mug from the rack and motioned her to have a seat. She thought to herself, *This is going to be bad. He's probably going to fire me because I'm nothing more than a basket case, and I can't possibly be useful or able to stay abreast of all the stuff I need to know here.*

But Charlie took Suzanne by surprise, "I've got some news for you, Suzanne," he said. "You ever hear of a Sanctuary satellite office?"

She answered quickly, as if *anyone* would certainly know what a Sanctuary satellite office was: "Uh, sure, Charlie, I know what a Sanctuary satellite office is: 'course, there aren't any for this Sanctuary, yet anyway," she answered.

"Well, I spent about an hour on the phone with the Stellwagen manager this morning, and he and I think it would be a good idea to establish one here in P'town, what you think about that?" Charlie waited for a reaction.

Somewhat dumbfounded, Suzanne sat speechless for a moment then, finally, she asked, "Are you serious, Charlie? I mean, in many ways, it makes sense, since Provincetown is at the southern limit to the Sanctuary boundary, and as you know, is a pretty major tourist attraction by itself," she added. Gathering strength in her response, Suzanne added, "I mean, you could certainly kill a couple of birds with one stone, so to speak, by having both the Cetacean Research Center *and* a Sanctuary field office here, don't you think?" she concluded.

"Couldn't have said it better myself," Charlie answered. "That's why I told your manager up there in Scituate to get the go-ahead from Washington, and we'll start looking for possible office locations; how's that sound to you? I figured since you can't seem to stop talking Sanctuary all the time, we might as well make it officially okay, right?" Charlie winked at her. It was the first time she'd seen Charlie crack a smile since the whale entanglement ordeal.

"Do you mean *here*, near the Center?"

"Yep, 'cause I still expect you to help with fund-raising for the Center. Otherwise, you're gonna be your own show, kiddo," Charlie said, as he finished his coffee and got up from his desk.

She didn't know what to think; she didn't even now *how* to react to this suggestion: was Charlie suggesting that she run a Sanctuary field office? It was too much to digest and decide upon immediately. "Can I think about it, Charlie? I mean, it's a huge responsibility, you know? Are you, in fact offering me a job as manager of a Sanctuary field office?"

"Nah, Suzanne, I can't offer you any kind of Sanctuary

job; I'm the private sector, not the federal government, remember?"

"I don't want to be a field office manager. I moved up here to get a simpler life, you know, Charlie?"

"What on earth makes you think life is simpler here than in Washington, darlin'?" Charlie asked, although it was clear he didn't really expect an answer. "We just have a different set of complications here, that's all," he added.

The statement couldn't be argued with, that was for sure. *I'd rather be researching the potential environmental impacts of some proposed federal action than trying to rescue a whale from nylon fishing gear,* she thought. "No, you're right, Charlie; I just don't think I could be a good manager," Suzanne concluded.

"I think you underestimate yourself, kid; but think about it overnight, okay?" Charlie grinned at her and picked up some papers from his desk and started downstairs.

Okay, I'll think about it, she thought to herself, as she also headed downstairs and for the door. *Maybe; maybe I can; maybe . . . but all that responsibility . . . ugh, who needs it?* It was a lot to think about.

When she got home (and after discussing it with Barney), Suzanne called Natalie and asked her how she felt about the possibility of being an office manager (and photographer) for a Sanctuary satellite in Provincetown.

"What in the *hell* are you talking about, Suzanne? Are you jumping ship, or something?" a surprised Natalie responded.

"Nah, don't worry, Nat; I wouldn't *think* of leaving you and Charlie, but there's maybe an incredible opportunity coming up in the near future, and I'm pretty sure it can be a great thing for all of us. Want to hear more? How long have you worked at the Center, anyway, Nat?" Her thoughts were racing; she felt like she had to get Nat on board with this; this could be a great team: great for both the Center and the Sanctuary.

"Charlie had a long discussion with the manager at the Sanctuary this morning, and the two of them apparently decided that it would be a grand thing to establish a satellite office for the Sanctuary here in Provincetown. The two offices have much to share in resources, and in information for the public and scientific communities," Suzanne started, only to be quickly stopped by Natalie.

"Whoa, partner! You're losing me fast. Can this really happen? I mean, doesn't it take a long time for the federal government to establish something like that?"

"Yeah usually, but since the Sanctuary is already established, what really remains for this new, smaller office to be established, is for funding to be 'earmarked' from the NOAA budget, and office location and staffing processes started, through public notices in the Federal Register," she continued, until she had to come up for air. After a short minute, Suzanne again asked, "So as you were about to tell me, how long have you been at the Center?"

Natalie sat down at her kitchen table, and didn't say anything for a moment. "Almost six years, if you can believe that," she finally said. "I was kind of between jobs; I used to manage that little book store on the north end of Commercial Street, 'til it went out of business. Not much of an endorsement is it?" she sighed. " 'Course, the closing was not *my* fault; a big book store outlet swamped any competition in New England," she added with a small measure of disgust.

"But, Charlie's an old friend, and I ran into him one morning while I was running down near the wharf, and he offered me a job at the Center right away; really needed someone to keep tabs on the office, you know? We kind of agreed on hours, money and responsibilities, and that was that. Been here ever since," Nat concluded.

"Wow, you'd be perfect. 'Course, we'll have to wait for the Register notice to come out, send in our applications and wait for NOAA to respond. Knowing the government, shouldn't take more than a couple of months," Suzanne smiled and chuckled quietly to herself. "So, partner, whadya think?" she asked.

"Benefits? Some vacation? Yeah, I guess so, Suzanne; it sounds pretty good," Nat replied happily. "I could do this; no problem. Manager Ward; I like the sound of that," she practiced. "Can I get a uniform?" she added.

"I think Sanctuary employees all wear uniform-type shirts, with NOAA and the name of the Sanctuary embroidered on them," Suzanne replied. "They're really pretty cool," she added.

"What color?" Nat pursued.

"Hey, don't push it, smart-ass," Suzanne laughed, "tan and dark blue."

The two friends hung up their phones happily, and it looked like life was beginning to improve. Although it was late, Suzanne felt invigorated by the conversation with Nat, and she stepped outside onto the small deck at the back of her house. Barney trailed closely behind her. An almost-full moon glowed quietly through the scrub pine trees at the back edge of the yard. With an audible sigh, Suzanne gazed at the moon, and said to herself, "Life has just *got* to get better now, don't you think, Barn?" Her query was met with his soft "woof" as he pushed close and leaned into Suzanne's legs. She sat down on the small bench running along the edge of the deck and held her hands out for Barney's soft muzzle. *I am so lucky,* she thought; *maybe being single isn't so awful after all, so long as I stay busy with something I really care about.* "Still, I wouldn't mind some company now and then; sorry Barn," she concluded.

Next morning Suzanne could tell Natalie was beginning

to scope out possible locations for the satellite office. "Don't get too far ahead of yourself, Nat. The Register notice hasn't even come out yet," Suzanne admonished playfully.

"Yeah, but it can't hurt to look for the perfect office location, right?" Nat responded.

"How about getting some of the *Center's* work done this morning?" Charlie piped in, in a less-than-playful voice.

"Grump," Suzanne muttered and glanced at Nat, while nodding toward Dr. Baio.

The office routine continued as usual that morning, but Suzanne was beginning to think about her conversation with Charlie yesterday, and beginning also to think that her first instinct about being a Sanctuary satellite office manager was correct: she really didn't want to be a manager at all. What she really wanted was to be able to talk and discuss the importance of protecting "special" ocean environments for future generations, so that their resources could be used by a large variety of public interests in ways that would not jeopardize their long-term vitality. *God, I'm still thinking like a bureaucrat,* she thought. *I think working for the federal government has ruined me forever,* she muttered to herself as she glanced over at Natalie and noticed that she had a series of real estate ads spread out on her desk.

"Find anything promising?" she asked.

"There's a couple of possibilities here," Nat replied, "See these?" she pointed to two listings which were within a half-block of the water. "This one looks pretty good," Nat continued. Suzanne came over to Nat's desk and looked more closely at the ad in the local paper.

"So, beyond figuring out where the office will be located, and how many staff members we should have, how do you feel about being a Sanctuary satellite office manager?" Suzanne asked Nat.

"I'm not sure I know what you mean, Suzanne. I thought

187

we were just talking about someone to keep the office running, you know," Nat looked at her with some surprise.

"Nope, I think at least for the immediate or startup of this office, you would be, in effect, the satellite Sanctuary manager, complete with all the responsibilities *attendant thereto,* darling," Suzanne replied. "Charlie asked me to think overnight about being the satellite office manager, but having had a little time to mull it over, it's not what I really want to do, Nat," she smiled apologetically back at Nat. "I don't want to be a manager of *anything,* really; I have enough trouble trying to get myself managed," she smiled.

"Well, I'm not sure I can handle all of that," Natalie said.

"Oh, yeah, you can, Nat you just have to know the basic rules and regs for this site, and something about what makes Stellwagen Bank so 'nationally significant', as NOAA has deemed it; you'd be great," Suzanne coaxed.

"Well, what do *you want* to do?" Nat asked.

"I just want to be able to talk to folks, all kinds of folks, about why the Sanctuary is important to all of us, not just to the whales," Suzanne smiled. "I want to learn much more about the people who live and work in Massachusetts, and the rest of New England. I want to understand their frustrations and fears of the federal government. I guess I really want to understand what's important to them, and try to get them to believe that this Sanctuary, and *any* sanctuary, for that matter, is not just another federal layer of regulation," Suzanne continued.

"Glutton for punishment, aren't you?" Charlie was standing at the back of the front room. Neither Suzanne nor Nat had even noticed him there. "Suzanne, I wish you every good fortune in your endeavors, but you'll never convince everyone, you know? There are actually people out there who are not as enlightened as all of us; can you believe that? But

I'm with you all the way in your efforts, kiddo," Charlie stepped forward and put his arm around Suzanne's shoulder.

"Well, I guess all we have to do is wait for the Federal Register notice to come out, huh?" said Nat, heaving a big sigh.

"No, all we have to do is continue the Center's work *while* we wait for the Register notice to come out. Now let's get to work, okay?" Charlie concluded.

Suzanne felt a big sense of relief, since it looked like Natalie would apply for the satellite office manager position. She sure hoped so, anyway. Now all she had to do was concentrate on fundraising for the Center, and what the future might hold for her, as a single woman. For the time being, anyway, she felt reasonably sure that *something* would surface and become a fabulous idea.

As the week went on, Suzanne encouraged Natalie to contact the Sanctuary manager, and to get to know the other staff members there. Of course, it helped that she knew Karen and through her, Bud, who was very helpful to Nat in getting her familiar with who did what at the Sanctuary, and who to go to for information. By the end of the week, Suzanne could tell Nat was getting a little more comfortable with the whole idea, and this made her feel happy for Nat; Suzanne felt that Natalie didn't get the recognition she deserved for all she did at the Center's office.

On Friday afternoon, as the researchers and volunteers closed up for the evening, Suzanne lingered around Natalie's desk until the front office was empty. "You know, Nat, I think it might be a good idea if you could go to the Scituate office, and kind of introduce yourself and get to know the manager and Bud and Mason, and the other staff members up there, and get to know what their routine duties are, and all that kind of stuff," Suzanne suggested. "The current Sanctuary manager is a NOAA Corps officer, and his tour of duty there is only for three years. That's partly why NOAA is looking for a permanent manager, and why *I*, at least, think you'd be great there," she concluded.

"Oh, gee, I don't know, Suzanne. I don't think I can; it seems kind of presumptive, don't you think?" Natalie hesitated.

"No, Nat, I think that's exactly why you should go. And besides, Karen can be a huge support and help to you," Suzanne replied. "C'mon, "I'll go with you, Nat; tomorrow's Saturday; we could leave the Center early and head on up to the Sanctuary and spend the day there. Whadda you think? I bet Karen and Bud could put us up for the night if we want to stay over. It's a *road* trip, let's go, it'll be fun and we *both* will learn a lot, okay?" Suzanne pushed.

Natalie hesitated for a while, and finally said, "Okay, Suzanne, if you come with me."

"Great," Suzanne responded. "You'll see, Nat; it'll be a blast," she added. "Can we take your car? Mine's a rental, and I'm about to go over the mileage limit on it," Suzanne asked.

"Sure," Nat answered, and then added, "Can Barney come along?"

"If you don't care about dog hair all over the seats; he's a 24/7 kind of shedder," Suzanne smiled and nodded.

Saturday morning came, and Suzanne put Barney on a leash and walked up to Natalie's house. Natalie met them out front, carrying a coffee thermos jug, plastic coffee cups with covers, and a thick stack of papers.

"Hey, partner, ready to roll?" Nat nearly bounced up and down with excitement. As she put the coffee jug and cups in her car, she bent down to greet Barney. "Hey, Barn; I'm so glad you're coming along for the ride!" she said while giving Barney a big hug and ear rubs. His rapidly wagging tail almost knocked Suzanne over, as she tried to load both the freshly baked cross-buns and herself into the passenger seat.

"Guess someone's pretty excited, right?" Suzanne laughed, and Natalie grinned back.

"Does Charlie know about this trip?" Nat asked almost as soon as they got under way.

"Nope, not as far as I know, anyway," Suzanne replied. "I figure there's no point in telling him; you know how Charlie worries about everything," she chuckled. "Boy, I'll tell you, this trip is a real treat for me, Nat; it really helps clear my mind from a lot of junk, know what I mean?" she said as she gazed out the window.

It looked like it was going to be a beautiful day; already the sun was shining full in a sky completely void of clouds. Suzanne breathed deeply, and offered coffee to Nat. "So, what's the big stack of papers for?" she asked as Natalie took a long, appreciative draw on the coffee.

"Oh, you know, I'm just brushing up on my Sanctuary regulatory knowledge. Just in case the manager or anyone asks me any questions," she quietly replied.

"I think I already know most everything, but there's always some little detail or rule that slips my mind," Nat continued, as she turned off of Route 6A, and headed north toward Boston.

"I don't think anyone's going to be interviewing you today, Nat; you can relax. Just make a really good impression on the staff up there, and I think that'll more or less seal it when the time comes for a selection to be made," Suzanne said, as she bit into a still-warm cross bun and took a sip of coffee.

"Do you think a lot of people are going to apply for this position?" Nat asked. "I'm not very well-qualified, you know," she added.

"Oh, you underestimate yourself, Nat. Your knowledge of the program and the way you relate to people are two very strong advantages," Suzanne replied. She looked at the back seat and Barney, who had very happily draped his snout over the half-rolled-down window, and was taking in all olfactory sensations as quickly as they came at him. "You're just in hog heaven, aren't you, old boy?" she cooed as she gave him a gentle tug on the ear closest to her.

It was close to 11:00 A.M. when they rolled into Scituate, a pretty little town not far from Cape Ann. They had made good time, but Barney, as well as both Nat and Suzanne, were ready to get out and stretch their legs a bit before pulling into the Sanctuary parking area and entering the long, low building formerly used by the Coast Guard.

"You mean the Sanctuary has *all* this space?" Nat marveled as they walked toward the entrance.

"Yep. Neat, isn't it?" Suzanne answered. "And they have an option in future years, to take over the building out back, too," she added.

"Sounds like at least at *this* Sanctuary, there is an expectation that the staff and operations will expand," Nat cheerfully observed.

"That's exactly right; we *will* get bigger and do more things," came a deep voice from the side of the main building. Striding toward them, dressed in his usual black, was Mason. He still looked fantastic; Suzanne noted silently. *How come all the good ones are taken?* she thought; *it just isn't fair.*

"Mason! How the hell are you?" Suzanne exclaimed excitedly. "I didn't really expect to see you here, buddy," she said, as she got up close to Mason and shook his hand. Probably at hearing Mason's voice, Barney was at the car's rear window, barking and whining almost frantically. "I think he remembers you," Suzanne smiled broadly, as she let him out of the car. Barney went galloping to Mason, who met him with extended arms. "Barney! Good boy! Man, it's good to see you again!" Mason hugged the big dog, and "wrassled" him to the ground. The two were like long-lost friends, rolling around on the ground, who couldn't get enough of each other.

"So, Mason . . . done many necropsies lately? Wasn't that fun? I sure hope we can do that again sometime soon," Suzanne gushed.

"Not me, it's not exactly my favorite activity," Mason responded. "Nat, it's good to see you again, too; what are you guys doing up here, anyway?" he asked.

"Well, truth is, Mason, we came up to kind of get a little better acquainted with the staff and their various responsibilities," Natalie said.

"Because . . . ?" Mason looked intently at her.

"Because when the vacancy announcement comes out for the Sanctuary satellite office manager position, I want to apply for it," Nat asserted with a good deal of bravery, Suzanne thought.

"Ah, *good* idea," Mason smiled. "You'd be good at it, too," and he gave her a hug. Nat blushed. "You're going to have to get used to that," Suzanne said in a lowered voice to her friend.

So after a good deal of schmoozing, everyone went inside the Sanctuary office, where, as usual, there was plenty of activity going on. Being Saturday morning, plenty of volunteers moved around from table to table, and office to office. Soon after they entered the office, the Sanctuary manager came out of his office to say hello and greet Suzanne. Suzanne was, after all, well-known and appreciated for her work in getting the Stellwagen Bank Sanctuary designated, after almost ten years of effort.

"Suzanne Douglas! It's great to finally meet you; welcome to the office. Have some coffee, and let me show you around," NOAA Corps Lieutenant Miles Nelson smiled broadly as he extended his hand. "Is this your dog?" he asked, as Barney sidled up and sat down directly on the Lieutenant's left foot.

"Uh, yeah, this is Barney, Miles; he thinks everyone loves

him; I'm sorry he's not better trained," Suzanne said, as she pulled Barney off Miles' foot.

"No problem," Miles said. "I love dogs; unfortunately, we don't get too take them on the vessels much with us. Does Barney swim?" he asked.

"Only every time he gets the chance," Suzanne laughed.

Suzanne put Barney on a leash, and asked if it would be alright to bring him along on the office tour. "Sure, that's fine," Lt. Nelson answered. As they walked around the office, Suzanne was amazed at the increased technological approaches to measuring, monitoring and counting the myriad components—both living and inanimate—of the Sanctuary environment.

"Wow, this is really impressive. How long have you been here, Lieutenant?"

"Please call me Miles, Suzanne; things are pretty informal around here, and I like it that way. You know, you're a legend around these parts; did it really take almost nine years to get this site designated, and you were the only project staff member working on Stellwagen Bank?"

"Well, at the beginning, I had a lot of help from someone from the Massachusetts Office of Coastal and Ocean Resources," she replied. "But, as the project got more and more complicated and controversial, I was pretty much on my own. I'm not sure I'd ever want to go through it again; there were times dealing with the Army Corps of Engineers, and even the Environmental Protection Agency, when I felt like I was alone trying to scale a brick wall with only my bare fingers and no rope."

"And at some point, you discovered that on the other side of the brick wall, there was a moat filled with alligators," piped in Natalie.

Suzanne laughed, nodding her head, and said, "*And* I discovered that I didn't know how to swim!"

"Somehow, I find that hard to believe," Miles commented with a smile. "Seriously, anyone who can survive nine years of working with and against the ACOE *and* the EPA, to say nothing of getting through the mind-numbing bureaucracy of the National Oceanic and Atmospheric Administration, while staying focused on the goal of convincing all parties of the importance of creating a national marine sanctuary with some 'teeth' in its regulations has my undying admiration and respect," and Miles Nelson came up, at last, for air.

"Whew, I'm exhausted!" Suzanne said, wiping her brow for effect, and smiling all the while. "But thank you very much; I appreciate your kind and glowing words."

Lieutenant Nelson now turned his attention to Natalie, who was eagerly hanging on his every word.

"So, Natalie, or do you prefer 'Nat'?" Miles asked, "Do you think Charlie can get along without you at the Center? How long have you been there anyway?" he continued with the friendly questions.

Nat was clearly a little flustered, but Suzanne knew she had to handle these questions by herself, so she kept quiet. "I've been working at the Center with Charlie for about six years," Nat said, "and, as much as I love it, I'm pretty sure Charlie could get along without me, after some serious withdrawal training," she laughed.

"Well, the word about you that *I've* heard, anyway, is that you are nearly indispensable to the Center, and probably to Charlie, as well," Miles continued.

"Well, Lieutenant, I don't know about that," Natalie murmured quietly but, as Suzanne noticed, she also smiled.

"Relax, Natalie it's all good news about you; maybe you're on your way to being a legend, too," Miles said. "You guys come on in to my office; I've got something to show you that I'm pretty sure you'll want to see," he said as he led them into his small office in the rear of the building. With the office door closed behind them, the Lieutenant handed Nat and Suzanne two advance copies of vacancy announcements. Nat's eyes grew wide and she caught her breath, as she uttered to Miles, "But, but, aren't these supposed to be kept under cover until the official publication date?"

Miles smiled at the apparently naivete that Nat so sweetly demonstrated and said in response: "Yeah, but the notice will be published on Tuesday, and give applicants three weeks to respond, so I figured, among friends, what's an extra couple of days to allow some *really well-qualified* individuals to prepare their applications?"

While Natalie was obviously excited and overjoyed at the Lieutenant's generous preliminary gift, Suzanne just smiled and kept her thoughts to herself, at least for the present. She had no idea whether Miles could get into some trouble for giving out these vacancy announcements before the publication date, and she didn't want to be involved if there was going to be any inquiry into possible improper actions taken by a NOAA employee. *Ah, you overanalyze things too much; loosen up*, she thought.

"Wow, Lieutenant Nelson, thanks a lot," Suzanne said. "Natalie and I will be giving these applications a *lot* of attention in the next few days. And, you can be sure that neither of us will let on to others that we had this information in advance of publication of the Federal Register."

It was close to 2:00 P.M. before their discussions with Lieutenant Nelson were completed; Suzanne indicated to Natalie that she was pretty much ready to start back to P'town. "Anything else you want to see, or anyone else you want to talk to, Nat?" Suzanne asked.

"Nope, I think I've seen enough for now," Nat replied. "Do you want to get some lunch before we leave Scituate?" she asked.

"Yeah, that'd be great," Suzanne answered. "Oh, you

know what else?" Suzanne asked. "We should see Bud and Karen before we leave town; are they around today?" she asked Miles.

"Yeah, sure, Suzanne; they're in the back office, I think," Miles responded. So Suzanne and Nat poked their heads into the back office, where Karen and Bud were deeply involved in going through and categorizing the day's mail. "Gosh, Bud, can't you get someone else to do that stuff?" Suzanne joked as she put her arms around Bud and reached out to shake Karen's hand. "How are you guys, anyway? Seems like forever since I've seen you, you know?"

Bud looked up from the rather large pile of mail and smiled broadly at Suzanne and Natalie. "Did you ever think a former D.C. police detective would end up here, keeping track of violations of a Sanctuary's rules and regs? What did you think I'd end up doing here, anyway? Nah, I'm just kidding, Suzanne; I'm really glad we took that trip up here to see the whales and stuff, and thanks to you, I got to meet Karen, so life's great now," Bud responded happily.

"What about you, Suzanne?" asked Karen. "Did you really finally get that house in P'town?" she asked.

"Yeah, took almost every penny I had, and it needs some work, but I love living in Provincetown," she answered like a true non-native. By this time, Barney had found his way into the back office, and went directly over to Karen. He sniffed her briefly, then, as though he had gotten his "targets' confused, trotted with gusto over to Bud. *Karen's probably a "cat" person*, Suzanne thought, as she reached down and pulled Barney a little closer to her.

"Well, Nat and I just wanted to see you both and ask how things are going, and whether or not you like it here," Suzanne said.

"And when you're getting married, so we can mark the date on our calendars," Nat added, grinning.

197

Karen actually blushed, and Bud didn't say anything, but a moment or two later, he pulled Suzanne aside and said, "In answer to your question, no time real soon." Suzanne looked at him with some surprise and started to ask why not, but decided better of it, and just nodded her head and smiled knowingly in Nat's direction. Karen asked Suzanne how things were at the Center, and how she liked fundraising.

"I'm not sure I'm any good at it," Suzanne replied, "but it's really interesting and fun being there."

"Well, I'm glad for you," Karen said. Suzanne felt like she didn't really mean it, but she didn't much care. She just hoped that Bud was happy with her.

Finally, Nat and Suzanne left the Sanctuary headquarters, and headed out for somewhere to eat, before getting back on the road back to Provincetown. After a quick grilled tuna and cheese, and a little time for Barney to take care of business, they settled into Nat's sports sedan and left, full and happy.

"Well," smiled Nat, "I, for one, know what I'm going to be doing when we get back."

"And that would be?" Suzanne asked knowingly.

"Well, gee, isn't it exciting? We can be the first ones to get our applications in to NOAA: neat, huh?"

"Yeah, I guess so," Suzanne smiled in response; "I'm looking forward to going over the application documents." It was pretty clear to Suzanne that Natalie had really embraced the idea of being a manager at the satellite office in Provincetown, assuming such an office was to be established. *And it will. This is a good thing,* she thought to herself, as they sped their way back from Scituate. Even though Suzanne was quiet on the trip back, Natalie couldn't seem to cease with her unending stream of questions and comments about both the Sanctuary Program, and the potential satellite office.

"Gosh, Suzanne, do you think the new satellite office will

be established within, say, the next couple of months?" was the first question.

"You've never worked for the federal government, have you?" Suzanne teased.

Natalie started to apologize, but Suzanne stopped her in mid-sentence. "Nat, Nat, don't get upset; I'm teasing. No one who starts working for the feds can ever get over *how long* it takes to get *anything* done; it's very frustrating. You can't let it get to you; you know that old saying about having the grace to accept that which you cannot change, or something like that. 'Course, I can't *tell* you how many times I'd get so mad at some of the stupid rules and regulations I wanted to scream and quit," she said.

"How come you didn't, then?" Nat asked tentatively.

"I guess because the larger goal of getting this Sanctuary designated kept me from it," Suzanne answered. "But it definitely aged me, I can tell you," she smiled as they drove on.

By the time they got back to Provincetown, Suzanne was ready to call it a day, even though it was only about 3:30 P.M. They pulled into the Research Center and started answering phone calls and checking messages. It didn't take long for Charlie to bound downstairs, asking how their "day trip" to Scituate had gone.

Surprised, but not really, Suzanne responded, "Great, Charlie, just great! You really should meet Lieutenant Nelson; he's very excited about the possibilities for expanded cooperative efforts between the Sanctuary and a new Sanctuary satellite office," she exclaimed.

"I feel I *have* met him, after all the time he and I have spent on the phone lately," Charlie responded. "He and I are on the same page when it comes to cooperative data gathering and dissemination to the public and other research institutions of information and policy development results," Charlie smiled.

And so it was that Suzanne and Natalie spent the rest of the afternoon working on public information pieces, trying to incorporate the latest Center findings on individual whale species population figures, migration patterns, and interaction with human activities, including fishing and recreational boating. It was interesting, but tedious, work.

"You know what? I think I can work on these at home this evening," Suzanne said, as she closed up a medium-sized pile of papers and reached for her jacket. On the walk home from the office, she fell victim to the sweet aromas drifting out of the P'town Bakery and stopped to purchase a half dozen chocolate chip cookies. *Gotta keep your strength up for this intensive imaginative work,* she rationalized to herself as she entered the cottage yard through the front gate. Barney, as always, thumped his tail and woofed his greetings to her as she came inside the front room. "Boy, am I glad to see you, pal," she cooed as she rubbed and scratched the golden's head and shoulders. She added, "Time for dinner, right, old boy?" At the mere mention of the word "dinner", Barney's full attention focused on her and every move she made. As always, these actions and reactions brought a broad grin to Suzanne's face. *This dog brings me such happiness and peace; how can I ever take him for granted?*

Once she got finally and comfortably settled in, Suzanne found, somewhat to her surprise, that writing the information pieces came easily. For four or more hours, the words just kept coming into her brain and onto the computer screen, *Wow, this must be the writer's equivalent of the runner's "high" that you hear so much about,* she thought to herself as she finished a piece on why the proposed sand-and-gravel mining of Stellwagen Bank was rejected, and the effects such activity would have on both the living resources and the structure itself of the bank environment. She found it was difficult not to editorialize, but she figured reviewers of her work would be able to "clean up" her writing. *I've got no particular pride of authorship in this;* she thought; *I'm just telling the facts, just the facts.* She worked through and finished her draft copy for four additional issues or resource status discussion, and finally stood up to stretch and crack her knuckles. *Man, I'm beat,* she thought. *Think I'll wrap up for the night.* And so she sank gratefully into Angela's bed, where she always slept well.

Twelve
Swimming Free

Next morning at the office, the mail arrived early, and among the dozens of letters from whale lovers looking for jobs were three or four copies of the Federal Register notice of vacancy announcement. "Wow! It came early, Suzanne, look at these!" exclaimed Natalie. "I can hardly wait to fill one of these out and mail it in! Okay if I copy one of the applications to use for practice?" she asked.

"Sure, Nat; go wild. I'm doing nothing until I've had a cup of coffee," Suzanne replied. She kind of smiled as she sat down and started to go through the rest of the mail. *God, it's just amazing how many people think they can save the world by "donating" a summer's work to the satellite office for the Stellwagen Bank Sanctuary,* she thought as she rifled through twenty or thirty resumes from high school or college students willing to work for "minimum" pay, say, $300 to $500 a week on Cape Cod during the summer months. *What a world; what a world,* she thought as she drained her second cup. "Man o' man," she muttered toward Natalie, "Wouldn't it be nice if the world was this simple?"

"Never happen, darling; never happen," Nat replied. "The older the world gets, the more complicated and more crowded it gets," she added.

"Ain't *that* the truth?" Suzanne replied. "I still haven't figured out how to program a VCR; fortunately, I don't really care about that stuff," she continued. The morning passed pretty slowly, and shortly before lunch time, Charlie came downstairs and asked Suzanne to come up to his office and go over some fundraising ideas with him for the next interview with a local corporation interested in promoting its public support of cetacean research. With a slight look of confusion directed at Natalie, Suzanne climbed upstairs to Charlie's office.

"Charlie, I thought we didn't have any corporate donor interviews until next week; did I miss something in scheduling?" she asked. She turned around from closing the door to his office, and couldn't help staring. It was almost like she had never seen this great-looking man before. Suddenly, she felt very excited, and very nervous.

Charlie, to the contrary, looked completely relaxed. This only made Suzanne more uneasy. She sat down in the canvas director's chair opposite Charlie's desk. Nervous or not, she decided to bite the bullet, and asked, "So, what's up, Charlie? Did you spend all night thinking up great ideas for raising research funds for the Center?"

"Nope; I had a couple of truly *great* ideas, but they have nothing, or very little, to do with research funding," he smiled.

"So?" Suzanne looked at him quizzically; "Wanna give me a hint, or a clue of some kind, old pal?"

Charlie leaned forward on his desk and said to Suzanne, "One of the whale-watch boat captains just radioed in a few minutes ago and said they're spotting a couple of fin whales out near Tillie's Bank; I thought maybe you'd like to go take a look with me," he stood up, smiling.

"Oh, man, *would* I?" she gushed. "Isn't this kind of unusual timing for fin whales?" she asked.

"A little late in the year, maybe, but it's sure worth the trip out there to see them," Charlie replied excitedly.

"Couldn't agree more," she replied. "Their behavior is so unpredictable; and I know they're difficult to track. So when do you want to go?"

"Now, of course; before they move too far northeast," Charlie answered.

Suzanne had kind of forgotten that Tillie's Bank was located near the northeast corner of the Stellwagen Bank feature, a good distance offshore. "How long will it take to get out there, do you think?" she asked

"Probably two hours, if we don't waste any time," Charlie replied. "I'll grab a heavier waterproof jacket; meet you at your boat, okay?" Suzanne beamed and turned to change coats.

"It's *not* a boat, you dummy!" exclaimed Charlie. Suzanne turned and smiled calmly at him, as she put on her jacket and dashed down the stairs to let Natalie know she was leaving with Charlie, and to ask her to please take care of Barney this evening.

"No problem, amigo," Natalie responded. "So what's up with you two, anyway?" she pressed for more information.

"Ah, nothing much; Charlie wants to go out to Tillie's Bank to see a couple of fin whales," Suzanne answered succinctly. "I've never seen a fin whale; I thought it would be fun."

"Sounds like a date to me," Natalie muttered half to herself.

"I didn't hear that," Suzanne lied, and smiled broadly as she dashed out the front door of the Center. The "boat" (otherwise known as the research vessel, *Ever Barbara*) was docked within several hundred yards, and looked ready to go. She didn't know why, exactly, but she always had kind of a funny feeling stepping onto the boat Charlie had built for his beloved, deceased wife. She didn't have much time to think about that feeling, as Charlie arrived minutes behind her and nearly knocked her over in his hurry to get on board and start the engine.

"Oh, sorry, Suzanne; I didn't mean to run you over! Just excited, I guess. Need some help getting aboard?" He turned and held out his hand to Suzanne, and, although she didn't need any assistance, she grinned and took his hand. Once aboard, they set out at a reasonable clip, moving smoothly in a northeasterly direction. It was chilly to be sure, but the sun was bright, and the waters quite conducive to a quick passage through the north end of the Sanctuary. About an hour into the trip, Suzanne thought she saw some activity of the leeward side of the *Ever Barbara*. "Charlie! Look! Aren't those fin whales over there?" she asked as she pointed to the left of the sturdy research vessel. Charlie immediately turned to the left and cut the engine, allowing them to drift slowly and silently in the direction of what now appeared to be three or four fin whales.

"Oh, I wish we could see more of them; I mean see more of the body above water, you know?" Suzanne exclaimed excitedly.

"Well, if we're lucky, we may see them breach," Charlie said, as he raised his binoculars close to his eyes and scanned the horizon.

"Oh, man; you think so, really?" Suzanne asked excitedly.

"Did you know that fin whales are the second largest of the great whales? They average between sixty and seventy feet long. And they're a lot more streamlined than the humpbacks or the northern rights. I call them the 'steel gray bullets with half-white faces,' " Charlie expanded.

"What do you mean, 'half-white faces'?" Suzanne asked.

Charlie moved closer and passed the binoculars to Suzanne. "Well, I know it sounds really weird, but all fins, as far as we can tell, anyway, exhibit a characteristic white right side of their jaws; I don't think we're sure about the purpose or function of this trait. Baffling, isn't it?" Charlie grinned at her. Suzanne returned the grin, and moved a little closer to Charlie. She was feeling some sort of special closeness to Charlie, knowing that Charlie did not typically share any feelings of confusion. She treasured this private moment with him. Switching to a conversational area that she knew Charlie would respond to, Suzanne asked him, "So, isn't this kind of south of where you usually find fin whales, Charlie?"

"Yep, the fins are usually found in feeding areas further north of here, in Canada. But they feed on the same stuff as other whales found here, like krill and small schooling fish," he answered.

"So we just got a little lucky, huh?" Suzanne said and smiled, as she put the binoculars closer to her face and searched the horizon. "They sure are elegant-looking" she observed, "but somehow to me, anyway, they don't have the intriguing appeal of the humpbacks or even the northern right whales; they seem rather aloof, know what I mean?" And with that, rather suddenly, Charlie leaned over close to Suzanne and put his arms tightly around her. It was a scary but magical moment for the highly nervous Suzanne. "Charlie!" was all she could immediately utter, but inwardly, of course, she was thrilled. It seemed like nothing more needed to be said, for now. It was just one of those rarely occurring instances that somehow would be shattered if there were verbal attempts at explanation.

Just then, the water's surface on their left broke with splashes, and two fin whales breached, exposing clearly the right white sides of their jaws. And just as suddenly, the water became still again, as the whales disappeared below the surface.

"Wow! Did you see that? God, that was fantastic, Charlie! I didn't even know that fin whales ever breached at all.

That's so cool!" she exclaimed while leaning over the side of the research vessel. "How often have you seen fins do that?" she asked Charlie.

"Not that often, kiddo; not very often at all," he responded.

The remainder of the trip remained exciting, as they saw additional marine life on their way back to the Center, dolphins and several pelagic seabirds. But for Suzanne, the air remained full of further excitement and promise. She could hardly believe it, and she really didn't want the trip to end. It was close to 5:00 P.M. when they docked back at the Center's berth, and the air was starting to get chilly. As they unloaded onto the dock, and Suzanne was gathering her extra raingear, Charlie stopped whatever he was doing, took her by the arm and said, "You know, this is going to change a lot of things, kiddo."

Trying to keep the banter light, but failing badly, Suzanne replied, "Whatever to you mean, Dr. Baio?" She could feel that she was going to lose control of this conversation shortly, and this was confirmed when Charlie took firm hold and kissed her gently. "Whoa; I never thought it would be like *this*. Charlie; it's almost a *fantasy!*" Suzanne stammered and blushed.

"Do you know this is the first time I've felt something like this since Barbara died?" Charlie said quietly, as he pulled away and looked deeply at Suzanne. "I guess I thought I would never feel this way about anyone again," Charlie continued.

"Me neither, Charlie; me neither," was all she could get out.

"Let's not rush it, okay?" he whispered, as they made their way back to the Center. By now, it was dark, the Center was empty and it seemed like a very good time to think about getting some dinner. "How about dinner and a drink down at Nappy's?" he asked.

207

"Sounds good to me," she quickly replied. As they moved together toward Commercial Street, where almost all the restaurants seemed to be located, Suzanne's fear disappeared and she added, "Maybe *two* drinks, you think?" Charlie just smiled and put his arm around her shoulder. They made their way, arm-in-arm, to Nappy's, situated near the end of Commercial Street, overlooking the boat-filled harbor. The aromas spilling out onto the narrow street were, as always, almost overwhelmingly rich and tantalizing. Until just then, she hadn't realized just how famished she really was.

"So, Charlie, what's the specialty of the house here?" she asked.

"The seafood chowder, without question," Charlie replied with a little chuckle.

"And does anyone in this township eat beef?" she teased.

"Blasphemy! We intend to strip the ocean completely of edible fishes and shellfish," Charlie laughed. He was kidding, of course, but the thought of an ocean barren of seafood was, indeed, a sobering thought. "No, seriously, maybe that's why the idea of farm-raised fish makes some sense, you know?" he continued. "It's also why I personally feel like this Sanctuary may be the last real hope for the recovery of the northern right whale species. If only everyone plays by the very flexible Sanctuary rules, maybe the whales will get the chance they need," Charlie concluded.

"You sound kind of doomsday, Dr. Baio," Suzanne said quietly.

"Well, it *is* kind of doomsday, considering the present status of this species' population, but I haven't lost all hope," Charlie smiled at her.

Smiling and hand-in-hand, they walked into Nappy's, where almost everyone there seemed to be a friend of Charlie's. Several people came up to them and welcomed Charlie, in particular. It apparently had been a long time since Charlie had been to Nappy's. Nappy owner Bill Preston called out, "Charlie! Hey, man; boy, it's sure good to see you here again. Where you been hiding all this time, anyway?" It being a small town, of course all the local residents knew of Charlie's loss, and how tough times had been for him. Charlie looked up in Bill's direction, and smiled in gratitude. Bill came over closer to them, and steered them to a corner table, overlooking the harbor. "Seriously, Charlie, it sure is good to see you out again," Bill said as he placed two menus on the table and lit the large candle between them.

After several minutes, the local pub crowd drifted back to wherever its members had been before Charlie and Suzanne arrived, and they were left to themselves, to make menu choices and exchange meaningful looks and pithy comments. "Oh, Charlie; can you believe this? I mean can you believe it?" Suzanne sighed heavily as she sat down. Charlie was very quiet and just stared at her. It was like the two of them had made some giant discovery, and they weren't quite ready to share it with the rest of the world—not just yet. If she had been asked later, Suzanne would have said that there's something wonderful about sharing a deeply personal secret between two people who have found each other without ever looking. Finally, Suzanne reached across the table and took Charlie's hands and said, "This is so cool; it's just so cool, Charlie! Don't you think so?" As though snapped out of a trance, Charlie replied, "I could not agree more; couldn't agree more." After several minutes, Bill Preston quietly reappeared and offered to take their orders. He just stood , grinning, as though he too, had some great secret to share. "I'm just so damn glad to see you back, Charlie; and your girlfriend, here, she's a knockout! Where'd you find her anyway?"

By now, Charlie had had about enough of the glad-handing and pats on the back; he was ready to get a drink and some chowder. "This is Suzanne Douglas, Bill; she's helping me out with fundraising for the Center. Now, could you bring us each a large bowl of chowder, and a beer? Thanks, Bill." Looking a little chagrined, Bill mumbled "sure" and quickly disappeared. The much-praised seafood chowder was everything Suzanne hoped for; hot, delicious, and rich with very discernible flavors blended into a thick base sauce. "Ymm; this is great, just great," Suzanne exclaimed happily between spoonfuls. "Didn't realize how hungry I was," she finally said when she had swallowed the last spoonful. As they both happily downed their second beer, Suzanne sat back slowly and gave a very contented sigh.

"God, what a day, huh? Charlie, I can honestly say I've *never* felt so happy and fulfilled," she beamed.

"You're just happy to be *filled,* Sunshine; I can maybe *fulfill* you later," Charlie winked.

Glad to see you haven't lost your touch, big guy, she thought to herself. She felt an overwhelming urge to get lost in the dark somewhere with Charlie, for a long, long time. Their bellies full and their hearts happy, Charlie and Suzanne left Nappy's and walked back in the direction of the Center. Charlie was the first to speak. "You know, kiddo? As much as I would really love to take you back to my place for the night, I'm pretty exhausted, and I don't want to disappoint you, know what I mean? Can we make a date for tomorrow?" he asked as he pulled her close to him and softly stroked her face.

"Oh, Charlie, sure we can make a date for tomorrow. I just don't know if I can wait that long," she said breathlessly. "But at least it will give me time to do my nails," she teased.

"Women," Charlie snorted, "Listen kiddo: I want you to understand that I really want this to be perfect for both of us. Let's give it the time and attention it needs, alright?"

"Yeah," she answered quietly. Inside, she was churning with anticipation, but somehow, she had to keep her composure; lose that when the magic moment arrives. She thought

210

quickly about inviting Charlie back to her place, but he had made it pretty clear he really was tired, and besides, she didn't want to ruin these moments. "You're right, Charlie, let's wait; see if both of us can remember the fine points of lovemaking," she whispered to him.

"Hey, smart-ass, it hasn't been *that* long; I still know a trick or maneuver or two," he whispered back. They reached the front parking area at the Center, and Suzanne pulled up the zipper on her rain jacket; she said to Charlie, "I guess I'll see you in the morning, boss, okay?" That was certainly as "neutral" a tone as she could muster at this point, and she almost hoped he would just say "fine" or "okay, fine" and turn around and head for home. Which he did, but not before he pulled her close to him again and kissed her long and hard.

It was almost more than she could withstand, but she kind of got the last word in when she handed over exactly half of the dinner tab, shoved it into his pocket, turned on a dime, and walked quickly away toward her cottage, with Charlie exclaiming loudly, "No way, Suzanne!" behind her. Truth was, she was sort of relieved when she got inside the front door. Although she missed Barney's usual enthusiastic greeting, she was also kind of glad that Barney was with Natalie, where he was well cared for, and she could have the time to contemplate the day's events. She still tingled from Charlie's kisses, and it was a glorious feeling. After catching a bit of the late news, she decided to take a hot shower and roll into bed. *What am I going to tell Nat?* she wondered, as she finally drifted off to a wonderful sleep.

As they almost always do, the next morning came too fast, and Suzanne on this morning was still on a high, still wondering how to answer Nat's inevitable questions. Oddly, however, the question did not start with the first cup of coffee. Nat was deeply engrossed in the completion of her resume and application for the vacancy at the still-to-be built Sanctuary satellite office.

"Hey, good morning! Have you had a chance to start filling out your application for the satellite office job yet? I'm having a little trouble with some of these questions; think you could give me a hand sometime today?" she asked eagerly.

Incredible, she thought, *she doesn't seem to have a clue about yesterday afternoon, and me and Charlie. Oh, well; I'll tell her later.*

"Sure, Nat, let's get together over lunch, okay? I haven't started on my application yet," Suzanne smiled and grabbed a cup of coffee.

"You *haven't?*" Nat shot back in surprise. "You know, there's only two weeks left to get these suckers in the mail," she said.

"Oh, there's plenty of time," Suzanne said; "I'm not worried." It seemed to Natalie that Suzanne was being unbelievably blasé about what *she* viewed as a once-in-a-lifetime opportunity. But, of course, she thought, she has actually worked for the federal government; maybe it's not as golden as some people think it is.

During their lunch break, Nat and Suzanne sat at the large table in the back room and went over Nat's answers to the questions on the application. "These are pretty good, I think," observed Suzanne. "Did you include all of your relevant experience?" she asked, as Nat briefly expanded her response to the questions on organization of the office.

"Yeah, I think, so, " Nat answered. "Everything I could think of, anyway," she added. Suzanne smiled and encouraged Nat to finish up the application.

"Really, Nat; it looks very good" she said with praising finality.

After picking up Barney, Suzanne walked home slowly, thinking about her "date" with Charlie, sort of scheduled for later this evening. *Damn,* she thought, *it's been a long time since I did anything like this; I hope I don't screw it up.* As she showered and thought about the evening ahead, she couldn't help smiling to herself and wondering what Charlie was feeling at this very moment. Barney almost "purred" with his soft growl, as she stroked his head and shared some private thoughts with him. "It sure is good to have you back, Barn; I think life is about to get a little more complicated, but you're always going to be with me, pal. Forever, okay?" she said quietly. The phone downstairs rang, and she dashed to answer.

"Hello?" she answered breathlessly. For a moment or two, there was no answer. She repeated "Hello?" and waited. Softly in the background, there came music that reminded her of a favorite song from many years past—"All in the Game" by Tommy Edwards. She smiled and knew, of course, it was Charlie. "I had no idea you were such a romantic," she said quietly. "I like that about you, Charlie," she added.

"Are you ready?" he asked.

"Now you're making me nervous, you know?" she answered tentatively.

"Me, too, if it makes you feel any better," Charlie responded. "I'll pick you up around seven, okay?" he asked.

"Sounds perfect," Suzanne answered. "Can I bring some wine for dinner? I've got some pretty good merlot here," she offered.

"Sure, bring it," he said. 'I'm going to cook some rib-eye steaks; sound alright to you?"

"What? No seafood? Oh, Charlie, I don't know; it seems so *unusual.* Does it go with merlot?" she smiled to herself. As nervous as she was about the evening to come, she was enjoying herself, and she dabbed on some of her favorite perfume.

"Has anyone ever mentioned to you that you're a smart-ass?" he chided. "I'll see you soon, sunshine," he hung up with a soft laugh.

213

What to wear? What to wear? God, I'm working myself into a frenzy, she thought, as she paced around her bedroom and stood before her open closet. There were already three days' worth of clothing piled on the bed; she couldn't decide on anything as being "just right." Finally, she gave up trying, and decided on clean faded blue jeans and a favorite purple shirt. Barney hovered around, like he was expecting someone to show up at the door. "No, I'm sorry, Barn; no out for you tonight; I've got a date, can you believe that?" she said wondrously to her faithful friend. And to add to her inner tension, he was right on time. *Gulp,* she thought, as she grabbed the bottle of wine and went to answer the door. As Barney quietly woofed and stood wagging his tail, Suzanne opened the front door and gazed smiling at Charlie. She couldn't believe it: Charlie was wearing a fitted dark purple shirt, and it looked great on him.

"Hi, boss! Boy, it's good to see you again; it's been too long, huh?" she chuckled. "Did you check with the wardrobe monitor? Or are we on some kind of same wavelength?"

"And I get a comedian in the act," Charlie replied, almost grinning and starting to laugh. "Are you ready for some beef steaks?" he asked.

"Let's go," she responded, and they headed for Charlie's Jeep, which had apparently been washed for the event. With Barney quietly whining back in the house, Suzanne hopped in, and they took off slowly toward Race Point, near Charlie's house. It was a beautiful night, just as Suzanne had fantasized it would be: the sky was dark and clear, with about a gazillion stars lighting their way and fueling Suzanne's excitement. Within ten minutes, they pulled onto the gravel road leading to the Baio cottage. It was modest but utterly charming, everything Suzanne thought it would be. Once inside, its feeling was clearly that of people who cared very much about the oceanic world so near them. There where pictures and carvings of

214

whales, dolphins and seabirds everywhere; and though she was no longer among her legions of peers and friends, Barbara Baio was still very present in this house. On several walls, there were many presentations and awards, neatly framed and hung with care in prominent positions.

"Wow," Suzanne exclaimed. "This is beautiful, Charlie. I feel honored to be here," she went on.

"The house is honored to have you here," he answered softly and put his arms around her. Charlie ushered her into the living room, where there was a small fireplace already lit and crackling with good cheer. "How about opening that bottle of merlot?" he suggested, as he disappeared into the kitchen and reappeared quickly with two wine glasses. Suzanne was already making herself comfortable on the small sofa and gazing into the fire. She could feel herself beginning to unwind and relax; *this is a good place to be,* she thought.

As Charlie poured the wine, she asked him, "When's the last time you saw fin whales like that? I never expected to see any here near the Sanctuary."

"To tell you the truth, those are the only ones I've seen this season down here. They must have heard you were coming up to visit," he smiled. He filled up his glass, and joined her on the sofa. "Let's drink a toast," he suggested, and lifted his glass to touch hers lightly on the rim.

"To all fin whales everywhere," Suzanne started, when Charlie interrupted her with "and to all right whales, and Sanctuary-makers everywhere." Suzanne beamed with the praise given. After a few minutes, they went outside onto the small patio, where Charlie had already started a charcoal fire, and had laid out the steaks on a thick cutting board. Charlie showed Suzanne to a porch easy chair, and started seasoning the steaks. "There's a big salad bowl in the kitchen; want to help? Pick out a salad dressing and start tossing," he smiled.

Suzanne was actually beginning to feel a little more at ease and at home almost.

"How do you like your steaks, Suzanne?"

"Bloody, Charlie; bloody," she responded.

"Doesn't surprise me a bit," Charlie answered, as he turned the steaks and removed them from the fire. "That being the case, I think these are done," he chuckled. He pulled the steaks onto the dinner plates, as Suzanne opened the bottle of chunky blue cheese dressing and poured it into the tossed green salad. With the addition of hot fresh rolls, freshly buttered, the meal was complete. They both pulled up their chairs close to the long porch table, and Charlie lit two candles.

With a long sigh of contentment Charlie said, "Whew, I could get used to this kind of dinner, you know?" Suzanne smiled and leaned back in her chair. "These steaks look and smell wonderful, Charlie; you done good," she praised.

"Here's to you, Suzanne," he toasted as he raised his glass to her. "You really deserve a lot of praise for all your hard work on the Sanctuary; it is amazing to me and a lot of others, I'm sure, how you managed to get this thing designated," he said as he stared deep into her eyes.

"Ah, Charlie, what's ten years of your life? Although there were times when I felt like resigning in almost total disgust, now it seems like a monumental effort that was *well* worth it," she said, as she dug into her salad. "And as you have said, this may be the last real chance for recovery of the northern right whale," she observed through her first bite of ribeye steak. "*God* this is great; thanks, Charlie."

"No thanks necessary, trust me," Charlie smiled. As they lingered over the meal, and spoke vaguely about the right whale population fifty years ago, Suzanne began to think to herself about what a dumb idea it was (for her, anyway) to have a big meal before engaging in a long, wondrous lovemaking session. *Gee, I hope I don't get sick in the middle of things;*

that would be so embarrassing! With noticeable hesitation Charlie almost whispered: "So, sunshine, are you ready for this?"

She took a deep long breath and held it for several seconds. "Of course not; I don't mind saying I'm very nervous, Charlie, but I really want to make love to you; I just hope I'm good enough for you," she stammered. "This is so monumental for me *and* you; I just want it to be perfect, you know?"

"Yeah, I know, Suzanne; it's going to be fine. Come here; make it perfect," Charlie said as he held his arms open and gathered Suzanne in to his chest. And it was. It was a lot more than fine; it was, as Suzanne later described it to Natalie, *magical.* Charlie led her into his bedroom, and very carefully and slowly unbuttoned her shirt and unbuckled her jeans. Almost simultaneously, Suzanne opened Charlie's shirt and unbuttoned his jeans. And so, in the quiet privacy of Charlie's bedroom, they made love, long and soft and hard, until they could love no longer. And much to Suzanne's happy surprise, she found out that, when your heart's in it, making love is something you never forget how to do.

When they first were completely undressed, Suzanne was almost struck motionless by what a breathtaking man Charlie was; although he was perhaps ten to twelve years her senior, Charlie was lean and firm all over, a testament to clean living in pursuit of greater knowledge being spread through the scientific, commercial and public communities throughout the country. *Clean living, hell; he's just a great-looking guy and I want him,* she swore to herself. She was perhaps struck motionless for a quick moment, but within minutes, she was all over him, and every move she could remember flooded back to sweet memory. Charlie, also, did not appear to be at a loss for action, and they shared and enjoyed each other for what seemed like eternity, or at least, until they were both physically spent. As they both laid back, sort of gasping for breath, they gazed at each other and smiled contently.

Finally, she rolled over to him and asked, "Did I miss any spot? God, you were incredible, Charlie. I have *never* been loved like that before, ever," she said breathlessly. Charlie pulled her close to him, and whispered, "I didn't think I would ever feel this way again, ever, Suzanne."

"Let's try to keep it that way always, okay?" she replied.

"Deal, Sunshine, deal," Charlie smiled and rolled over on his back.

"I don't think I've ever seen you look so relaxed," Suzanne observed, as she stretched out over the pale beige and thoroughly rumpled sheets.

"That's because I'm extremely happy right now," Charlie sighed. She reached over to the curtained window closest to the bed, and pulled back the curtain, so she could look at the now-dark and star-filled sky. 'God, it's beautiful out there; can you see the sky, Charlie?" she whispered. There was no immediate answer, but there was a very quiet snore emanating from the pillow next to her. *Just like a man,* she thought and smiled, as she slowly got up and went into the bathroom. Glancing at the small alarm clock next to the sink, she realized it was close to twelve o'clock midnight. *Whew,* she thought, *like they say, time sure flies when you're having fun. And we sure did have fun, huh, Charlie?* When she finished a short cleaning job on herself, she returned to the bedroom, where she quietly rejoined the now-sound-asleep Charlie.

Although she was really tired, Suzanne could not fall asleep right away; there was way too much to think about: *Was this the start of something big and meaningful? How did Charlie* really *feel about her? Should I really jump into yet another relationship again? How cautious should I be, anyway? And how do I really feel about this guy?* Probably because she was *so* tired, Suzanne decided there were no definite answers tonight, and that maybe things would be clearer in the morning.

As always, morning came too soon but as the sun broke through the curtains, Suzanne was first to open her eyes and have a quiet second or two to think about what a great night it had been. She rolled slowly onto her back and raised her arms to stretch. Charlie began to stir into consciousness and moved toward Suzanne. "Hmm; morning, Sunshine. How'd you sleep?" he mumbled through a slow smile.

"Great, boss, and you?" she answered. "Got any coffee around here?" she added, as she reached over to kiss him.

"Yeah, there's coffee, but there's one thing you absolutely have to stop doing, Suzanne." Charlie now looked rather serious.

"What's that?" she asked.

"Stop calling me boss, damn it!" Charlie half sat up and grabbed her around the waist.

She giggled, and hugged him back. "Okay, okay," she laughed, "I promise, Charlie."

"What time is it, anyway?" Suzanne asked.

"Time? Hell, what *day* is it?" Charlie countered. "All I know is that yesterday was pretty cool, and I really enjoyed having you here overnight," he smiled and hugged her again.

"I think it's Sunday, Charlie, and I, too, had a pretty cool time last night; you are the *best*," she exclaimed

"Ready for coffee? Ready to face the world?" she asked.

"Yeah," he chuckled, "soon as I get a shower. Join me," he said, as he undressed, grabbed a towel and pushed her in the direction of the bathroom.

"Okay, so the secrets underneath the clothing are revealed, once and for all," Suzanne blushed as she stumbled into the shower stall.

"Women," he snorted. "Suzanne, your body is gorgeous,

trust me," Charlie said, as he adjusted the water temperature and lathered a soft soap on her back.

"I guess we have no secrets anymore, Charlie, at least with regard to clothes, huh? I mean, what you see is what you get, lover," she smiled huge.

"Bingo, darlin', you're right on, and I like what I see, honest," he passed the shampoo and they *both* got lathered, cleaned and invigorated for the day; it was a great start to a wholly new relationship.

When they finally got dressed and sat down at the kitchen table, Suzanne asked Charlie if he was going to the Bank today. He leaned back in his director's chair, and groaned slightly, as he stretched his arms to the ceiling. "I think I'm getting too old for this," he said, as he wrapped one hand around the other's wrist and rested both at the back of his head. As Suzanne poured two cups of coffee, Charlie gazed in her direction and answered her question: "You know? I think I'll take the day off; maybe go into the office a little later and finish up some of those files I've been neglecting. Want to help?"

"Sure, I'd be happy to, Charlie; what do you need me to do?" she asked. Suzanne was beginning to feel the need to unwind some by herself; kind of try to get a grip on what was happening between them, and to herself. *I want to be alone,* she thought; *check that; I want to see Barney.*

As she finished off her second cup of coffee, she said to Charlie: "You know what? I think I'd really like to finish going through all those applications the Sanctuary and the Center have received for summer employment. Karen, Bud and I have seen some promising candidates I think we could make good use of," she offered.

"Nice grammar, pal; but sure, go ahead and see what you can find. Keep in mind we can't afford more than two or three, okay?" he smiled and reached across the table to kiss her.

"Thanks, Charlie. You're the *best,* in more ways than one, but you knew that already, didn't you?" she hugged him and got up to leave. Once outside Charlie's cottage, she slowed to turn around and take a lasting look at what was now almost an enchanted place for her. *Charlie, Charlie, Charlie,* she thought, *this could really be so wonderful.* Within a few seconds, her mind returned to reality, and she turned back to the cottage and opened the kitchen door.

"Yo, Charlie! Can I get a ride home?" she smiled sweetly.

"Yep; I was wondering when you'd be back," Charlie grinned, as he rose from the kitchen table. They went out together and got into Charlie's Jeep.

"You ever have days when you think you're losing your mind, Charlie?" she asked. "Sometimes I think things are just supposed to be a certain way, and when I discover they're not, somehow I feel gypped, or something." It was a feeble explanation, but all she could come up with. Already he was becoming someone to whom she could make small, intimate comments. Was this a good thing? She had no idea, but it was interesting, if nothing else.

The Jeep got off to a slow and noisy start, and putted down the gravel lane leading from Charlie's house to the main road, and from there to Suzanne's cottage. Being Sunday, things were very quiet; Suzanne was convinced they never got out of second gear the whole trip.

When they arrived at Suzanne's lane, Charlie pulled into her short driveway and turned off the engine. Suzanne had just started to ask Charlie if he wanted to come in when Barney nosed his way out the back of the kitchen, through the doggie door. As always he was happy to see her, as well as her new friend. "Barn! Did you miss me, boy?" she asked, as she dropped to her knees and hugged the big golden.

"You really love that dog, don't you?" Charlie asked.

"Yeah, I do," she smiled. "I imagine he's pretty hungry by

now," she said, as she stood up and headed for the large canister holding the dry kibble, filled a large cup measure and poured it into his personalized dish next to the refrigerator. By the time she changed and filled his water dish, Barney was done eating. "There's nothing like predictability," she smiled, and Barney is *always* predictable. Sometimes, for fun, my friends and I will time him to see how long it takes for him to clean the bowl," she laughed. "I think the record is twelve seconds."

"Wow! That's some appetite," Charlie was pretty amazed. "You know, Suzanne? He's a pretty great dog; I can see why you're so devoted to him. Maybe I *will* let him on the research vessel sometime," he mused, as he bent down to scratch and rub Barney's ears. Barney, of course, responded as he always did, with focused attention and neat placement of his rear end on Charlie's shoes.

"Well, gorgeous, I gotta go relax for the remainder of Sunday afternoon. Think I'll fix some eggs benedict and sit on the deck. See what you missed by insisting on getting back to your beloved mutt?"

"Ooo, you better be just kidding Charlie, I was just beginning to think you were the nicest guy in the whole world. Don't prove me wrong here, handsome," Suzanne was beginning to feel more at home now. "I'll stop calling you 'boss', if you stop referring to Barney as a 'mutt', okay?" she said. She smiled and waved as Charlie pulled out of the driveway. *Whew, what a night; what a night,* she thought to herself in the very quiet of her own house.

Thirteen
Waves and Undertow

Late Monday morning, Suzanne got a phone call from the Sanctuary office in Scituate; it was Karen. "Hey, Suzanne, how's it going? You have a good weekend? I've got a couple of interesting applications here; I thought you might like to review them yourself," Karen said. Suzanne took a long, deep breath and leaned back in her chair.

"Hey Karen, it's good to hear from you. So, how many applications has the Sanctuary gotten altogether, anyway? Seems like the most popular place on the east coast for a summer job, huh? Yeah, I'd like to review some of them; can you fax copies to me here, or do you need me to come up to Scituate?"

"Yeah, sure, I can fax you some of these. There's one in particular I thought you would like to see. Seems she used to work directly with you in Washington at Program headquarters," Karen responded.

"Oh, yeah? And who might that be?" Suzanne asked.

"The return address is from a 'J. Cranson' in Plainview, New Jersey. Ring any bells?" Of course she knew who it was; frankly, just the mention of her name made Suzanne's blood run a little cold. *I thought that bimbo was still in jail; how could she be applying for a federal job or any job for that matter?* Suzanne's thoughts raced back in time to when she had learned Jodie's terrible secret: that she had killed that hand-

223

some young intern just because he wouldn't have lunch with her. *God, what a mindless, selfish idiot,* she thought.

"Sure, Karen, fax those apps on down here; I'll be glad to review them and give you guys my assessments," Suzanne smiled as she leaned over to grab a cup of coffee. Suzanne sighed deeply and strolled out onto the deck; Barney, as usual, followed closely behind. As she sat at the small round table next to the wall, she couldn't help feeling smug; she had slept with Charlie! How big a deal was that? Was her whole life going to be different now? God, she hoped so. As Barney lay quietly at her feet, she felt lost in questioning contemplation that had no answers. It was a nice kind of lost, though; despite all the questions, she felt happier than she had for a very long time.

Within a few hours, Suzanne's fax machine started making familiar incoming noises, and with some uneasy anticipation, Suzanne went to retrieve what Karen had forwarded to her. Not too surprisingly, there were five or six applications sent for review. *Always lots of students looking for "glamorous" summer jobs,* she thought, as she rifled through the approximately twenty pages of resumes. *Even some non-students,* she observed as she reached that of Jodie Cranson. Suzanne took the small pile of papers and retired to the deck with a second cup of coffee. A couple applicants could be eliminated immediately, at least as far as Suzanne was concerned. When she got to Jodie's resume, she kind of came up for air and spent some time thinking about days long past, when she considered Jodie the best of friends. That past had ended abruptly though, when Jodie had insisted on telling her that she had killed Justin Kennard, then sworn her to secrecy. *Why on earth had I ever agreed to not say anything about this incident to anyone?*

She quickly reviewed and made notes on the four or five applicants looking for employment at the new Sanctuary satellite office in Provincetown. Only one, maybe two of them were worth bringing in for interviews. She put Jodie's application aside, deciding to look at it later. Wandering into the kitchen, she pulled the tuna salad she had made earlier from the fridge, gathered some fresh Portuguese bread and a little mayo and lettuce, and started compiling the ingredients into a large sandwich. Despite everything, this bread was the best she'd ever tasted. *P'town is still a good place to be,* she reminded herself, *and I'd like to stay here with Charlie.*

The next day's mail at the Center included a letter addressed to Suzanne and marked "personal." she noted the return address as Plainview, New Jersey, and knew immediately the letter was from good old Jodie. *What in the hell does she want, anyway?* Suzanne thought, as she rather slowly opened the envelope. And what Jodi wanted was this:

Hey, Suzanne: Guess you know where I've been lately. Yeah, holed up for the last couple of years. I'm not saying I didn't deserve it, but I've paid my debt to society, and I'm ready to come back to the Sanctuary Program. You know as well as I do that I know everything about the Program, and I deserve to be hired as the manager for the new satellite office in Provincetown. So how about putting in a few good words for me when the applicants are reviewed. Thanks, pal. Jodie.

The nerve, she thought. *What unmitigated gall. If she thinks I'm going to put in* any *good words for her, she's crazier than I thought she was. Oh, I'll put some words in for her, but she's not going to like them,* Suzanne thought, as she stomped around the office.

"Hey, Suzanne, what's wrong?" Nat asked. Not answering immediately, Suzanne thought to herself, *I wonder if Bud knows about this. He should be as pissed as I am, since he's the one who arrested her.* She decided to put off calling Bud until she had a little more information, and maybe had the pleasure of communicating directly with Jodie. Nat was still standing there, waiting for some sort of explanation for the stomping.

"Oh, Nat, I'm sorry; I just got some very unpleasant news from someone that used to work it the Sanctuary Program headquarters office in Washington, D.C. It seems the young woman in question has recently talked her way out of jail, where, by the way, she belongs, and is now applying for the manager's job at the satellite office in Provincetown," she finished quickly. "Believe me, Nat, this woman is not to be trusted, and she most *certainly* is not qualified for any Sanctuary position; as far as I'm concerned, you are the ideal candidate for the job," she finished. Nat blushed a little, like she almost always did when people complimented her, and it was clear she wanted to know more about what was going on. But she decided to not pursue it for now, anyway; Suzanne seemed too upset.

When Suzanne got home that evening, she decided to call Bud, and see what his take was on Jodie's application. As soon as the phone started to ring at Karen and Bud's place, she knew somehow Karen was going to answer. Karen recognized Suzanne's voice immediately, and started asking questions about Jodie. Before she could get too deeply engaged in analysis of Jodie's intentions relative to the Sanctuary Program, Suzanne interrupted and asked if Bud was there.

"Sure, Suzanne; hang on; I'll get him," Karen responded.

"Hey, Suze, what's up? Are you calling about Jodie Cranson? I thought she was still in jail; please don't tell me she's out! How? How'd that happen? Jeez, I can't believe, this," Bud railed on.

"Well, she apparently *somehow* got out on parole, or something; I don't know. I don't understand it, either," Suzanne responded. "She always *was* a little devious," she added.

"Well, it just plain pisses me off, Suze; it almost makes me wish I was still a D.C. cop, you know?" Bud continued.

"Don't get drastic on me, Bud; you're much better off here with Karen, don't you think?" Suzanne asked.

"Yeah; you're right, as usual," Bud chuckled. "I really think this job has mellowed me."

"Anyway, I just wanted to kind of get your read on Jodie's application, and to let you know that she has asked me, in a separate letter, to endorse her for the satellite office manager position," Suzanne relayed. "Not that I would even consider it," she added.

"That dumb bitch," Bud responded.

"Not immediately, but I will respond to her letter, and make it very clear that she will *not* be considered for any Sanctuary Program position, based on her past history," Suzanne concluded. "I'm glad we're in agreement," she sighed with satisfaction.

"Sounds good to me, and I am in complete agreement," Bud answered.

"Thanks, Bud; I'll talk to you soon, okay?" Suzanne smiled as she hung up the phone.

Later that evening, accompanied by a large bowl of rocky road, Suzanne sat down and started to compose a moderately civil response to Jodie's ridiculous request. It was almost more than she could stomach, even with Barney's unfailing attention (and limited assistance). Finally around 11:00 P.M., she had banged out a rough draft, which included everything about how she really felt about Jodie's deceptions and complete lack of fairness. *Well, at least I got it out onto paper,* she thought, *I guess the "real" letter can be written tomorrow sometime.*

The next morning, Suzanne almost couldn't resist the temptation to immediately sit down and compose the real letter back to Jodie. But she put it off until late in the afternoon, after she had had plenty of time to think about how deceitful Jodie had been, and how *little* she deserved even the most cursory consideration for the job at the Sanctuary satellite office. When late afternoon finally rolled around, and things were quiet at he Center, Suzanne cleared her desk and put these words to paper:

Hi, former good friend Jodie. It was interesting to hear from you after all this time. Knowing you as well as I thought I did, it was nonetheless astounding to me that even you would have the gall to think that I would ever consider promoting your name for the manager position at the new sanctuary satellite office in Provincetown. Did being incarcerated cause you to lose all sense of right and wrong, of any sense of fairness? Or did you ever have any sense of fairness?

Many months ago, I thought that you, like me, believed in the rightness of the National Marine Sanctuary Program. And yet you chucked it all because some "pretty boy" intern wouldn't have lunch with you, and you took out your petty jealousies by shooting the poor kid and concocting some lame story about where you were at the time. In retrospect, I was wrong to hide your secret from investigators. Yeah, you did your time, Jodie, but I don't think the Sanctuary Program will ever want a convicted killer on its payroll.

I hope you learn from your mistakes, and will take care of yourself.

Suzanne

Once finished, Suzanne quickly put the letter in an envelope, added postage and slipped the letter into the outgoing mail box. Frankly, she couldn't wait to get rid of it, and all things connected to Jodie Cranson. She hoped she would never hear from her again But even though she was pleased with what she had written to Jodie, she had an unpleasant

228

feeling that she had not heard the last from her. Suzanne knew she was capable of anything. *Now there's a comforting thought to keep you warm at night,* she thought.

In the meantime, the search for a satellite office location had progressed, and there appeared to be two or three potential buildings with real possibilities. Lt. Nelson telephoned Suzanne early in the week to ask if she would be interested in helping the Sanctuary staff and NOAA officials in Washington make a decision. After checking with Charlie to make sure he could "spare" her for an afternoon or two, Suzanne happily said yes and agreed to meet with the Lieutenant and Karen to assess and rank the sites against the needs of the new office.

"Since the buildings are obviously in our backyard, we thought you'd probably know them, and could give us an honest appraisal of their usefulness to the Program," Lieutenant Nelson explained on the phone.

"Yeah, I'm pretty familiar with the buildings you're considering, and I'd be happy to help out," Suzanne replied enthusiastically. "When are you planning on coming down to P'town?" she asked.

"As soon as possible," Miles replied. "How about this coming Tuesday morning, around ten o'clock?"

"I'll line up a local realtor to get us into the places," Suzanne offered.

"Great, Suzanne; we'll meet you at the Center and go from there," Miles responded. When Miles and she had hung up the phone, Suzanne immediately called Mitsy Blair, of Outer Cape Reality; despite the cutesy name, Mitsy had the most successful real estate business in the entire southern New England region. The success of the business was largely due to Mitsy's reputation as a first-rate deal closer. Suzanne was looking forward to meeting her.

"Good afternoon. May I speak, please, with Mitsy Blair? This is Suzanne Douglas calling," she asked.

"This is Mitsy Blair. How can I help you, Ms. Douglas?" a very efficient voice answered

"Ms. Blair, I work with Dr. Charles Baio, over at the Cetacean Research Center. Are you familiar with their work?" she asked.

"Oh, a little. I know everyone in P'town *loves* them. They are an incredibly positive influence on the entire community, and the whole region, for that matter," she answered.

"Well, the reason I'm calling you is to give you some advanced notice that tomorrow morning, the manager and a couple of staffers from the Stellwagen Bank National Marine Sanctuary will be here to start looking at potential office space for a satellite Sanctuary office here in Provincetown," Suzanne started to explain.

"Oh, the Stellwagen Bank Sanctuary! I thought that office was located up in Scituate," she asked.

"It is," Suzanne replied, "but the real need, given the anticipated visitor and outreach activity levels, an additional, or satellite, office located in Provincetown, is an absolute necessity."

"So how much room do you anticipate needing?" Mitsy asked.

"The Sanctuary manager can fill you in on details, but in general, I think they're looking for office space to accommodate four of five staff members with individual offices, a conference/public meeting room for at least a couple hundred people, and open office space for volunteers. And of course, everything must meet ADA requirements," Suzanne finished.

"Of course," Mitsy murmured, thinking while Suzanne was rattling off figures. "There are two, possibly three offices that I think would meet the Sanctuary's needs; why don't I get these offices open for your folks to see tomorrow, around eleven A.M. sound okay?" Mitsy asked, quickly regaining her stride. "Now, who's going to be here? Their names?"

"As far as I know, Lieutenant Nelson, the Sanctuary manager, Karen Clapham, the outreach and public information coordinator, and possibly Mason Weisner, the Sanctuary research coordinator; and possibly one or more NOAA staffers from Washington," Suzanne answered.

Unflustered, Mitsy replied, "So, probably six or seven, if you and Dr. Baio also attend, right?"

"Right," Suzanne answered.

"Sounds like a great full day; we'll plan on having lunch somewhere in town," Mitsy offered.

"This all sounds great; the Sanctuary folks will meet us at the Center around ten-thirty A.M.," Suzanne finished, thanking Mitsy for her time before she hung up the phone. *Whew, looks like things are going to get a little more frenetic,* she thought, as she sat down and dialed the Scituate number. Mason answered the phone.

"Stellwagen Bank Sanctuary; Mason Weisner," the deep voice said.

She still got that slight flip in her stomach whenever she heard Mason's voice. She sat up a little straighter, and answered in a mock deep, throaty voice: "Mason, darling! Suzanne here; just wanted to inform you that we're all set up for tomorrow morning to office shop. The gang is expected by ten-thirty A.M., at the Center, and will be met by Ms. Mitsy Blair, of Outer Cape Reality."

"Super, Suzanne; good work in a hurry," Mason responded immediately.

"Thanks, darling; see you then," Suzanne cooed. She knew she was shameless, but didn't really care. She kept her thoughts about private feelings to herself, and went quickly into Charlie's office and asked if he was interested in joining the Sanctuary office hunt tomorrow morning. She hadn't noticed that Charlie was on the phone when she entered his office, but realized it in a hurry when he shot her a sharp look

231

and waved her out of the room. Firmly chastised, Suzanne returned to her desk and started reviewing the Center's schedule for the week. *Boy, I think I overstepped some serious boundaries there,* she thought. Although Natalie had not witnessed this sharp reminder of who was the boss, she cheerfully asked Suzanne how she was, and what was new.

"Well, Nat, in case you hadn't heard, Sanctuary folks are going to be in town tomorrow, looking for space for the satellite office," she happily relayed to her friend.

"Wow! That's cool; can I tag along and watch?" Nat asked excitedly.

"Nat, technically, you're not part of the office search committee. So, yeah, you can tag along and watch, but no comments or suggestions, right?" Suzanne answered.

"Okay, I understand," Nat sighed and smiled.

About then, Charlie emerged from his office and said quietly to Suzanne, "Hey, I'm sorry about shooing you out of the office; I was having trouble hearing Ms. Blair on the phone," he explained. "Next time, let me know you're coming before you start talking, okay?" he added.

"I'm sorry, I didn't even think before I started talking; it won't happen again, promise," Suzanne smiled and shrugged. "So, are you coming along on tomorrow's office search?" she asked.

"Wouldn't miss it," Charlie answered. He shot a broad smile in Suzanne's direction.

Tuesday morning broke clear and sunny; a perfect day for checking out available Provincetown offices. Suzanne was excited, in part because she had been through this exercise before, when NOAA was finding an office space in Sciutate. They got lucky then, as they were able to lease a former Coast Guard station, giving them plenty of room to expand in the future. She fixed a quick cup of coffee, gave Barney an equally quick walk, and headed for the Center.

232

Somewhat to her surprise, Mitsy Blair was already there, ready and waiting. She wouldn't have known who it was, except for the cute little BMW convertible parked in the driveway. *Realtors,* she thought, *the least she could have done was bring a big car.* However, within a couple of minutes. Lieutenant Nelson, Karen Clapham and Mason Weisner arrived together in a large NOAA van, kicking up a bit of dust from the Center' gravel driveway.

"My, this is quite an entourage!" exclaimed Mitsy, who was obviously impressed, particularly with Miles' uniform. Directly after the Sanctuary folks arrived, Charlie pulled up in his Jeep. Suzanne trotted up to Charlie's Jeep and smiling broadly, said "Hi, there Dr. Baio; ready for some office hunting?"

Charlie winked back, and when no one was looking their way, said, "I sure have missed you, Sunshine."

Suzanne walked Charlie over to Lieutenant Nelson and introduced him. "Lieutenant Nelson, as I've said earlier, this is the best of opportunities for you and the rest of the Sanctuary staff to get to see and know the Center's work, and the many connections with Sanctuary programs and objectives," she went on. Lieutenant Nelson looked around at his Sanctuary staff present and observed, "Ms. Douglas, unless I'm badly mistaken, I believe these particular staffers are very familiar with the Center's work, but I agree with you that the opportunity is ripe for strengthening the cooperative ties that serve the goals of both programs." Charlie stepped forward and extended his hand to Lieutenant Nelson, saying, "It's great to meet you, Lieutenant, I hope you'll stick around long enough this afternoon to take a look at our labs and learn more about the connections between the Center's work and the Sanctuary's goals."

"I'd be delighted, and thanks for the offer," the Lieutenant answered.

"Well!" exclaimed Mitsy, "Let's get this show on the road, shall we? The first office site, in fact all three sites, are within easy walking distance, but I think we should probably take the vehicles so we can easily break over lunch at Moonakis Café, alright with everyone?" she fairly beamed with excitement. And with that, the entourage loaded themselves into Mitsy's BMW and the Sanctuary van, and took off for the first of three office sites.

Partly because it was just her nature and partly because somebody had to take comprehensive notes, Suzanne was able to quickly assess the three office sites. Although much of her assessment was laced with personal reactions, there were accurate data entered on each of the sites. In discussing the sites over lunch, Suzanne advocated strongly for the office building located directly across the street from the water (big surprise). She did not have to push hard for her favorite; Miles, Karen, Mason, and Charlie all agreed that the small office building located near the McMillan Pier at the north end of town was a perfect location. And by the end of a very long day, even Mitsy, although tired, was extremely pleased at the relatively easy consensus.

As the group continued talking informally about the attributes of their proposed office selection, Suzanne noticed someone hanging around the parked vehicles in the parking lot, who seemed very interested in what the group was discussing. She thought the person looked familiar, but she couldn't be sure, since the figure wore sunglasses and a large floppy hat. She decided to just keep an eye on her, to see if the person would make herself known, or ask questions of the group. As it turned out, Mitsy solved the mystery by approaching the woman and asking directly who she was. *Realtors have a lot of guts,* she thought. At Mitsy's question, the sunglasses came off, and Suzanne felt disgusted: it was Jodie. She felt she had to go over and say something to her, and at least find out what she wanted, although she was sure she knew what that was.

"Jodie, what are you doing here?" she asked.

Jodie looked at Suzanne and said simply, "Like I said in my note, I'm looking for a job with the Sanctuary, of course."

"Did you get my letter back to you? I thought I made it pretty clear that, although I don't make the decisions about hiring, it would be very unlikely that someone with your record would be hired by NOAA for anything," Suzanne answered.

Trying to change the subject, Jodie asked, "What are all these people doing here?"

"This is a preliminary group looking at potential office sites for a satellite office for the Stellwagen Bank Sanctuary in Scituate," she answered rather succinctly.

"Well, I still want the opportunity to apply for a job at this office when it opens," Jodie said.

"You may still be able to get an application from the Sanctuary Manager, Lieutenant Nelson, or from Karen Clapham; they're over there by the Sanctuary van," Suzanne offered.

Jodie immediately turned around and headed for the Lieutenant. Charlie took Suzanne's arm and started to ask what was going on, but she stopped him and said, "Don't worry, Charlie; Miles knows all about Jodie's background; he'll dissuade her from pursuing this, I hope."

"Is she the one who killed the White House intern in your office back in D.C.?" Charlie asked.

"Yeah, that's her," Suzanne nodded.

"Incredible; you just never know about people, do you?" Charlie muttered.

"Never," Suzanne answered as she moved away from the vehicles.

It appeared that Miles had effectively talked Jodie out of causing a scene by finding an employment application form to give her, and informing her that she had only five days to get the form mailed in to NOAA headquarters in Washington. Placated for the time being, Jodie left the parking lot and quickly disappeared. Breathing a huge sigh of relief, Suzanne went over to Miles and asked if there was anything she should do or be aware of during the next week.

"Nah, I don't think so, Suzanne; I made sure she was aware that even if her application is accepted, there will be a security check conducted on her as a routine matter. Hopefully, that will put an end to the whole thing," Miles said.

"Good work, Lieutenant! I hope you're right," Suzanne exclaimed.

The mini-distraction resolved, Mitsy closed in on Miles to wrap up the informal decision made by the Sanctuary group. "I think you've made a great decision on an office location, Lieutenant Nelson; I will present the offer to the owner, and you can make your desires known to NOAA," she said, as she closed her files and handed Miles copies of descriptive brochures on the office.

"Thanks so much for your assistance in guiding us around these offices," Miles responded warmly and added, "I'm so pleased that this group came to consensus quickly on a perfect location and facility for the satellite office." As Suzanne looked on, she could see that Mitsy was closing in on Miles for more than simply handing him some papers. *It's always the uniform; always,* she thought. As amusing as it might have been to watch Mitsy try to get Miles' attention, Suzanne had had about enough of office hunting and of Mitsy's flaunting maneuvers.

"What do you say we all head back to the P'Town Bar and Grill for a happy hour send off for the Scituate folks and further relaxed discussions for the P-town folks?" Suzanne offered.

"What a fine idea," Mitsy said, "I'm going to contact the

owner of this office building and convince him he couldn't have a better purchaser than the federal government. I'll join you at the Grill, okay?" she asked excitedly. So the Sanctuary folks headed down to the Grill (only a block away from their proposed new satellite office site, Suzanne noted with a good deal of comfort). Once settled in at the Grill, and after placing orders for the local beer all around, Miles sighed happily and said, "What a day, huh? Suzanne, you did a great job picking the best office site; I really appreciate your help. By the way who's your friend hangin' out in the back there?"

"That's my very good friend, Natalie Ward; she works at the Center and had helped in more ways than I can even count, Miles," Suzanne said, smiling broadly at Nat.

Hearing her name mentioned, Natalie came over to where Miles, Suzanne and the rest of the group were sitting, at a large round table. Displaying a previously unknown amount of courage, Nat sat down at the table and said to Suzanne. "So, Suze; talking about me again, huh? You know I'm an open book; ask me anything you want, go ahead."

Caught momentarily off guard (but only momentarily), Suzanne laughed and responded: "Nat, this is Lieutenant Miles Nelson, Sanctuary Manager, Karen and Mason you know, and of course, your boss, Charlie Baio."

Nat displayed her renowned blush, and tried to join the conversation about the office site which had been preliminarily chosen by the group. Somewhat against her own better judgment, Suzanne went ahead and announced that Nat was very interested in the manager's position at the satellite office.

Karen immediately piped up and said, "Natalie would be great as the office manager; she knows everything about the Sanctuary and its rules and regulations. You couldn't make a better choice," she concluded. There appeared to be general agreement around the table, even though Suzanne was quick to point out that the folks here gathered did not have the responsibility for making that decision.

"So who *does* make the decision?" Karen asked.

"I think what NOAA will do is bring together several of the existing Sanctuary managers to interview the candidate applicants, probably either in Scituate or here in Provincetown, but it's only a somewhat educated guess," Suzanne offered.

"Sounds like a plan," Mason piped in, stating the obvious. Mason looked over in Natalie's direction and winked. He leaned over to her and whispered, "Don't worry kid, you're a shoo-in."

Nat whispered back, "I sure hope you're right."

By the time a second round of beer had been ordered for the group, Mitsy returned with the happy news that the owner of the office building the group had picked as the perfect site had accepted NOAA's offer to lease the site for an initial period of five years. There was loud clapping and cheers all around the table, and genuine appreciation shown for Mitsy's efforts.

"We could not have found this without your help, and are very grateful, Ms. Blair," Miles said, as he shook hands with the real estate agent.

So the necessary paperwork and forms were forwarded back to NOAA headquarters in Washington, D.C., and agreements among NOAA officials, the Sanctuary manager and the property owner in Provincetown were signed. Almost immediately, plans related to the renovation and furnishing of the satellite office were formed, discussed, finalized and initiated by local designers, carpenters, painters and publicity personnel. It was a very exciting time for not only the Sanctuary, but also the residents of Provincetown. As Suzanne mentioned to Nat, it never failed to amaze her how quickly the federal government could make things happen when there was a particular push to get something accomplished. And it certainly seemed to her that the desire to get the satellite office established and set up was undeniable.

"Just think Nat, in just a few weeks, probably, this office will be open for business, hopefully with you as the office manager, and just in time for the tourist season. Can you stand it?"

"Oh, Suzanne, you don't have any idea who's going to end up with that job, you know?" Natalie asked.

"Oh, I think it's a pretty good bet, but of course, all the applicants will have to be interviewed first. But face it, you've got a definite inside track," Suzanne continued.

Within weeks, the Federal Register notice was published, announcnig NOAA's intention to open a satellite office for the Stellwagen Bank National Marine Sanctuary in Provincetown, Massachusetts, and that the period for receiving applications for the Manager's position and necessary start-up office staff positions had closed. The notice further explained that interviews for these positions would be conducted in Provincetown by a panel of Sanctuary managers and office staff from other existing National Marine Sanctuaries during the second week of May, at the Provincetown High School building, on Butler Avenue. Specified times for the interviews would be provided by mail to the applicants chosen by the National Marine Sanctuary Program.

At the Center's office, Nat was almost uncontrollably excited: she had received written notice from NOAA that her application had been received, and she was invited to an interview for the manager's position on May 8th at 1:00 P.M. at Provincetown High School on Butler Avenue.

"Oh, God, Suzanne! I'm so excited and nervous; what should I wear for the interview?" Nat asked her good friend.

"Wear what you would wear on the job, Nat what else?" Suzanne replied. "I mean, you've got to look the part, you know? Oh, Nat, you're going to do fine, believe me; you'll be great and they will love you," she assured her friend.

After Nat's excitement died down (a little) sometime shortly after lunch, she walked over to Suzanne's desk and asked her quietly, "So Suzanne, did you get an invitation letter, too? What does yours say? What position are they interviewing you for? I can't wait to be working with you directly at the satellite office, you know?" Nat went on and on.

Suzanne took a deep breath, and guided Nat to a quiet spot outside Center office, where they could sit down and talk together sort of privately for a few moments.

"Nat, we're still going to be working together at the satellite office, but I'm mostly going to be continuing to work with Charlie at the Center on fundraising efforts. I'll be helping out at the satellite office as a volunteer educator and outreach person. It's what I want to do," she concluded.

"Didn't you apply for a job at the satellite office? Are you crazy?" Nat exclaimed. "I don't get it, Suzanne; I thought the Sanctuary was your *life*!' Nat seemed almost close to tears.

"Nat, the Sanctuary *was* my life, for more than ten years. You know, I think I finally realized that change is a good thing, once in a while, you know? It doesn't mean that I don't care about the Sanctuary—I do. I always will. It's just time for me to do some different things. We will always be connected by the Sanctuary and our friendship, okay?" Suzanne reached over and hugged her friend.

Fourteen
Natalie's Interview

May 8th finally arrived, and Nat could not have been more excited and nervous. Sanctuary managers and educational/research staff from the Florida Keys, Channel Islands, Gray's Reef, The Monitor, Thunder Bay, and of course, Stellwagen Bank assembled in Provincetown for the scheduled four days of interviews for the first manager and staff at a National Marine Sanctuary satellite office. The weather that day in Provincetown was perfect: clear, crisp and full of excitement for the visiting managers and their staff. It was almost like a "mini-managers meeting"; for some of the staff, this was the first opportunity for meeting personnel from other Sanctuary sites.

As Sanctuary folks gathered at the high school for the day's interviews, there was a great deal of hugging, hand shaking, story swapping and even some griping about budget restrictions imposed by Sanctuary Program headquarters in Washington. But even to the casual observer, there was no questioning the fierce loyalty and determination of the on-site staffs, and the same intensity would be applied to the applicant's interviews.

Natalie was relieved to discover that she was not the first applicant interview; she was the third. All of the applicants gathered in the small room adjacent to the auditorium; as Natalie counted, there were a total of ten, and she didn't even know six of them. She did notice, though, that one of the applicants was wearing a uniform of some sort. *That's not fair,* she thought. Upon a little closer gaze, she discovered it was a National Park Service uniform. *Gosh, I hope she isn't before me,* Nat thought. Manager Nelson welcomed them all to the interview session, and presented some brief remarks on what NOAA was hoping to establish at the satellite office.

"Thanks for coming, all of you. This is the first of four days of interviews for the manager's position at the new satellite office here in Provincetown. We've asked all the applicants to come today so we can present you with kind of an overview of this first, but we hope not the last, satellite office established to further support the goals and objectives of the Stellwagen Bank National Marine Sanctuary. Whew, that sounded a little like a canned speech, huh? But seriously, folks, this is an exciting new venture and expansion of Sanctuary programs, so that more of the interested public learn what Marine Sanctuaries are all about.

"I expect that we'll get to three individuals a day, and finish on the twelfth. Gathered here with us are Sanctuary Managers from six established National Marine Sanctuaries around the country, representing half of the entire system of Sanctuaries. I don't want to go on at great length here, but each of you was assigned a number when you came in. That number is your interview number. So there's no reason for all of you to stay; just pick up your number and return here on the date and at the time indicated, okay? Are there any questions so far?"

One hand went up from the back of the room.

"And what is *your* name, sir?" the questioner asked.

"Oh, crap; what a jerk, huh? I am Lieutenant Miles Nelson, NOAA Corps; I'm very sorry. Clearly, public speaking is *not* my forte. But I look pretty good in a uniform, don't you think? At least, that's what my mom tells me," Lieutenant Nelson smiled and shuffled a bit. There was gentle laughter around the room.

By now, folks had started to stand up and prepare to leave, while checking their interview numbers and date. Natalie was very relieved she wasn't first, at least; but she was scheduled to interview on the first day. Soon the room had cleared of all but four applicants and the Sanctuary Program staffs. Two conference tables had been set up with several chairs placed around them, but as Manager Nelson walked around the room, he quickly decided this arrangement was, at the very least, not overly inviting for the applicants to be interviewed. So in an effort to make the environment more comfortable, Nelson rearranged the tables and chairs in a semicircle.

"Much better, don't you think?" he asked. The visiting Sanctuary staffs nodded in agreement, and the first applicant was asked to join them at the table. Natalie and the other two applicants waited outside in an adjacent room, where Natalie became more and more nervous. She wondered what kind of questions were being asked, and if she'd have any answers when her turn came. She still did not recognize any of the applicants; the Park Service person had left after the orientation, so maybe wearing a uniform wouldn't make such an impression on the interview staff after all. As the second candidate came out of the conference room, he looked completely wiped out.

"Tough one, huh?" Natalie offered, silently hoping that this guy was just stupid and had failed miserably at the questioning. Even though she was known as quiet and normally shy, she had a deep belief in the Sanctuary Program's goals and regulations. By the time the second candidate had left the building, she was ready but scared to death. "Natalie Ward?" Manager Nelson asked, and she stood up and moved into the conference room, taking a seat where she faced all the managers and staffs.

"It's still a little intimidating, isn't it? We don't mean it to be at all, Natalie; okay, if I call you Natalie, or do you prefer Ms. Ward?" Miles asked.

Surprisingly even to herself, Natalie answered, "Please, call me Natalie, or Nat; the more informal the better, as far as I'm concerned, anyway."

"Me, too," Miles assured her.

The other Sanctuary managers and staff members introduced themselves, as they went around the semi-circle of chairs, several making friendly comments about the great work done by the Cetacean Research Center, and Dr. Baio's contribution to greater understanding of large cetacean populations. Natalie began to feel a little more comfortable.

"Natalie, we're all familiar with the invaluable work you've done at the Center. As you know, the satellite office to be established here in Provincetown is a first for the Program. We're very interested in how you envision such an office functioning, and its value to both the Program and the community around it. And that's pretty much the entire interview question; we *know* you're qualified." Miles smiled broadly at her and sat down.

Natalie took a very deep breath and smiled. She was among friends, she could tell.

"Wow," she sighed, "where to start?"

"I guess I would start by saying that the overriding objective of a Sanctuary satellite office is to provide a regional center for Sanctuary programs to be carried out, and for a Sanctuary's rules and regulations to be enforced. But none of this can be accomplished without the understanding, support and direct involvement of the community surrounding it. Any successful Sanctuary program is dependent on community, as well as national, support. Like that old song says, 'You can't have one without the other,' particularly as that applies here in New England. As Dr. Baio has often said, the Stellwagen Bank Sanctuary may be the last hope for recovery of the northern right whale. So I see the Sanctuary satellite office as a place where people can take an active part in helping the National Marine Sanctuary Program establish a firm and ever-growing understanding of this special marine world, and spreading that understanding can be accomplished through active educational outreach efforts, as well as focused research to support them."

As she glanced at the wall clock, Nat realized she had been talking non-stop for almost forty-five minutes. No wonder her mouth felt dry. But the more she talked, the more she realized that there were dozens, if not hundreds, of creatures now protected by Sanctuary status that she had not even touched on. So in closing she added, "Of course, any Sanctuary's staff has to be complete with appropriate personnel to reach its objectives."

"Agreed, of course," Miles said, as the staffs awarded Nat a much-appreciated round of applause.

"Could I have some water?" Nat asked in a small, now-scratchy voice.

There was appreciative laughter all around the table, and Miles winked at her, as he put a glass of ice water in front of her.

When she got home late that afternoon, the first thing Nat wanted to do was call Suzanne. She could hardly believe the ordeal was over, and wanted to know if Suzanne had any inside information on when the panel of Sanctuary managers and staff would make their decision.

"Suzanne, I'm so glad I caught you at home! My interview is over; God, I'm so glad! There were some really strange-looking applicants there; I didn't know any of them. Guess there were some from out of town. There was even somebody there in a Park Service uniform, can you believe that? Man, what a day!" Nat spewed into the phone.

"Nat, Nat! Slow down, buddy; you're making my head spin," Suzanne answered when she could get a word in edgewise. "Hey, I'm glad things went well for you; sounds like you said all the right things, Nat," she said.

"Hey, how do you know things went well for me? *I* don't know that; how come *you* know?" Nat exclaimed.

"Because I talked to Miles Nelson after today's interviews were finished, and he told me that you did a really great job and that the Sanctuary folks there really liked you and your responses to questions. See? I told you they would love you, Nat," Suzanne answered, smiling.

"So when do you think they'll make a decision?" Nat asked.

"Well, I assume it will be some time shortly after the twelfth, when everyone has been interviewed. You know they want to get this wrapped up quickly, so they can get new staffing hired and in place as soon as the office is furnished and ready. It's only a guess, but I'm thinking they will have the manager hired and ready to take office, so to speak, by the end of the month," Suzanne concluded.

"Wow," Nat exclaimed. "What about uniforms?" she pushed.

"So Nat, I assume you really want this job?" Suzanne chuckled at her friend's anxious enthusiasm. "*If* you are offered the job, someone from NOAA will be asking what size shirt and slacks you wear, and they might fit you for a jacket, too," she continued.

"Size eight, size eight all around; I'm easy," Nat was almost laughing and shouting at the same time.

"Calm down, Nat; don't assume everything at once. Don't forget; I'm not a NOAA employee anymore. I'm just giving you my best guesses here," Suzanne replied in her best soothing voice.

"You're my best friend, Suzanne; I don't know what I would do without you," Nat answered.

"I do, Nat. You'll be a really good satellite office manager, *if* you get the job," Suzanne smiled, "talk to you later, okay?"

As she hung up the phone, Suzanne had kind of a sense of regret that she had not applied for any job at the new satellite office. In a way, she felt a little left out of all the excitement surrounding the establishment of this new office, although she didn't know why. *You can't really be thinking you'd like to go back to work for the federal government. You idiot! Think of the paperwork! Think of your sanity! Get a life!* she reminded herself over and over. *There were certainly more pleasant things to think about than a return to the federal government; there was Charlie, and who knows where that could go?* she thought. *I know where I'd **like** it to go; I think we could be a really good team together.*

In the end, she wound up thinking about how great it had been to make love with Charlie; there were no particular inroads made into saving the northern right whale population, or gaining the trust and support of local fishermen for the new management plan of the area surrounding and including Stellwagen Bank. Even though the Sanctuary was finally designated, there was still a great deal of work to be done—mainly, getting the local and regional users of the Sanctuary to buy into their "stewardship" role in protecting the area's resources. She sort of felt like that colossal job was now the work of others; she had done her part, and wanted to move on into other things. Things with Charlie, she hoped.

Rather quickly after the conclusion of the four-day interview process, NOAA headquarters in Washington notified each of the applicants that a final decision would be made by the end of the following week, May 20th. Suzanne didn't think Natalie was going to last that long; she was one nervous young woman. What Natalie had forgotten in all the excitement leading up to the interview itself was the fact that all those interviewed had to have a background check completed on them before a final decision and the offer of employment could be made. Checking the backgrounds and previous employment records of all the applicants was tedious and detailed work, and was conducted and reviewed by several Sanctuary staffers, as well as a number of NOAA employees in Washington. The last thing NOAA wanted was an employee in a managerial position with an unstable or otherwise questionable background. Suzanne realized that these standards would definitely eliminate Jodie Cranson, and she relaxed a little.

Following the departure of all applicants and Sanctuary staff from other locations, life at the Center returned more or less to normal, except for the rapid progress being made on the satellite office building and Nat's constant inquiries regarding expected completion dates. While she waited impatiently for NOAA's final decision to be made, Nat continued to review the regulations and management priorities pertinent to Stellwagen Bank Sanctuary. Suzanne came to the belief that Nat knew more than any one of the applicants about not only the Sanctuary's regulations, but its resources as well. Within three weeks, the satellite office had been refurbished, and carpeting, furniture and office equipment installed. All it awaited was the satellite office personnel. As soon as the Stellwagen Bank National Marine Sanctuary/NOAA sign went up in front of the revitalized three-story office building situated half a block from McMillan Pier, there was increased and continuing excited conversation throughout Provincetown. Included in the excited conversation were Charlie's increasingly frequent reminders to Nat that she pay attention to the Center's workload.

"Sheesh!" Nat quietly complained to Suzanne, "He can be such a grouch sometimes, you know? I mean, I'm just trying to better myself, and working at the satellite office would be working for many of the same goals as the Center, for cryin' out loud."

"Are you through, Nat?" Suzanne whispered back so that Charlie could not hear. "You know, you're going to have to temper your language a little, at least when you're speaking to the public; just a suggestion, kiddo," she smiled at her friend.

By everyone's measure except Natalie's, the next several days passed quickly; there was a ton of work to do at the Center. Finally, at the end of business on May 20th, the phone rang at the center, and Nat's life changed in ten minutes.

"I won! I got it! Oh, gosh; I'm going to be the manager at the satellite office! Suzanne, I'm so excited," Nat gushed her thrill to all within hearing. "I gotta call my folks in Maine," she said and disappeared into the back file room of the Center.

Fifteen

Dropping Anchor in Settled Waters

Despite the excitement all around the Center, Charlie had lined up a couple potential corporate donors, and Suzanne was busy helping him prepare presentations. She found working directly with Charlie surprisingly easy; although she was totally attracted to him, often finding herself watching his every move, she focused intently on the preparation of the Center's presentations.

"Suzanne, do you remember those guys from the Fleet Bank that we met with several months ago?"

"Yeah, have they ever gotten back to you about supporting some of the Center's research on northern right whales?" Suzanne responded.

"Kind of. They phoned yesterday and would like for us to come up to Boston and make our case directly to the Bank's board of directors. So I'd like for you to come with me on a short trip to Boston, where you can make the presentation and hopefully help me close the deal, okay?"

She gulped. "Oh, Charlie, I don't know if I can do it; I mean, I get so nervous especially with you watching and having to correct me every fourth word or something," Suzanne said.

"Hey, buck up, kiddo. You know more than any of them about northern right whales *and* the Stellwagen Sanctuary. You'll be great, and I promise not to make any corrections unless it's absolutely necessary," Charlie smiled and winked at her.

"Gosh, I guess I can't refuse your request, Charlie," Suzanne said.

"Not if you want to stay with me," Charlie chuckled and came close to her and rested his hands on her shoulders. "Not if you want to stay," he whispered.

And stay with him she wanted to do, but Suzanne couldn't help feeling that this was kind of a bribe. Probably against what was left of her better judgment, she decided to play the game.

"Okay, Charlie, I'll go with you to Boston, but what makes you think that I'm doing this just because I want to stay with you?"

"Because I know you do, Sunshine; I know you do," Charlie answered without the slightest hesitation.

Damn, she thought. *I guess I forgot I'm dealing with a pro. I think I can live with that,* she smiled to herself, as she walked home and began to pack for Boston.